Forgiveness Trilogy
Book Two

Petals Beyond the Bend

© 2016 by Eva C. Maddox
All rights reserved

No part of this book may be reproduced, stored in a retrieval system, or transmitted by any means without the written permission of the author. Petals Beyond the Bend is a book of fiction. Any resemblance to actual events and persons, living or dead, is coincidental.

All scripture quotations, unless otherwise indicated, are taken from the Holy Bible, New International Version (NIV). Copyright ©1973, 1978, 1984, 2011 by Biblica, Inc.™

ISBN-13:978-1534888807
ISBN-10:1534888802

Published by WE Ink, Seaford, Delaware, 2016

Acknowledgements:

I am thankful for the editing skills of Kristi Wile and Wilma Caraway who helped make this book possible. I am also indebted to the members of Delmarva Christian Writers Fellowship, Georgetown, Delaware and Kingdom Writers Fellowship, Seaford, Delaware, for their constant encouragement and support.

For assistance with the book cover, I'm grateful to Wilma Caraway, author of: *101 Surprises! Sayings with Scripture You Didn't See Coming. (Available on Amazon.)*

Petals Beyond the Bend

by

Eva C. Maddox

Connections

Chapter 1

August 1981

A man's heart plans his way, but the Lord directs his steps.
Proverbs 16:9

Dani sped along I-75 toward Brady City, Tennessee, in her new car. Well, not exactly new, but new to her. Field after field showed the effects of the brutal August weather, and heat rose in glimmering circles from the baked pavement. Carter's words in the card he had sent scrolled through her mind.

"I can't wait to see you again. I'll call as soon as I get to campus."

Carter Matthews had called several times over the summer, and even though their conversations consisted of small talk, her heart twittered at the sound of his voice.

This is the first time that Dani had driven herself to school. She recalled her parents' insistence that she attend an out-of-state college and her complete lack of interest in going to college at all. The death of her beloved sister, Betts, had smacked Dani into deep despair that almost cost her own life. She praised God for giving her parents who loved her through those dark days.

The car in front of Dani slammed on the brakes, but she managed to stop inches before she crashed into its rear. Her heart raced and blood rushed to her face. *Oh, God, can I do this? What if I cause another accident? Pay attention to your driving, Dani.* She detested the high-speed, monotonous turnpike driving and how it could change in an instant to a crawl. She saw the cause of the slow-down a half hour later as she inched past the emergency vehicles and mangled automobiles. *Some other family is going to get tragic news today. God, be with them.*

Dani pulled into the parking lot of the same dorm she had been in previously. The campus buzzed with the excitement of students unloading vehicles and bidding farewell to parents. She removed her sunglasses, took a deep breath, and opened her car door. The air felt as if she had opened a hot oven.

It took her a half hour to check out her room and lug almost everything from her car up the stairs and down the hall to Room 213. "Whew!" she said as she fanned with her hands, grateful for the air conditioning. She rummaged through one of her bags, found a scrunchie, pulled her hair into a pony tail, and headed downstairs for her final load.

Her parents had given her a microwave oven so that she could prepare snacks in her room, something the college had not allowed previously. She hoped to carry it up along with the remaining bag in one final trip. As she reached into her trunk, a tall and very blond young man appeared beside her.

"Here, let me get that for you," he said.

"Oh, that's all right. I can handle it."

"What?" he said with muscled arms on his slim hips, "and allow chivalry to die right here in a parking lot at Brady-Jaxson College?"

"Well, since you put it that way, I know I couldn't live with the guilt." Dani smiled, and stepped aside. "Go for it."

The handsome volunteer easily lifted the microwave as if it were made of cardboard. "Lead the way, Miss . . ."

"Krieg. Dani Krieg."

"Nice to meet you, Dani. I'm Steve Foster."

"It's nice to meet you, too." Dani grabbed the last bag from her car, locked the doors, and headed for the dorm again as Steve followed behind.

"You new here, Dani?"

"No, I was . . . I am a sophomore. You?"

"I transferred here last year from Berea College in Kentucky. I'm a junior."

"Cool."

Dani had been so deep in depression during her last semester she barely remembered her closest friends.

"I saw you around campus a few times," he said.

"Oh?"

"Yeah, you always seemed . . . kind of sad."

"I had a rough year." She was thankful Steve dropped the subject.

He whistled the whole way up the stairs, and Dani thought that any moment he would toss the microwave as if he were about to shoot a basketball.

By the time they reached Dani's room, her leg that been broken in the car accident throbbed. The ache triggered thoughts about all she had been through over the last two years—death of her sister and her own battle with depression—but she had learned the hard way not to allow these thoughts to sabotage her progress.

She held the door open for Steve as he stepped inside.

"Where shall I put it?"

Dani pointed to a small stand. "On that little stand will be great."

"There you go," he said.

"Perfect. Thanks so much, Steve."

"You're most welcome," he said as he bowed and turned to go.

Dani grinned.

In didn't take long for Dani to put away her things and make her bed. She stretched out on the bright yellow comforter her mom had bought her. *I wonder if Carter is on campus yet?* She glanced at her clock radio. *Hmm . . . five o'clock. We're all supposed to be on campus by eight. For crying out loud, Dani, he's just a friend, and you've got other things to think about besides Carter Matthews.* A tap on the door ended Dani's musings.

"Yes?"

A smiling girl stepped inside. "Hi, I'm Courtney."

Dani hopped up. "Hi, Courtney. I'm Dani. Do you need help with anything?"

"No thanks. My brother is bringing up the rest of my stuff." She scanned the small room and headed for the bed with the bare mattress. "Guess this one's mine, huh?" She dropped a duffle bag on it and adjusted her glasses.

"I'll switch if you'd rather have this one," Dani said. "Really, I don't mind at all."

"Thanks, but this one's fine." She slicked her short sandy hair behind her ears. "Whew! Climbing these stairs should help me shed a few pounds." Her joyful laugh filled their room.

"You'll get used to the stairs," Dani said with a smile. She liked Courtney immediately and silently thanked God for her.

"Court? You in there?" A voice sounded from the hall.

"My brother," Courtney said as she pulled open the door to a teenage boy loaded with bags.

"Come on in, Bro."

After he had placed Courtney's things on her bed, he pulled a handkerchief from his back pocket and wiped his dripping forehead. "Man! It's hot today." He glanced at Dani and smiled.

"Kyle, meet Dani, my roommate," Courtney said. "Dani, my big, strong brother."

"Nice to meet you, Kyle."

"You, too." He turned to Courtney. "See you at Thanksgiving, Sis."

She hugged him. "Thanks, Kyle. I appreciate you helping me out."

After Kyle left, Courtney attacked the piles of clothes, books, and supplies.

"Excuse me, Courtney, but I desperately need a shower."

Courtney appeared not to have heard her. "You have a microwave!" Courtney said.

"Yes, and you're welcome to use it anytime you like."

"Thanks!"

After her shower, Dani changed into a sleeveless blue top and white capris.

"Cute outfit, Dani."

"Thanks. I'm starving. Would you like to go to dinner?" She had hoped Carter would call and ask to have dinner with her, but the phone didn't ring, and her stomach cried for food.

"Absolutely! I haven't had a bite since breakfast. Let's go, roomie," she said as she linked her arm with Dani's.

Dani felt as if she had known Courtney forever.

❅❅❅

Dani piled cheese, lettuce, and tomato on her tostada, and memories of her sweet mother crept through her mind. Lindy Krieg, a native of Mexico, regularly served their family her spicy dishes.

"I'll save you a seat, Dani," Courtney said as she finished filling her plate.

"Okay," Dani said.

Moments later, she heard Courtney's jovial laughter as she met up with some friends.

Someone tapped on Dani's shoulder, and she turned to find Steve Foster smiling at her. "Having dinner with anyone special?"

"Hi again. Uh . . . Courtney, my roommate and I —"

"Courtney Cook?"

"Yeah. You know her?"

"Everybody who has been on campus for any length of time knows Courtney."

"I pretty much guessed that. You're certainly welcome to join us."

"You sure?"

"Why not? Have a seat."

When Courtney saw that Dani was sharing a table with Steve, she gestured that she would eat with her friends.

Dani learned that Steve planned to become a youth pastor. The youth director of his church had taken him under his wing when Steve experienced some rough teenage years. Steve felt that God wanted him to do the same for other troubled youth.

While she enjoyed the pleasant chat with Steve her mind returned several times to Carter, and she wanted to get back to her dorm in case he called. She downed the last of her iced tea and stood to leave. "I think I'll head back to the dorm now, Steve. Thanks for sharing dinner with me."

"How 'bout I walk you back?"

"Oh, that's okay. You probably have plenty to do tonight. Getting settled in and all."

"I insist."

Dani waved goodbye to Courtney and left the cafeteria with Steve Foster. She hoped she hadn't missed Carter Matthew's call.

"See you tomorrow, Dani," Steve said when they reached the steps to her dorm.

"Thanks again, Steve."

As soon as Dani reached the top step, the hall phone began ringing, and she raced to get it.

"Hello?"

"Dani?"

She tried not to sound disappointed. After all, she loved her mother.

Chapter 2

For it is God who works in you to will and to act in order to fulfill his good purpose. Philippians 2:13

Dani winced at the concern in her mother's voice. "Oh, Mom, I'm so sorry I forgot to call, but I'm fine. I ran into a slow-down on the turnpike, but otherwise, no problems."

"Thank God. We've been concerned."

"I got busy putting things away and just forgot."

"Oh, okay. Have you met your roommate yet?"

"Yes, I did, and we hit it off right away . . ."

After she hung up, Dani returned to her room, pulled the drape aside, and peered into the mutual parking lot between Carter's dorm, Baker Hall, and hers. *Where is he?*

Moments later, Courtney tapped on the door and stepped inside. "Hey, Dani. How was dinner with that cutie, Steve Foster?"

"Fine. He's very nice."

"Nice?"

"Yeah, why?"

"Just about every girl on campus would give their eye teeth to date Steve."

Dani grinned and dropped onto her bed. "Without their eye teeth he may not be interested."

"Well, I'll be a monkey's uncle if I don't have a comedian for a roomie."

"Takes one to know one."

"Guess we're like two peas in a pod, huh? Seriously, Dani, did you connect with Steve?"

"Connect? I don't know. We just had dinner together, thanks to you, I might add."

"You're very welcome. He already likes you."

"Don't be ridiculous. He doesn't even know me."

"We'll see. I can read people pretty good, if I do say so myself."

Dani laughed, and tossed a sofa pillow at Courtney.

Courtney caught the pillow and tossed it back. "Hey, it's still early. You up for a game of ping pong?"

"Ping pong? Where?"

"In the basement. Last year they put up two ping pong tables and opened a little snack bar they call The Oasis. It's a great place to hang out."

Wow, I was here last year, and I had no idea.

"Okay. I'm warning you, though, I'm no good."

"Then we're a perfect match."

The girls played two games and then decided to enjoy a Coke and relax in the small lounge.

A group had pulled two tables together in one corner and from the aroma of sauce and pepperoni, Dani knew they were enjoying pizza. Her mouth watered, and she toyed with the idea of ordering one.

Courtney must have read her mind. "We can order one," she said. "It's not too late."

"Sure is tempting, but I need to watch my money."

"And I need to watch my weight!"

"Courtney, you look fine."
"Hey, look who just walked in."
Steve Foster waved to the girls, winked at Dani, and turned toward the menu board.

❄❄❄

As Dani stood in the registration line on Monday morning, she heard someone calling her name.
"Dani! Dani Krieg!"
She turned to find Jessica at the end of the line waving furiously. Dani smiled and returned her wave. Jessica was part of Carrie Adams' Bible study last year. *I wonder if she will be having the study this year since Carrie graduated.*
After Dani changed her major to special education, she wandered over to the bookstore to purchase the books she needed for her classes. She glanced toward Baker Hall hoping to see Carter's car in the parking lot. *No Carter.* Someone suddenly grasped her shoulders from behind.
"Dani!"
"Oh! Bobbi! What a nice surprise."
"How are you, Dani?"
"I'm doing very well. Certainly a lot better than the last time you saw me."
"We were all so worried about you."
"Thanks for your prayers and your friendship."
"By the way, Jess is starting up the Bible study again, maybe you'll come?"
"I'd love to. Just let me know where and when."
"I sure will."
"It'll be nice connecting with everyone again."
"Are you still going for a degree in elementary education?"
"No, I switched to special ed."
"That's great. Did you get your books yet?"
"No, I'm heading there now."

"Me, too. Let's go spend our parents' money."

Dani laughed and picked up her pace. *I have missed out on so much over the last two years.*

After purchasing the books and supplies she needed, Dani headed to her dorm room and spent several hours perusing her books and working out her schedule. When her stomach rumbled, she stood, did several toe touches, and decided to eat a granola bar rather than bothering with lunch. *I wish Betts were here.* She swiped a tear that escaped at the thought of her sister. She reached for her journal, curled up on her bed, and entered her first note since arriving on campus.

Dear Betts, I wish you could be here at college with me. It would be so much fun to share a room again. I do have a really nice roommate. Her name is Courtney, and it seems like we are going to be a good match. Carter Matthews is an amazing guy I met last year, but . . . well, you know what last year was like. Anyway, he phoned me several times this summer and told me he would call me as soon as he arrived on campus. So far, he hasn't arrived, and the students were supposed to be on campus by eight last night.

"Dani? You in there?" *Thump, thump.*

Dani dropped her pen and scooted to the door to find Courtney with an armload of books. She pushed inside and dumped them onto her bed.

"Wow! Textbooks get bigger every year!"

"I know. And more expensive. Why so many?"

"Supplementary reading."

"Couldn't you check them out from the library?"

"I tried doing that last year, but the books were usually not there when I needed them."

Dani strolled to the window, and her heart flipped at the sight of Carter Matthews unloading the trunk of his yellow 1981 Camaro.

Chapter 3

September 1981

And my God will meet all your needs according to the riches of his glory in Christ Jesus. Philippians 4:19

Since Dani had a whole day before her first class began, she decided to spend the time looking for a job. She had seen several posted on bulletin boards around campus and left with pen in hand.

She bounded down the stairs and headed for the Administration Building. Once outside, the combination of humidity and heat slammed her, and she felt as if she had stepped into a sauna. *Help me find a job, Lord. I don't want to be more of a burden on my parents than is necessary. They have sacrificed so much for me. It's a miracle I'm even here.*

Even though she had worked all summer and saved as much as she could, it scarcely made a dent in the cost of her tuition. Her parents had insisted that she go back to school and helped as much as they could in spite of Dani's protests. Even so, she would still have had to borrow enough money to cover the cost of her tuition along with room, board, and books. That is, unless God provided some other way, and the "way" had happened through her wonderful grandparents.

A verse she had learned recently crossed her mind. *Give, and it will be given to you. A good measure, pressed down, shaken together and running over, will be poured into your lap* (Luke 6:38). *That's so true of my grandma and grandpa Krieg.* It seemed to Dani that they no sooner heard of a need than they were meeting it.

Early on, Forrest Krieg's business had taken off and because he and Edith had decided to live simply and spend wisely, they had been able to save a considerable amount of money. Their plan was to pass on a sizeable estate to their children and grandchildren.

When Dani learned they had paid for much of her hospitalization, her old habit of self-condemnation set in. *I have cost my family so much grief. I don't deserve—*

Don't you dare go there, Danita Krieg! You're done with that kind of defeatist thinking.

Dani remembered the day her grandfather called to say he was sending money. Her dad picked up the phone . . .

"No, Dad. You've done enough. My goodness, you helped with Dani's hospitalization after all. This is my responsibility, not yours. I'm going to be coaching some this fall, and that will help—"

"Son, I want to do this."

Cameron sighed. "Dad, I could never win an argument with you." Dani watched him blink away tears.

A week before she was to leave for school, her mom brought in the mail, sorted through it, and handed her a letter. "It's addressed to you, honey."

A letter from Gramps? Hmm . . . he's never written me. Her grandmother had sent her notes from time to time, but not her grandfather. Dani tore open the letter and pulled out a picture of a red sports car that had been cut from a magazine. *What?* She unfolded the note and watched a check float to the floor.

Dear Dani, your grandmother and I would like to help you get another car of your own. This check won't buy a new car, but if you and your dad shop around, you will probably fine a good used one. We love you.

How can I accept this after all they've done? How will I ever repay them? She picked up the check and gasped at the amount. *Two thousand dollars?*

"What is it, Dani?" Lindy asked as she saw the shock registered on her daughter's face.

"It's a . . . a check from Gramps."

"A check? He's already helped us way too much."

"He wants me to buy a car."

"Oh, my goodness. Dad Krieg is the kindness, most generous man I've ever met. I don't know what we would have done this past year without his help."

"I know he wants to help again, but I'm going to send this check right back to him."

"Why don't you talk to him before you do that?"

Needless to say, Forrest would not hear of Dani returning the check and assured her that the Lord had inspired him to send it.

Dani didn't feel as if she should argue with the Lord and accepted the check with humble gratitude.

"I only ask one favor, Granddaughter."

"Anything."

"Send me a picture of you and your new car."

Dani laughed. "I'll surely do that. Thanks again. I love you and Grandma so much."

❄❄❄

By the time Dani arrived at the stately old Administration Building, perspiration beaded on her forehead, and she was glad to be inside where the air conditioning welcomed her. As she rummaged in her purse for a tissue, a familiar voice greeted her.

"Well, if it isn't Danita Krieg."

"Mr. Warren!"

"How are you doing?"

"Much better than last year, I'm happy to say."

"Well, welcome back."

"Thank you. It's good to be back."

She enjoyed Mr. Warren's English class, and regretted that she hadn't completed it. *It's too bad I won't have him this year.*

Dani jotted down three possible job openings that would fit with her schedule: cleaning and stocking restrooms in the Student Union building, library file clerk, and daycare assistant. She didn't relish the idea of cleaning restrooms and decided to check into that one last. Since she would be spending a great deal of time in the library, she thought working there as well might get old. The daycare assistant job held the most appeal for her, and she decided to go for it first.

A few years ago, the college had started a daycare for married students and faculty with infants. They were looking for someone who could work from 6:30 to 9:30 in the morning. If she got the job, she would have plenty of time to get to her 10 o'clock class.

She whirled around to head for the daycare and smacked right into Steve Foster. "Oh, sorry, Steve. I didn't know you were standing there."

"That's quite all right. You checking out jobs?"

"Yes. I'm hoping this one at the daycare will pan out. See you around." Dani dashed for the door.

"Dani! Hold on a sec." Steve scrambled to where she stood with one foot already out the door.

She turned in Steve's direction.

"Would you like to go to a concert with me tonight?"

"Uh . . ." *A concert with Steve? What about Carter?*

"A friend of mine will be one of the featured artists. What do you say?"

"I don't think so, Steve. I need to check into this job and—" *Why hasn't Carter called? He's on campus.*

"Okay. If you change your mind, just call my dorm. I'm in Baker Hall." Steve grinned at Dani and two dimples completed his all-too-perfect face.

"Thanks, Steve."

Dani left the daycare and felt as if she could leap and click her heels together. She not only landed the job, but it was exactly what she was planning on making her life's work. Her primary responsibility would be working one-on-one with a little girl who has Down syndrome. *Thank You, Lord!*

Since it was almost noon, Dani decided to head to the cafeteria for lunch before returning to her room.

At first, she barely noticed the couple sitting on a bench under one of the many crepe myrtle trees scattered about the campus. *Could that be . . . Carter? Surely not, but it certainly looks like him.* Her heart rattled oddly, and she diverted onto a sidewalk that passed several yards behind the bench, but close enough for Dani to be sure it was him.

Well, Carter Matthews, it appears you have forgotten that you couldn't wait to see me. Guess the red head stroking your forehead helped you forget.

Dani harrumphed as the girl pulled out a tissue and wiped Carter's forehead. *Oh, brother.*

Chapter 4

But the wisdom that comes from heaven is first of all pure; then peace-loving, considerate, submissive, full of mercy and good fruit, impartial and sincere. James 3:17

After seeing Carter with another girl, Dani was in no mood for lunch. *I sure misunderstood Carter's interest in me. Even so, he could at least have called.* Anger replaced Dani's disappointment, shock, and confusion. *Fine, Carter Matthews, you're not the only fish in the pond.* She strode back to her dorm ignoring the beads of perspiration escaping down her back, picked up the receiver on the second floor phone, and called Baker Hall.

It shocked Dani that Steve answered. "Baker Hall."

"May I speak to Steve Foster, please?"

"This is Steve, Dani."

"How did you know it was me?"

"I recognized your voice."

"Oh. Is the invitation for tonight still open?"

"Of course. How about I meet you outside your dorm at six-thirty?"

"Sounds good."

"See you then. I'm glad you called."

"Bye, Steve."

As soon as she closed the door of her room, Dani plopped on her bed, grabbed her journal and a pen from her night stand, and jotted an entry.

Dear Betts, I must admit I'm pretty angry right now. Carter arrived on campus last evening and hasn't tried to call me. Not only that, I just saw him with another girl and she was all over him! I guess I misjudged him. So, sister dear, I am going to a concert tonight with Steve Foster, and from what I hear, he's a very popular guy with the girls.

Dani dropped her pen and stretched out on her bed. The anger she felt moments ago evaporated into sadness and regret. *Father, I don't want to begin this year with angry thoughts. Help me to move on with my life and accept that Carter already has a girlfriend.*

Courtney tapped on the door and shuffled into the room. "Just me, Dani."

"Hey," Dani said without sitting up.

"You okay?"

"Fit as a fiddle."

"Fine as frog's hair, huh?" Courtney dropped onto her own bed and studied her new friend.

"Happy as a clam," Dani said with no smile evident.

"Okay, spill it, roomie."

"Well, there's this guy, Carter Matthews . . ."

Dani poured out her heart to Courtney. "So, tonight I'm going to a concert with Steve."

"I see. Hmm . . . do you think you're really interested in Steve?"

"Well, why not?"

"Can I just give you a teeny bit of advice, Dani?"

"Sure."

"Don't use Steve."

Dani sprang upright and scowled at Courtney. "Use him? How am I using him?"

"I mean, don't go out with him for any reason except you genuinely care for him."

"I do care for him. I mean, I don't know him that well, but he seems nice. Besides, he's the one who invited me, Courtney. How is that using him?"

"If you're going because you are angry with—"

"I don't think that's what I'm doing. I don't want Steve to get hurt. That's for sure."

"Well, that's my advice for today." Courtney hopped up. "Did you have lunch?"

"No, I'm not really hungry."

"Well, I'm starving. So, I'll see ya later."

"Wait a sec." Dani stood and held out her arms to Courtney. "Thanks."

Courtney chuckled and hugged Dani. "All's well that ends well?"

"Good as gold."

After Courtney left, Dani picked out an outfit for her date and reviewed her schedule. She pulled out her *Introduction to Special Education* book and began reading ahead. *Am I doing what Courtney said, "Using Steve?"*

❄❄❄

Dani glanced at her image in the floor length mirror. Her simple, sleeveless coral dress with a contrasting belt felt right for the occasion. She fluffed her hair, grabbed her purse, and left to meet Steve.

As she descended the steps, it surprised her that Steve was not there. She checked her watch. *Hmm* . . .

"Hello there, beautiful."

She whirled in the direction of Steve's voice and then rolled her eyes at the sight. He was sitting above her on one of the huge pillars that framed the entrance to Livingston Hall. "Hi Steve. Is this how you usually meet your date?"

He jumped down to a lower level and then to the sidewalk beside her. "No, only special ones."

"I see. I am duly impressed."

Steve offered her his arm. "Shall we go m'lady?"

"We shall." Dani linked her arm through his.

He covered her hand with his free hand and smiled down at her. She returned his smile. *He is certainly handsome. That's for sure.*

Steve's friend, Justin, was first on the program and played a number of piano pieces. He was definitely a talented young man.

I wonder if Carter and his girlfriend are here? She resisted the urge to scan the room.

By the time a classical guitarist and a soloist had performed, Dani shivered and wished she had brought along a sweater. *They really have the AC set awfully low.* She shivered again.

"You cold?" Steve whispered.

"A bit."

"We can leave if you like."

"I'll be all right."

Steve slipped his arm around her where it remained for the rest of the concert.

"Would you like to grab a snack at The Oasis?" Steve asked as they exited the auditorium.

"I don't think so. I have some things I need to do."

"Okay. Thanks for going tonight. I hope you enjoyed the concert."

"I did. It was very nice."

"Wasn't Justin amazing?"

"He's very talented, for sure."

I can't believe how cold it was in there!

Chapter 5

For the Lord gives wisdom; from his mouth come knowledge and understanding. Proverbs 2:6

By the end of the second week of classes, Dani had her routine of her job, class attendance, and homework down pat, and she loved it all.

Little two-year-old Mandi captured Dani's heart the first day she worked with her in the daycare. A puff of brown curls as soft as velvet crowned her tiny rosy-cheeked face, and her small brown eyes sparkled with curiosity.

Since Mandi could not walk without assistance, and her language development was delayed, Dani's primary job would be working with her on these two skills. That suited Dani just fine. Thoughts of little Joey back home and the progress he made over the summer filled her heart with joy. She hoped to do the same for Mandi.

Dani had seen Carter a few times but so far had managed to avoid him. She worried about how she would handle a face-to-face encounter.

When she entered the cafeteria on Thursday evening, she spotted him with his girlfriend and quickly turned around and left.

It's hard to believe Carter couldn't at least have been honest with me.

Dani and Steve had shared several unplanned lunches together since he always seemed to be in the cafeteria when she arrived. On Friday afternoon, he caught her between classes. "Dani, how would you like to grab dinner at The Oasis rather than the cafeteria tonight?"

"Okay. Sevenish?"

"Yeah. See you there."

She spent the afternoon in her room writing the rough draft of a research paper for one of her classes, wrote a note home to her parents, and decided to take a shower and change before dinner.

Steve had arrived early and beckoned to her as she entered the snack bar. *He is such a nice guy.* She smiled and waved. She felt comfortable with him and enjoyed their friendly banter.

"My Greek class is going to be a challenge . . . "

I suppose Carter is with his girlfriend tonight. Thoughts of Carter continually invaded Dani's mind much to her dismay. Each time it happened, she scolded herself, to no avail.

"Dani? Earth to Dani."

"I'm sorry, Steve. Guess I was zoning out there for a moment. What were you saying?"

"Oh, it wasn't really important. What do you say we order now? You ready?"

"Sure."

"Before we do, I'd like to ask you a question."

"Okay."

"How about going to the homecoming dance with me."

"Uh . . . when is it?"

"October 19th."

"I don't know, Steve. I have so much reading to do for my classes."

"Come on, Dani. All work and no pl—"

"I know. I know. Makes Dani a dull girl."

"That's not what I was going to say."

"All right. Let's have it."

"Makes Steve a sad boy." He hung his head, frowned, and stuck out his lip.

Dani laughed. "All right, I'll go."

"Great! Now what would you like to eat? A pizza? Hamburger? Hot dog?"

Dani stared at the menu board. Um . . . how about a chili dog?"

"Okay. I'll be right back."

Dani spotted a couple of students that she vaguely remembered from last year and smiled at them. She pulled a napkin out of the holder and wiped up spills and crumbs that someone had left behind. She organized the salt, pepper, mustard, and ketchup containers around the napkin holder, and then drummed her fingers on the table.

Steve returned with two Cokes and hot dogs piled high with scrumptious looking chili.

"Yum," Dani said.

"Yeah, they make good chili dogs."

The two chomped on their meals and enjoyed small talk about their classes.

"Tell me, Dani, what you find so compelling about special education? Do you have experience working with special needs kids?"

She started to reply to Steve's question, but her breath caught in her throat. She stammered and flushed red as she watched Carter Matthews saunter alone into The Oasis. As if she had snapped a picture of him, Dani captured the image of Carter impeccably dressed in gray slacks and a pale pink sweater. *Stop my throttling heart, Lord!*

Steve noticed her embarrassment and turned to see the

reason. He waved at Carter who smiled and pointed at him, and mini-saluted her.

She nodded, feeling as if her face would catch fire at any moment.

"You know Carter, Dani?"

"Uh . . . I met him on campus a few times." *Not exactly the truth, Dani.*

"He's a good guy."

"Steve, if it's all right, I'd like to call it a night." She ignored her thumping heart.

"You sure? It's early."

"Sorry. I need to get to the library before it closes. Let me pay you for —"

"I got it."

"Thank you."

Dani tidied the table as Steve dumped their trash. As the two left The Oasis, she refused to train her eyes in Carter's direction.

"See you later, Steve. Thanks again."

"You're very welcome. I think I'll go for a quick run before they turn out the lights on the track." He kissed her cheek and sailed down the sidewalk toward the track leaving Dani in shock.

He kissed me? Lord, I need your wisdom. I like Steve, I really do, but do I like him enough to be his girlfriend?

She spent two hours in the library and estimated about a fourth of that was spent trying to sort out her feelings and silently asking God to give her wisdom.

Maybe I should call Carter and confront him. After all, he owes me an explanation. Don't be ridiculous, Dani. He didn't promise you anything but a phone call for crying out loud. I do like Steve. He's handsome, funny, and so easy to be with. And he's a Christian who takes his faith seriously. What more could a girl want in a guy? I can easily picture us together. Maybe I should go out with him for a while and see if I develop romantic feelings for him. That is, if he asks me. I know he already has feelings for me. But, what if I hurt him? Lord knows I've hurt enough people in my life already. I don't know what to do. Maybe I should just forget about guys altogether!

She dropped her books into her bag and headed for the door aware of a nagging headache.

"Hey, Dani! How are you?" Jessica Jenkins caught up with her as she headed outside.

"Jess, how nice to see you. I'm fine. When is the Bible study getting together?"

"Next Tuesday night. My room. You coming?"

"Sure. Will it be every Tuesday night?"

"Yep. Seven o'clock. So glad you're coming again."

"I'll try and keep my Tuesday nights free."

Finally, the hot summer temperatures had moderated, and a pleasant breeze met the girls as they stepped outside.

Dani found Courtney lying on her bed, arms under her head. When she saw Dani, she grinned, and the grin grew into a smile that exploded into laughter.

"Okay, Courtney. You look like the cat that swallowed the canary. What's going on?"

"I'm walking on air," Courtney said as she kicked her legs in the air."

"It's obvious you're as happy as a pig in mud. You going to tell me the good news or keep me in the dark?"

"Sure as shootin'. Better sit down."

Dani dropped her book bag beside her bed and plopped down. "Spill the beans, girl."

"I have a date for the homecoming dance."

"That's great, Courtney. Why are you so shocked? You're a great gal."

"You know, Dani, I have a lot of friends, but I have never had a boyfriend. I didn't even get asked to my high school prom."

"Sorry, Courtney. Who are you going with?"

"Michael Williams. Do you know him?"

"I don't think so."

"He's older than me, but is only a freshman. He is soooo handsome!"

"I'm happy for you, Courtney. I'll be going, too."

"You are? That's great. Maybe we can double."

"Doubling would be fun, but we have to ask the guys. Must have our ducks in a row."

"Dani, you're smarter than the average bear."

Dani loved the cliché jousting with Courtney.

Chapter 6

He holds success in store for the upright, he is a shield to those whose walk is blameless, for he guards the course of the just and protects the way of his faithful ones. Proverbs 2:7-8

The following Monday, Steve was not in the cafeteria when Dani arrived for dinner. *Good, maybe I can do some reading.* She had checked out a book on Down Syndrome in hopes to learn more about the disability.

Dani picked at her salad as she poured over the book. It offered a number of strategies she thought would work with Mandi. *I need to get back to the dorm, so I can jot down some of these ideas.*

"Oh!" Dani jumped as someone tapped her shoulder.

"I'm sorry I startled you," Carter Matthews said.

Dani risked eye contact with him, and his radiant smile made her feel as if the sun had winked at her.

"Hello, Carter."

"How are you?"

"I'm fine," she said as heat started in her toes and made its way to her face. "Would you like to sit down?"

"Are you expecting Steve?"

"He's usually here, but so far I haven't seen him."

Carter pulled out the chair opposite her and sat.

"No girlfriend this evening, Carter?"

"Girlfriend? What do you mean?"

"Well, I saw you with a girl, and I—"

A frown wrinkled Carter's forehead. "You saw me with a girl? What did she look like?"

Dani pulled a napkin from the holder and busily wiped the table. "She had long, reddish hair as I recall." Dani struggled to sound nonchalant.

"Oh, you probably saw me with my friend, Amber. She's not my girlfriend."

Harrump! Didn't look that way to me.

Carter grinned and ran both hands through the mass of dark curls that crowned his head and spilled slightly over his ears caressing his collar.

"Amber Wheeler and I have been friends since kindergarten. Our parents are best friends, and Amber is like my little sister."

Dani forced herself to look into his steely blue eyes as she tried to hide the unnerving feelings that were coursing through her body. *Friends?* "Oh, I'm sorry. I shouldn't have jumped to conclusions."

"That's quite all right."

Why is he grinning? I am such an idiot.

"May I ask *you* a question, Dani?"

"Certainly." She clasped her hands together under the table to stop them from trembling.

"Are you and Steve an item?" He narrowed his eyes and sought hers.

"An item? I don't think I would call us that."

"I see you together a lot, so I thought—"

"Steve and I have become friends."

Ask him why he didn't call.

"Carter, I have been wondering why you didn't call when you arrived on campus? You made a point of saying that the last time we talked."

"What do you mean? I *did* call you."

"I didn't get any messages that you called."

"As soon as I arrived on Monday evening, I called your dorm and left word with a girl on your floor. She said she'd give you the message."

Dani rolled her eyes. *Nobody on our floor would do that. We look out for each other.*

Impelled to convince her, Carter continued. "I woke on Tuesday morning with a temperature and sore throat and headed for the infirmary. The doctor swabbed my throat and gave me medication. I planned to try calling you again, but nausea set in, and I staggered outside to a bench. That's where Amber found me, and probably where you saw us. I felt a little better that evening, but when I tried calling your dorm nobody answered the phone."

The concert.

Hope eased into Dani's heart.

"I was sick all day Wednesday and Thursday. Couldn't keep anything down. Amber, who is an assistant in the infirmary, called to say my throat tested positive for strep. On Friday, I saw you with Steve and because I didn't hear from you, I figured you had fallen for him."

"I haven't 'fallen' for anyone, as you put it. When you didn't call, and I saw you with the redhead—"

"Amber."

"The two of you looked pretty chummy to me."

"Oh, I get it. You *did* see Amber and me on the bench together."

"Right. And the way she—" Dani didn't know how to express what she saw.

Confusion registered on Carter's face, and he suddenly burst out laughing.

"I'm glad you find this so amusing."

"It *is* amusing. The day you saw us, I was sick."

"So, Amber was helping you feel better?"

"No. She was concerned that my temp was so high. She is a nursing student."

Is he telling the truth, Lord?

"Trust me, Amber and me? Never!"

"I . . . I don't know what to say." Dani took a sip of water and continued. "When you didn't call, and I saw you with Amber, I accepted a date with Steve."

"So, are the two of you serious?"

"Actually, I feel Steve would like to be, but . . . "

"But you went out with him because you figured I wasn't interested."

"Something like that."

"Steve Foster is a great guy, and I will certainly understand if you want to continue dating him."

"I am not dating him."

"Well, what do you call it?"

"We're just friends. I went to a concert with him the first week I was here. *Should I tell him the real reason I went with Steve to the concert?*

"I've seen you together several times, Dani."

"I know. Steve always saves a place for me in the cafeteria. He has invited me to go with him to the homecoming dance."

"And you accepted?"

"I saw no reason not to. I like Steve. He's interesting and fun."

"I see. Hmm . . . . Well, if you don't really think he's the one for you, you need to—"

"Tell him. I know."

"Obviously, he's interested in you."

"I've just been so confused, and . . . well, hurt."

"I understand. We sure got off to a rocky start, didn't we? I do want to get to know you better, but I can't do that as long as you're seeing Steve. He's a brother in Christ, and deserves honesty."

"You're right. I don't want to hurt Steve either. I can see I need some serious prayer time over this."

"I'll pray, too. I only want what is best."

"Thanks, Carter." Dani tidied up the table, as Carter rose to leave.

"It was good to finally talk to you. Now, I'm off to study. I'm still behind in my reading after missing three days of classes." He patted her shoulder as he left, and warmth surged down her arm.

❄❄❄

After Carter left the cafeteria, Dani couldn't concentrate on her book. She dropped it back into her book bag, dumped the salad into the trash can, and headed to her dorm. Thoughts about Carter and their ridiculous misunderstandings swirled in her mind. *I should have called him, even if I did see him with Amber. Still . . . he is the one who said he would call.*

"Hey, where are you going so fast? Have you already had lunch?"

"Steve!"

"The one and only," Steve said as he bowed and doffed an imaginary hat.

"Oh, you weren't here, so I . . ." *Time for honesty.*

She looked into Steve Foster's smiling brown eyes and wished she could match what she saw there.

"The truth is, Steve, Carter Matthews and I had a talk, and I'm a bit troubled at the moment."

"Oh?" he said as he placed an arm around her shoulder and gently pulled her aside from the group of students entering the cafeteria.

Tears moistened her eyes, and she blinked them away. "We need to talk, Steve."

"Okay. Now?"

"No. I need some time alone first to think and pray. I hope you understand." She regretted the frown that wrinkled his forehead and erased his dimples, knowing she had caused it.

"Of course. No problem, Dani." He dropped his hand from her shoulder. "Well . . . why don't you call me when you're ready to talk?"

"Okay. I . . I guess I'll see you around." She turned from him and headed out the door leaving him standing as if he were frozen in place.

Chapter 7

Do not be anxious about anything, but in every situation, by prayer and petition, with thanksgiving, present your requests to God.
Philippians 4:6

Dani all but ran to Livingston Hall. By the time she reached her room, an intense need to pray gripped her soul. She had never experienced this before, and it drove her straight to her knees.

Oh, Father, I have been so foolish. Forgive me for making assumptions and judging Carter. . . .

Dani was unaware of how long she cried out to God, but when she rose, she knew exactly what she had to do. She sat for a moment on the edge of her bed and prayed again—this time, a prayer of thanksgiving. *I am so thankful, Father, that I can come to You, knowing You hear and will answer me. It is Your forgiveness, Your peace, and most of all, Your wisdom I needed, and You graciously gave them to me.* Dani felt as if she had been lifted and placed before the very throne of God surrounded by holy angels. This had happened to her once before when she had invited Christ to be her Savior, and the feeling remained with her for days. She had tried to explain it to her mother, but words failed her. Her heart nearly burst with love and adoration of her heavenly Father, and she remained transfixed until a knock wrenched her back to the present.

"Telephone for Dani Krieg."

"Amen" Dani whispered before responding.

❈❈❈

"Shannon! It's so good to hear your voice! How are you doing?"

Shannon was Dani's best friend from high school.

"How am I? Very busy these days!"

Dani laughed. "The baby's keeping you hopping, huh?"

"Oh, does he ever."

"I can't wait to see him."

"How is school going?"

"Well . . . I love my classes, and I'm working with the most adorable little Down Syndrome girl, Mandi, three mornings a week."

"Sounds like a perfect job for you. What about Carter Matthews? You couldn't wait to see him again."

Dani thought about telling Shannon the whole story about what had transpired between Carter and her but realized it wasn't the time or place. "Carter and I have talked, but . . . well, it's kind of complicated."

"Sounds mysterious."

"I'll explain everything when I get home for Thanksgiving."

"I want you all to myself one afternoon."

"You've got it, my friend."

When Dani returned to her room, she found Courtney sitting on her bed chomping on potato chips. "Hey, Court."

Courtney had learned to recognize Dani's moods by her tone of voice. "Okay, out with it and no beating around the bush."

"What do you mean?" Dani asked sinking onto her desk chair.

"A little birdie told me something's wrong."

"That little birdie was as right as rain."

Courtney closed the chip bag, dangled her feet over the side of her bed, and studied Dani. "I'm a good listener, you know."

Tears pooled in Dani's eyes, and she swiped them with the back of her hand. "I've been so . . so stupid, Courtney. It's about Carter."

"Okay. Did you ever get a chance to talk to him?"

"Yes, and I have been so wrong about him."

"Meaning?"

"Well, remember I told you he said he would call when he arrived on campus, and how excited he said he would be to see me again?"

"I remember."

"Well . . . that's what I believed until . . ."

Dani paced the small room as she shared the story with Courtney.

"Oh, I'm beginning to get the picture. You decided to go out with Steve to get back at Carter?"

Dani nodded.

"So, do you have feelings for Carter?"

"I do. I was angry and hurt when he didn't call, or I didn't *think* he called."

"Okay, so you feel like you were not being honest with Steve because you knew deep down you weren't really interested in him, right?"

"I do *like* Steve but only as a friend."

"What do you think Steve feels for you?"

Dani pursed her lips, returned to the chair, and looked into her friend's eyes. "I know he's . . . he's—"

"Falling for you."

"Yes. At least, he appears to be."

"What now?"

"I prayed a short time ago for the Lord to show me what I need to do."

"And?"

"I know I have to be honest with Steve."

"For sure."

"I hate to even think about that, Courtney. He's such a great guy."

"True. He does deserve honesty, though."

"I have to think about how to tell him."

"You'll do the right thing. I'm sure of it."

"Well, I'm sure of this one thing," Dani said, as a grin brightened her face, "You're a blessing in disguise."

"Ditto that."

Chapter 8

Be very careful, then, how you live—not as unwise but as wise. Ephesians 5:15a

On her way to breakfast Wednesday morning, Dani spied Steve running in her direction dressed in a tee shirt, shorts, and sneakers. *Out for his morning run.*
"Hey," he said as he halted and gasped for air.
"You're out bright and early."
"Yeah. Gotta keep in shape," he said with a smile.
"Uh . . . we need to talk, Steve. How about lunch today? You available?"
"For you, I'm always available."
Oh, brother. "Cafeteria at twelve?"
Steve swiped the sweat trickling into his eyes as his smile faded. "Sounds good."
Dani's stomach churned at the prospect of the meeting with him, and decided that toast was all she could manage for breakfast and headed to her job at the daycare center.

Working with Mandi didn't feel like a job to her at all, but today, thoughts of what she would say to Steve and how he would react made it hard for her to focus.

She decided to skip her 11 o'clock class and instead made her way to the small chapel that had recently been completed thanks to a wealthy alumnus. She needed to be alone with the Lord. For the next hour, she simply prayed and rested before Him, as He stilled her mind. *Help me, Father, to consider how I treat people. I have hurt so many over the last two years—my parents, Kurt, my friends—so many. I never want to do that again. Thank You for preventing me from entering into a relationship with Steve on a deeper level. Who knows how that would have ended since I knew my feelings didn't match his. You are a merciful and loving God.*

❄❄❄

The talk with Steve had gone better than she thought probably because she took time to pray about it. A few days later, Carter called and invited her to a movie the college was showing in the Student Union building. Her thought that this would be their first date skimmed her mind as she headed to the library.

❄❄❄

The moment Dani spotted Carter at the entrance to the SU, she caught her breath and froze in place.

He is so incredibly good looking!

Carter was standing with his hands in the pockets of tan trousers topped with a yellow sweater that perfectly complimented the dark curls that framed his finely carved facial features.

When he spotted her, he smiled and waved.

Dani returned his wave and wended her way toward him through the throng of students.

"Hi, there," he said as a smile lit up his face.

Dani fluffed her hair. "Hey."

She was glad she had worn her pink a-line dress that fell gracefully just below her knees. Combined with her simple white sweater, she felt she had dressed appropriately.

Carter guided her inside, and Dani felt the warmth of his touch even after he had removed his hand and found seats for them.

"Would you like a snack?" he asked. "I smell popcorn."

"No, thanks."

"I heard this is a good movie. I hope you'll like it."

"I'm sure I will. The college seems to be trying to provide more on-campus things for students to do. First, The Oasis, then pool tables, and now movies."

Carter nodded in agreement.

Dani had heard that *Raiders of the Lost Ark* was good, but she had trouble focusing on it. Sitting this close to Carter called for a whole new set of thoughts and emotions she was unaccustomed to. *Why is my heart thumping as loudly as if it were outside my body? Can he hear it? Probably thinks I'm a silly schoolgirl.* She dared not glance at him for fear he would confirm her doubts. She hugged herself to still her trembling hands, closed her eyes, and focused on Harrison Ford. When Carter sought her hand and eyes, she knew her heart wasn't the only one thumping.

❄❄❄

Following their first date, Carter and Dani spent as much time together as they could manage, given their heavy class loads and work responsibilities.

As Dani headed to the daycare, she was excited to see if Mandi had made progress. She peeked inside the playroom and spied Mandi sitting among colorful toys.

The moment she spotted Dani, she scrambled on all fours to meet her as she squealed, "Dan-nee, Dan-nee."

Dani scooped her up and kissed her chubby cheek. "Good morning, Mandi,"

Mandi giggled.

"Can you say, 'Good morning?'"

Mandi chuckled and hooked her finger in her mouth.

Dani stood Mandi on wobbly legs. "Let's walk, Mandi. Let's walk. Good girl!"

Looks like I'm losing my heart to two people here at Brady—a big handsome guy and a little charming girl.

Dani's singing, clapping, and encouraging words as she worked with Mandi spilled over to the other workers, and soon the playroom blossomed with excitement.

When she had to leave for class, she plopped down beside Mandi who was busy playing with blocks. "I have to go now, Mandi. Can you say, bye-bye?"

No response.

"Bye-bye, Mandi." Dani stood to leave.

"Bye-bye, Dan-nee."

Dani smiled as joyful tears blurred her vision. *I knew you could do it.*

She checked her watch, and decided if she hurried, she could check her mailbox before class.

Her breath quickened as she recognized Carter's impeccable handwriting on the envelope she pulled from the box. Excitement rippled in her chest as she read the enclosed note.

Dear Dani,
These last few days have been the most exciting time of my life. I believe God has brought us together and has a wonderful plan for us. Hope to see you at lunch. I have some good news. Carter

Dani smiled at the words. *The most exciting time of his life! Wow!*

Finding time to meet and talk had been a challenge for Carter and Dani. Even though they had been able to share dinner on most days, their time together was limited due to their studies and the fact that their classes were on opposite ends of the campus. Their stroll about the grounds on Sunday afternoons afforded them the most alone time. During their long, leisurely walks, Dani learned that Carter knew without a doubt that he was called to be a pastor. He grew up attending church, but refused to go when he reached his teen years. When a friend invited him to a youth rally at his church, reluctantly, he agreed. It was at that rally, that Carter gave his life to Christ. His zeal to serve God grew in the years that followed, and the Holy Spirit led him to study for the ministry.

Wow, if Carter and I get married, that would make me a pastor's wife! Can I do that? Slow down, Dani, you've just started dating, for heaven's sake!

Dani folded the note, stuck it into her purse, and checked her watch. *Late for class!*

❊❊❊

Dani hurried to meet Carter for lunch. She glanced down at her skirt wrinkled from her time with Mandi and smoothed it with her hands before greeting him.

"Hi beautiful," he said as his smile almost took her breath away.

"Hi yourself."

"Hungry?"

"Sure am."

"It's so nice out today, what do you say we grab something and eat on one of the benches?"

"Sounds great."

As they entered the cafeteria, Dani smiled at Carter's obvious growing popularity. She loved the way he took time to greet everyone with a smile or a handshake.

Dani unwrapped the thickly-sliced ham and cheese sandwich she had chosen and stuck a straw into her Coke. She watched Carter peel the seal from his yogurt container and asked, "Is that all you're having?"

"This and an apple," he said. "That's all I need."

Great. Wrinkled skirt and fat-laden lunch.

"I don't know why I ordered this big old sandwich. I'm not even that hungry."

"I try not to eat if I'm not hungry and choose what is healthy," Carter said. "After all, our bodies are God's temples, right?"

Although slender and healthy, Dani suddenly felt huge and took only two bites of her sandwich before wrapping it back up. Her tongue stuck to the roof of her mouth as she answered. "Yes, that's right. That's absolutely right." Dani made a mental note to choose her foods more carefully.

Carter munched the last of his apple, turned toward Dani, and placed his arm around her shoulders.

She lay back against him and inhaled deeply savoring the autumn-scented air. She loved this season when trees dressed themselves in God's colors displaying His majesty to the world.

With his free hand, Carter reached for her chin and gently turned her to face him. When his eyes met hers, warmth surged through her body, and she longed to have him pull her into his arms. If he did that, more than likely they'd both be expelled because of college rules about displays of affection. As it was, they were taking a risk.

Carter moaned ever so gently and leaned even closer to her. "I'm falling in love with you, Dani."

His words wrapped her in sunshine. *Is this what real love feels like, Lord?*

Dani closed her eyes, massaged her temples, and glanced at him with misty eyes.

"What's wrong, Dani?"

"I'm . . . I'm scared of making a huge mistake."

"You don't have to say anything you don't feel, Dani. I don't want to rush you." Carter removed his arm from around her.

Dani pulled a tissue from her pocket and blotted her eyes. "Carter, I know I am attracted to you, and I love being with you, but I want to be very sure it is love I feel."

"I totally understand."

"Remember I shared that I had been engaged before?"

"Yes. To Kurt, right?"

"Yes. We were high school sweethearts. I *thought* I was in love with him, but looking back, I'm not sure it was real love, and I hurt him terribly. I don't want to make that mistake again."

Dani checked her watch and shook her head to clear her mind and refocus on the present.

"Hey, you said you had good news. Let's have it."

"Well, I've been offered a position as an interim student pastor of a small church."

"Really? How did that happen?"

"I saw a note on the bulletin board and asked Mr. Wheeler, my advisor, about it. He urged me to apply."

"I thought you had to have your degree before you become a pastor."

"Yes, ideally. But according to Mr. Wheeler, this church has used student pastors in the past. My guess is that they would struggle to pay for a full-time pastor."

"Where is the church?" Dani asked.

"It's only a few miles from here."

"Will you be able to keep up with your classes?"

"I don't think that will be a problem."

"That's fantastic!"

"Oh, I almost forgot to tell you that my folks are coming this weekend."

"Coming here?"

"Yeah. They took my sister, Margot, to check out some interior design schools in the Chicago area. I guess she's interested in making that her career. Anyway, they're on their way home. So, they can only visit a few hours on Saturday afternoon."

"Brady will be hopping this weekend for sure. After all it is Homecoming."

"Oh, I forgot about that. You're sure you don't want to go to the dance, right?"

"Not really. I'd rather meet your folks."

"And I'm not interested in going to the football game." Carter glanced at Dani. "Unless you are?"

"No, it'll be great meeting your folks."

"We'll probably go out to lunch."

"Great."

"I told my dad that I met a fantastic young lady, and he is excited to meet you."

"Your dad? What about your mom?"

"When I called, Mom had a headache and I didn't want to bother her."

"What if they don't like me?"

"Why wouldn't they like you?" Carter sought her hand. "You're the best thing that's ever happened to me, except for my relationship with the Lord, of course."

"That's sweet. Thank you, Carter."

"I mean it."

"By the way, I want to hear more about that."

"About what?"

"About how God worked in your life to lead you to study for the ministry."

"Absolutely. And I would like to learn more about what drew you to love working with special needs kids."

Carter checked his watch. "Another time, though, because we're going to be late for our next class."

Chapter 9

October 1981

So do not worry, saying, 'What shall we eat?' or 'What shall we drink?' or 'What shall we wear?' Matthew 6:31

Dani checked her hair and makeup in the bathroom mirror. She smiled at the updo Courtney had created for her that morning. *I think Carter will like it.* She scooted to the window for the third time to look for the Matthews' car—a 1981 Cadillac Eldorado, according to Carter. *They said they'd be here by ten and it's almost noon. Guess I'll try and get some reading done.*

Dani pulled out her *Exceptional Children* textbook and flipped to the assigned chapter. Several pages later with no recall of what she read, Dani slapped the book closed and checked the parking lot again. *Finally.*

Wow, Carter looks so much like his dad. Mr. Matthews had the same dark hair as Carter, but splashed with gray. Carter's mother's Farah Faucett hair style fell around her shoulders and perfectly completed what could have been a *Glamour* magazine layout. She stretched catlike and held out her arms for Carter's hug.

Dani expected Margot to look like her stylish mother, but there was no resemblance as she squeezed her way from the back seat. Dani laughed at the picture of Margot in her cutoff jeans and oversized top that covered but didn't disguise her ample figure. *Wow, what an interesting family.*

Margot removed her baseball cap and swung it into a bow to her brother as she waited for his hug. It surprised Dani that Carter fake-punched her arm instead.

Dani saw that Carter was pointing to her window and she waved down at them. Her heart pounded with a combination of nerves and excitement as she grabbed her purse and flew down the stairs to meet the Matthews.

Carter smiled as Dani approached revealing his perfect teeth. "Dad, I'd like you to meet Danita Krieg, Dani for short. Dani, my father, Hugh Matthews."

She offered her hand to him, but he pulled her into a warm hug. "It's a pleasure to meet you, Dani." His smile crinkled the corners of his eyes.

Carter grinned broadly and draped his arm around his mother who smiled up at him with adoring eyes. "Dani, this is my mother, Sheila.

Carter's mom, who appeared to have noticed Dani for the first time, patted her hand. "Dani, it's lovely to meet you, dear."

"And my sister, Margo," Carter said as he nodded in Margot's direction.

Margot hugged Dani in an apparent attempt to compensate for her mother's coldness and said, "Great to meet you, Dani."

"I'm so happy to meet all of you."

"Carter. where can we get a coffee?"

"Since it's lunchtime, we can see what they're serving in the cafeteria. And they always have coffee available."

"The cafeteria? You're kidding, right?"

"The cafeteria will be fine, Carter." Mr. Matthews squeezed his son's shoulder affectionately.

"Yeah, let's do it. I'm starved." Margot said.

"You're always starved," her mother smirked. "I saw a restaurant a few miles up the road."

"Mom, for crying out loud, the cafeteria is fine."

"Margot, please."

"Yes, Mommie dearest."

Dani smothered a chuckle at Margot's use of the famous movie title.

Mrs. Matthews ended up convincing everyone to lunch at an off-campus restaurant. *Looks like Carter's mom is used to getting her own way about things.*

All through lunch, Dani watched and weighed the interaction between the members of the Matthews family. *Obviously, Margot has her father's warm and kind personality and detests her mother's obsession with looks. Her clothing clearly shouts that. Mr. Matthews is the perpetual peacemaker who I suspect has been trying to keep the peace for years. Then, there's Carter. Hmm . . . it seems he's closer to his mother? That surprises me a bit.*

"Carter, so you're determined to go through with this plan of yours to be a pastor?" Sheila asked.

"Sheila, would you please just drop it?" Hugh Matthews said.

"I've told you, Mom" Carter said, "I plan to study for the ministry. I'm sorry you don't approve, but—"

"Dani, my wife seems to have forgotten that our son is an adult with a mind and plans of his own."

Dani didn't know how to respond to Mr. Matthews' comment and remained silent.

Sheila rolled her eyes, dabbed her mouth, and tossed her napkin onto her plate.

"Well, I guess we had better get you two back to the campus," Mr. Matthews said with an embarrassed laugh.

"It's been a pleasure meeting all of you," Dani said in an attempt to lighten the mood.

❄❄❄

Relief flooded Dani as the Matthews' car sped away. She and Carter waved until the car disappeared from sight.

"So, you've met my family, Dani. I hope it wasn't too traumatic."

"I'm glad I met them. They are obviously proud of you, as I am, I might say."

"Nice save," Carter said with a chuckle. "Well, I need to get some reading done this afternoon so—"

"And I have a paper due Monday. See you at dinner?"

Carter squeezed her hand and winked. "Dinner it is."

❄❄❄

Dani retreated to her room and collapsed on a chair. *Oh, what a day!*

I wish you were here, Betts. The thought prompted Dani to grab a pen and record the exhausting experience in her journal.

Dear Betts, this day, so far has been taxing, to say the least. Carter's parents and his sister arrived on campus to visit with him and meet me. I was a nervous wreck. I couldn't decide what to wear, but thanks to Courtney's help, I finally decided on my corduroy skirt and pink sweater. I wanted Carter to be proud of me, and I think the outfit worked. Can you believe his mom thought eating in the college cafeteria was beneath her? She pouted like a spoiled brat until Mr. Matthews gave in and agreed on lunch off campus. So, we all piled into the car and drove into town to the Cascades restaurant. Our lunch probably cost a lot, but money seems to be no object for this family. I was on pins and needles the whole time trying to think of the right things to say to a family I had just met. You would like his sister, Margot.

She is smart and funny and way different from her mother. I liked her instantly. I should be reading, but I can't concentrate. How can a short visit leave me drained and exhausted? I am so tired...

"Dani? What in the world? You're gonna have one stiff neck," Courtney said.

"Huh? What time is it?"

"A little past four."

"Must have been quite a visit."

"It was." Dani yawned and stretched. "Thanks for waking me, Courtney. I'll tell you all about it later, but I really need to head to the library to do some research for a paper due on Monday. So, see you later, gator."

"After while . . . you know the drill."

Dani grabbed her book bag, and charged from the room in a whirl.

❆❆❆

Dani returned to her room a little before six. "It's me," she said as she tapped and entered.

"Come in," Courtney said. "Just ignore the mess." A pile of clothes lay on both beds. "I'm sorry, Dani. I just can't decide what to wear. I'll move those things in a sec."

"No problem. What's the big occasion?"

"Michael asked me out on a real date."

"Great. Where's he taking you?"

"Dinner and miniature golf."

"Tonight?"

"No. On Saturday."

"Oh, *next* Saturday. O. .kay," Dani said, puzzled at Courtney's anxiety over a date a week away. She moved some dresses aside and made room to sit on her bed.

"We're doubling with Kathy Warren and John Day. "Do you know them?"

"No, I don't think so."

"Kathy is nice, but I don't really know her *or* John, and I'm so nervous. I've only played miniature golf once and I was terrible. I'll probably make a fool of myself. On top of everything else, I have absolutely nothing to wear. And everything looks awful on me anyway—"

"Whoa! Hold on a minute."

Courtney plopped down on the floor, dropped her head in her hands, and sobbed.

Dani grabbed a tissue from a box on her night stand and slid down beside her friend.

Courtney sniffed and accepted the tissue Dani held out for her. "I'm sorry. It's just that, well, other than the homecoming dance, I've never had a *real* date, and I'm scared silly."

Dani scooted behind her friend. "I know just what you need," she said, "a good back massage."

"One hour to stop that," Courtney blubbered.

"Relaxing, isn't it?"

Courtney nodded.

"You need to know what a terrific person you are, and obviously Michael sees that."

"You think?"

"Courtney, you are friendly, warm, caring, wise, witty, and pretty."

"Pretty? What's wrong with *your* vision? Maybe you better borrow my glasses."

"Nothing's wrong with my vision. You are all the things I mentioned. God created you, and you're beautiful." Dani gave Courtney's shoulders one last squeeze. "After all, if Michael asked you out again, he obviously sees something lovely in you."

"You on the level with me?" Courtney asked as she blew her nose.

"You can take it to the bank!"

"I'll be a monkey's uncle."

Dani stood and glanced at the clock. "Gotta go."

"Guess you're meeting Carter for dinner, huh?"

"Yes, and I need to check my hair."

"Here, let me fix it." Courtney hopped up and fixed the stragglers that had come loose from Dani's updo. "There, pretty as a picture."

"Thanks so much." Dani turned questioning eyes to Courtney. "You sure you're okay now?"

"I'll be fine. Thanks for your pep talk."

Dani hugged Courtney. "I'll see you later," she said as she headed for the door.

As Dani neared the cafeteria, she spied Carter waiting for her on one of the benches near the entrance. Her heart fluttered at the sight of him. *He is the most handsome man I have ever seen!*

He glanced up from the paper he appeared to be studying, and their eyes met. His smile warmed her from head to toe like hot cocoa after a trek in the snow.

"Hey," she said as she approached.

"Hi, beautiful."

Dani's face reddened at the compliment. "Hope I didn't keep you waiting long?"

"As long as it takes is as long as I'll wait."

"Waxing poetic, are you?"

"Just being truthful."

Carter grasped her hand and pulled her down on the bench beside him.

She tried to still her heart that drummed at his touch. *Oh, my, I believe I'm falling in love with this man.* She felt color warm her cheeks as she squeezed his hand. The temptation to throw herself into his arms almost overwhelmed her. She was unaccustomed to such strong emotions and it almost scared her.

Carter sensed her unease and ended the moment. "How about we head inside. I'm hungry, are you?"

"Uh-uh," she said as she rose to her feet.

The two filled their plates and slid into chairs at an empty table.

"Carter, I don't think your mom likes me," Dani said before taking a bite of food.

Carter cut a piece of his roast beef. "Now, why would you say that, Dani?"

Dani sipped her iced tea. "Well, she was kind of . . . distant, I guess is the word."

"Well, Mom's got her ideas, but I'm sure she likes you. What's not to like?"

Funny way of showing it.

"I was amazed at how much you look like your dad."

"I take that as a compliment."

"It's true. And I really liked your sister."

"My sister?" Carter frowned and paused before taking the bite of green beans teetering on his fork.

"Yes. She's warm and funny and—"

"Fat."

"Carter! That's an awful thing to say about Margot."

"I know. I just wish she would take more interest in her appearance."

"Believe me, I'd give anything to have my sister back even for a day."

"I shouldn't have said that. I do love my sister."

"Speaking of family, do you think you might be interested in spending Thanksgiving with my family?"

"Well, I don't see why not. I have to let mom know I won't be home, but she doesn't cook anyway."

"I won't be able to stay the whole weekend, though."

"Why not?"

"I have to preach on Sunday."

Dani frowned and stuck out her lower lip like her brother, Davy, did when he was two, and Mom refused him a second cookie.

"You're cute when you pout."

❄❄❄

Dani scurried up the stairs to her room, relieved the hall phone was free. *Oh, brother, I should have checked with mom and dad before inviting Carter for Thanksgiving.*

"Mikey?"

"Dani! How are you?"

"I'm fine, but I hardly recognized your voice."

Micah laughed. "People are always sayin' I sound just like Dad."

A grin spread across Dani's face. *My little brothers are growing up.* "What's going on?"

"Not much. Won this years' art contest."

"That's wonderful. I think you're going to be a famous artist some day."

"Thanks, Dani."

"Mom there?"

"Yeah, hold on. Mo-om! Dani's on the phone."

Dani worked at untwisting the long phone cord as she waited for her mother to pick up.

"Hi, sweetie," Lindy said.

"Hi, Mom."

"Is anything wrong, honey?"

Of course, she would think something was wrong after what I put her through last year.

"No, I'm fine, Mom. School is going great."

"That's fantastic. Dad and I are so happy for you."

"I called to ask you a question."

"Okay. . . . "

"I have invited Carter to share Thanksgiving with us. I hope that's going to be okay with you and Dad. I'm sorry I didn't check with you first before inviting him."

"That's fine, honey. It will be nice meeting Carter after all the glowing descriptions we've heard."

"How's Dad?"

"He's fine. Always busy he is this time of year."

"Tell him, I love him."

"I sure will."

"Well, guess I better go. I have to finish up a paper, and I have some reading to do. It seems like all I do is read and write papers."

"Thanks for calling, sweetheart. We will be looking forward to seeing you and meeting that guy of yours."

Dani grinned. "Bye, Mom."

"Oh, I almost forgot to tell you," Lindy said. "Your grandfather is in the hospital."

A chill zipped down Dani's back.

Chapter 10

But he was pierced for our transgressions, he was crushed for our iniquities; the punishment that brought us peace was on him, and by his wounds we are healed. Isaiah 53:5

Several days passed since the news that Forrest Krieg, Dani's grandfather, had been hospitalized. When her mom called yesterday to say he was improving, Dani thanked God.

Forrest had always been so strong and capable, and Dani could not imagine him any other way. She admired his generosity, compassion, and faith more than anyone she had ever known. *Please watch over him, Father.*

Dani gathered her Bible and some notes she had prepared for tonight's meeting and headed to Jessica Jenkins' dorm room.

"Hey, Jess, it's me," Dani said as she pecked on Jessica's door.

"Come in," a chorus of voices sang out.

Dani squeezed onto a bed between Bobbi and Dawn. She loved the Tuesday evening Bible studies with the girls she had grown to love, but the first meeting without Carrie took some getting used to. Carrie Adams had led the group every year until she graduated. *I wonder if she went on to grad school. Thank you, Lord, for her example of love and commitment.*

"I hope you remembered you're supposed to share your testimony tonight," Jessica said.

Dani smiled and nodded. "I do remember."

"Great. How about we start with prayer?"

"Jess, could you please pray for my grandfather Krieg? He's in the hospital, but I don't know much more than that at this point."

"Sure thing. I'm sorry to hear he's ill. I know from what you've shared before that he has a special place in your heart."

Dani swiped her gathering tears.

As Jessica noted the various prayer requests the girls shared, Dani reflected on the events that had brought her to this point. Images of her beloved sister floated through her mind as she recalled that fateful night when Betts lost her life. She squeezed her eyes shut momentarily and winced at the memory. She couldn't count the number of times she regretted not pulling over and waiting out that awful thunderstorm, but she had learned not to dwell on things she couldn't change. Dani now understood how deep the love of God is for His children; how He longs for them to turn to Him, not away from Him when their lives are turned upside down; how He welcomes them to bask in His presence accepting His forgiveness for sinful and foolish behavior, and to simply trust His heart.

As Dani shared her testimony, she prayed God would use her experience to encourage the girls gathered there.

Whenever Dani and Carter had time to spend together, Carter talked continuously about Bethany Community Church where he had become a student pastor. As the two shared dinner Thursday evening, Dani smiled at Carter's enthusiastic description of Sunday's service.

"How satisfying it is to watch the congregation seemingly come alive, Dani." Carter's eyes sparkled with excitement. "Don't get me wrong, it's not *me*, but the Lord who is working through me. Did I tell you a man in his sixties accepted Christ as Savior last Sunday? I can't wait until I get out of school and become a real pastor."

"You are a real pastor," Dani said as she picked at the roast chicken on her plate.

"You know what I mean — a full-time pastor, not just a temporary position."

"This is where God has you right now. He's molding you and teaching you things that you need to know. God doesn't waste any of our experiences, Carter. If there's one thing I've learned over the past two years, it's that." She finished her mashed potatoes and buttered her roll.

Carter didn't comment as he drank the last of his tea and dabbed his mouth with his napkin. Dani noted that he left his mashed potatoes untouched.

"And . . . I talked to the head deacon about restarting their Sunday school."

"Oh, they don't have Sunday school?"

"They had stopped meeting over a year ago as their attendance dropped."

"Do you think you can get it going again?"

"I have some ideas. Mr. Phillips told me he would talk to the other deacon and get back to me."

"That's wonderful, Carter."

"How would you like to go with me Sunday?"

"To Bethany? Really? I . . . I guess I could. We're required to be in chapel on Sundays, but I could ask permission to go with you."

"Great. I'll meet you in the parking lot at nine unless I hear from you."

"It shouldn't be a problem."

"I'll walk you to your dorm if you're finished eating."

"Sure." Dani stacked their plates, swiped the table with her napkin, and carried the dishes to the counter, ignoring her uneaten roll.

❅❅❅

"Where are you going all dressed up?" Courtney asked.

"To church with Carter. How do I look?" She twirled and curtsied.

"Pretty as a picture. How did you make that happen? Going off campus to church, that is."

"I simply asked."

"Oh. I wonder if Michael and I could go with you some Sunday?"

"Courtney, that would be fantastic!"

"Say, you guys are getting awfully serious, aren't you?" She rummaged in a drawer and pulled out a pair of panty hose, examining them for runs.

A smile broke across Dani's face. "I think I'm falling in love, Courtney." She clasped her hands over her chest. "Be still my beating heart."

"Wow, that's kind of fast, isn't it?"

"Don't forget I met him when I was a freshman, and we talked on the phone several times last summer."

Courtney dropped onto her bed and tugged on the panty hose as she eyed Dani skeptically.

"Don't look at me like that. I know it really does seem like our relationship is moving fast, but—"

"But you better hurry if you're meeting him at nine."

Dani dashed to the window. "It's him! She grabbed her Bible and headed for the door.

Chapter 11

November 1981

"For I know the plans I have for you," declares the Lord, "plans to prosper you and not to harm you, plans to give you hope and a future." Jeremiah 29:11

Mrs. Albertson plunked the notes of the last verse of "Victory in Jesus," and rose to take her place in the small sanctuary of Bethany Community Church.

Oh, Betts, how they could use your piano ability here at this church.

Carter squeezed Dani's hand before heading to the podium. "Mrs. Albertson, thank you so much for playing for us this morning. How about we give her a hand?" He smiled at her and clapped in appreciation.

Mrs. Albertson's face colored a bright pink as the people clapped and a few "Amens" rang out.

Dani beamed as Carter stepped to the podium.

"If you have your Bible with you today, turn to the book of Ecclesiastes, Chapter three."

Dani flipped to the book and basked in the confident sound of Carter's smooth voice that older more experienced pastors would surely envy.

"There is a time for everything, and a season for every activity under the heavens . . . ."

There's something about him that causes people to want to listen to what he's saying. She tried to be inconspicuous as she glanced around from her second pew seat. *All eyes are on him. It's going to be interesting to see how God is going to use Carter in the years to come. People are drawn to him. I see it on campus, and I see it here with these folks.* The words to Jeremiah 29:11 floated through her mind as if written by a skywriter. *"For I know the plans I have for you," declares the* LORD, *"plans to prosper you and not to harm you, plans to give you hope and a future." Will I be part of Your plans for Carter, Lord?* Warmth eased from Dani's toes to her cheeks turning them rosy at the thought. She smiled at Carter. His eyes rested on hers for a brief second and then crisscrossed the small room to capture his listeners. Dani studied his eyes, intense with the desire for these people to grasp his vision for them. *His eyes reflect the pure innocence of his heart, his longing for others to know the Christ who claimed his heart a few short years ago.*

Dani could not harness her runaway thoughts that vacillated between dreaming of a life with Carter and then doubting it was what God wanted for her. She chided herself to focus on Carter's words, but soon retreated into her private thoughts.

"So, my question to you this morning, my friends, is this: what season of life are *you* in?"

Oh, my, I haven't heard a word he's said. What season, indeed!

❄❄❄

A cold November wind pushed into the area, and Dani pulled her jacket tightly around her as she headed for her car. *What a bummer that Carter and I can't drive together to Meadow Glen.*

Because Carter wanted to be faithful to his commitment as a student pastor, he refused to find a replacement for Thanksgiving Sunday. He insisted that Dani leave as soon as her last class ended on Wednesday so she would have plenty of time to visit with her folks. "I really need to work on my sermon, sweetheart," he had said. "I haven't had a minute, and I know I wouldn't be able to study at your folks'. I'll drive up Thanksgiving morning and should be there by ten without a problem."

She loved that he had referred to her as "sweetheart," for the first time.

I wanted to be with Carter for all four days. As it is, he'll get there Thursday morning and have to leave on Saturday to be back in Brady to preach on Sunday. Dani realized the selfishness of her thoughts, and reprimanded herself. *What's more important, getting my own way, or respecting Carter for his commitment?*

It was after 5 o'clock by the time Dani finished packing and lugged her suitcase to the car.

❋❋❋

Dani sped along the interstate as her thoughts turned from Carter to her family and friends in Ohio. *I can't wait to see the twins. I wonder if they will like Carter? Of course they will. Everyone seems to gravitate toward Carter, and the boys will, too. I just know Mom and Dad will approve of him. What more could they ask for in a son-in-law? They have told me many times that they have been praying for each of us kids to find a life-mate who loves God. My goodness, what am I thinking? I'm not a "life-mate" of Carter or anyone else for that matter.* She shook her head to clear her mind and scolded herself for her presumptuous thought regarding her relationship with Carter. *Courtney is right. We haven't known each other very long at all. Just slow down!*

Dani glanced at her gas gauge. *I should have stopped at that last exit. Too late now.* She was glad that her car was good on gas. *I'm so grateful for grandpa Krieg. Please continue to strengthen his body, Father.* Dani had rejoiced at the news that her grandfather had recovered enough from his heart attack to be home for Thanksgiving. *I have to remember to call him and grandma tomorrow. I hope I can work in a visit with Shannon and Jared, too. I'm sure their baby is really getting big.*

A state trooper parked alongside the interstate grabbed Dani's attention, and she let up on the accelerator. She breathed a sigh of relief when he didn't pull her over since she had been going well over the speed limit. *Focus, Dani!*

She tried to concentrate on her driving, but that only lasted a few miles when Carter crept into her mind again. Her pulse quickened as she recalled his warm goodbye embrace. *Oh, my, how I wanted to throw my arms around him. I wonder what Carter sees in me? Why did he pick me as his girlfriend? Any girl on campus would love to go out with him, that's for sure. He always has girls batting their eyelashes at him, finding a reason to sit near him, or engaging him in conversation. Lord, You know I try not to be jealous, but it's not easy.*

As Dani reached the exit to Meadow Glen, snowflakes spotted her windshield, and her gas gauge read "empty."

How could I have let this happen? She spotted a Pure Oil station about a mile from the exit and gratefully coasted to one of the pumps. The Pure sign that was lit when she pulled in suddenly darkened. *Oh, no. They're not open.*

Dani started to pull away just as a man exited the station and headed for her car. *Thank God.* She rolled down her window and smiled at the man leaning a bit too far into her open window. The heavy scent of grease drifted inside. "I know you're closed, but I really, really need gas. Can you help me?"

"I think I can help a pretty lady in distress," he said.

"Thank you *so* much."

"Regular?"

"Yes, please."

"Coming right up."

Dani ignored his wink as she rolled up the window, waited for him to pump the gas, and rummaged in her purse for her wallet. She studied him in her mirror, suddenly uncomfortable at the unlit and isolated location of the station and pushed down the door lock.

He set the pump to automatic and rested his long lean body against the pump and jammed his hands into his pockets. When finished, he returned the nozzle to the pump and replaced her gas cap.

Dani rolled down her window to pay him as a nervous bubble tumbled about her chest. She watched him hitch up his pants, adjust his black knit cap, and scan the area before sauntering past her window to the front of the car. When he tapped on the hood indicating for Dani to release the hood latch, she stuck her head out of the window.

"Oh, you don't need to check the oil. I'm sure it's fine."

"Don't you smell that?" he asked.

Dani sniffed. "Not really. I'm sure it's nothing."

"It'll only take a minute to be sure. Smells like you're burning oil, and that could wreck your engine."

Isn't there an oil light that's supposed to come on? She hesitated for a moment and then released the hood latch with shaky hands. Dani licked her dry lips, closed her eyes, and prayed as "Bob"— the name barely readable on his greasy blue uniform jacket—checked her oil.

Moments later, he strode to her window with the oil stick in hand. "I hate to tell you ma'am, but your oil is dangerously low. Shoot, it don't even register."

"I'm sure it'll be fine until I get home. I'm only a few miles away."

"Well, you can do that, but if it was me, I wouldn't drive a block with my oil that low." He held the dip stick for her to see.

Oh, God. What should I do? I can't risk ruining my car. This guy wouldn't try anything funny would he? She wrung her hands nervously. *I mean, he's obviously a hard worker by the looks of his uniform.*

"Well . . . okay," she said. "Put some oil in if you're sure about this."

He closed the hood. "Just pull up to the service bay and I'll open the door."

"Can't you just put it in here?"

"Nah, it's gonna take a lot of oil, ma'am. It'll only take a few minutes." He turned and walked inside.

Maybe I should call Dad. She scanned the area for a phone booth, but saw none. *Hopefully, there's a phone inside I can use. I just have to trust this guy, I guess.*

Light flooded the open service area, the door rattled up, and Bob signaled for her to drive inside.

Well, here goes. I need your protection, Father.

She started her car and drove into the garage as the door closed behind her, and all the lights went out.

Chapter 12

Rescue me, Lord, from evildoers; protect me from the violent, who devise evil plans in their hearts and stir up war every day. They make their tongues as sharp as a serpent's; the poison of vipers is on their lips. Psalm 140:1-3

Dani's hands tightened around the steering wheel, her mind awhirl in confusion and fear. Suddenly, a flashlight split the darkness.

Dani rolled down her window a few inches. "Sir," she said trying to summons a voice with authority, "I've changed my mind."

Bob strolled to her window as Dani rolled it back up. He tapped the glass with the flashlight.

"I have changed my mind," she repeated much louder this time.

"I can't let you leave here knowing you'll wreck the engine in your car. It's just not the right thing to do."

What should I do? I don't know what to do.

Bob aimed the beam of light at her and smiled. "You don't have to be afraid. I just need you to release the hood latch and I'll put the oil in."

Dani closed her eyes and licked her lips.

"Come on, miss. It's late, and I need to get home to my wife and kids."

He has a wife and kids? Maybe, I'm just being paranoid. "Why don't you turn on the lights?" she asked.

"Sorry, if I do that other people will think we're open, and then I'll have to wait on them."

She inhaled a shaky breath and released the hood latch.

She watched him remove a can of oil from a shelf and plunge an opener into it as the flashlight created eerie shadows on the walls. He opened a second can of oil and moments later, tapped on her window again.

She jumped and her pulse quickened.

"What?" she asked through the closed window.

"I need to get in there and check something."

"Check what?"

"I think it may not be the oil after all."

What could it be? My car was running just fine.

"Look miss, I'm trying my best to help you. This is getting ridiculous."

Yeah, he's right. This is ridiculous. Dani drew in a quick breath, unlocked her door, and eased outside.

"Could you hurry, please?"

"I'm tryin' to do you a favor, lady. We're not really open, you know."

"You're right. I'm sorry."

He aimed the flashlight on a grease-covered refrigerator in a corner. "Why don't you grab yourself a Coke."

"No thanks. Is there a phone in here?"

"Sure," he said, "right in there." He pointed the flashlight toward the main part of the station. "Watch your step. The phone's on the desk."

Dani's desperation to call her father overruled the fear

that made her light-headed. She followed the beam of light up the step and through an open door. She picked her way through the oppressive darkness until her hands found the counter. Suddenly, she realized she had not heard the car door close, and no sound was coming from the bay. *Oh, God!* Desperately, she felt for the telephone, knocking over something as papers spilled on the floor in front of her. *Where is the phone? He said the phone was*—She swiped her hands along the counter and finally bumped the phone relieved to hear its soft jingle. She lifted the sticky receiver to her face as nausea roared in her stomach.

Dani sensed his evil presence though she had not heard him enter the area. His hand crashed down on her fingers before she could dial and she screamed.

"Oh, no, pretty lady, we can't have you screaming." He jerked her into his arms and clamped a filthy hand over her mouth. She heaved, and the contents of her stomach rose and spilled onto his hand, staining her jacket and covering her shoes.

He swore a wicked oath and pulled a handkerchief from his pocket wiping his hand and swearing again.

Dani wiped her mouth on her jacket sleeve, bolted for the bay, but slipped on the spilled papers and the vomit.

Bob caught her arm, spun her around, and tore at her clothing. "You're not goin' anywhere, missy. Not until I say so. Whew, you *do* stink."

Dani brought one soiled and smelly foot up and connected with his groin.

Bob howled and released her as she scrambled toward her car, forgetting the step and tumbling to the concrete floor. She tried to stand, but a flash of pain coursed through her ankle.

Bob lumbered into the bay and stood over her. "So, you're a fighter, huh? Well, I love a good fight now and then." Before she could move away from him, he dropped to his knees.

Dani moaned in pain and knew she was fighting for her life. *If I could only see!* She felt around for something, anything she could use as a weapon. Her hand bumped something. *The flashlight!*

Bob straddled Dani just as she snatched the heavy flashlight and crashed it into his forehead.

When he howled and reached for his head, Dani swung the flashlight again and banged with all her might into the side of his head. Blood-curdling curses echoed in the bay and then nothing.

Dani twisted free of him and pushed to her feet, trying to rush in spite of the searing pain in her left foot. Still holding the flashlight, she hobbled to the car leaving Bob lying lifeless and sprawled on the floor. She slammed the hood down, tossed the flashlight, and slipped inside the car. She jammed down the lock and reached for the keys. *The keys!* She flicked on the interior light to see Bob leaning against the passenger window, blood dripping from the wound on his head. Her foot brushed against the keys where they had apparently fallen, and she retrieved them. The violent tremors of her hands made it nearly impossible for her to insert the key into the ignition, but finally the engine roared to life. She put the car in reverse and exploded through the closed bay doors!

Chapter 13

Keep me safe, my God, for in you I take refuge. Psalm 16:1

Dani flew down the highway toward Meadow Glen, her breath coming in short gasps. A few miles down the road, the darkness behind her confirmed that Bob had not followed her. *Oh, God. Help me calm down before I get home. I have been so stupid!* She tugged at the seatbelt to fasten it, but her trembling fingers refused to cooperate. After several glances to locate the buckle slot, she made the connection.

Blinding headlights split the darkness and a car appeared behind Dani. *Oh, no. It's him!* Her nausea returned and without thinking, she hit the brakes. She feared at any moment she would faint. *Oh, dear God, please help me.*

The driver laid on the horn after almost ramming into the back of her.

Her heart throttled at the blast as her trembling foot again found the accelerator.

Terror raced through Dani as the car pulled along beside her. When a man reached out of his open window and made a vulgar sign, she thought she might lose complete control of her car, but the driver roared ahead down the highway. Dani drew in a long shaky breath. *Thank you, Father.*

Dani clung to the steering wheel willing her body and mind to calm down as she aimed the car for home.

❄❄❄

Micah pulled open the refrigerator door and retrieved a jug of milk. *Glad Mom got Oreos.* He glanced out the window as headlights lit their driveway. *Dani!*

He pushed open the kitchen door and shouted to David , "Dani's here!" and then bolted out to meet her.

Dani hoped she could stand, as she freed herself from the seatbelt and stepped out into the cool night air. Her ankle throbbed.

Micah threw his arms around her. "Hi, Dani."

"Hi, yourself," she said, hugging her twelve-year-old brother. "Oh, my goodness, Mikey, I think you've grown since August. You're almost as tall as I am."

"Dad thinks I'll end up taller than him. Hey, what's all over your jacket? Man, it stinks, Dani. And your hair's a mess. Oh, sorry, I guess I shouldn't have said that."

"That's all right, Mikey. I *do* stink." She managed a chuckle and struggled to control the panic rising in her. "I think I caught a bug. It made me throw up."

"Maybe Mom will give you something to make you better. She's good at that, you know."

"I *do* know." She wondered how long she could control the panic whirling through her.

"Want to give me a hand with my bags?" she asked as she limped toward the trunk.

"Sure. Did you hurt your foot?"

"Yeah, it's nothing though."

Micah stared at the dents on the back of her car. "Wow! What happened to your car? It's all messed up."

"Yeah, I need to get that fixed while I'm home."

The dented trunk lid screeched as Dani opened it. "Think you can handle that suitcase, Mike?"

"No problem," he said as he headed inside.

Dani slammed the trunk closed and leaned heavily against it for a moment trying to summon strength.

"Where is everybody?" she asked as they entered through the door Micah had left open.

"Mom and Dad went over to the church to help set up for the community Thanksgiving dinner. They'll be home soon. Dave was listening to the radio, so he probably didn't hear me say you were home."

"Do you want me to take these things to your room?"

"Just one minute. I want to say a quick hello to Davy."

Micah dropped Dani's bag and returned to the kitchen. Dani tapped on the boys' door and limped inside.

David didn't hear or see her because his back was turned away from the door. Huge headphones blocked all hearing save that coming from the boom box sitting on the floor in front of him. Before creeping toward him, Dani watched him beat out a rhythm on the carpet with his eyes closed. Gently, she tugged on one of his untamable red curls and waited for a reaction. Nothing. She pulled a bit harder and laughed as he swatted the spot.

"Dani! Hey, I didn't hear you come in," he said as he pulled off the headphones and stood to hug her.

"I wonder why you didn't hear me," Dani teased.

David grinned. "Sorry. Hey, what happened to you?"

"I know. I stink. Got sick on the way home."

"Wow. Guess you're glad you're home, huh?"

"I sure am." *Understatement.*

"I'd like to know what mom's been feeding you guys."

"I'm probably gonna be taller than Mike."

"Think so, huh?"

He puffed out his chest and stood as tall as possible.

"Well, you're both still shorter than me so you better just watch out." She scrunched her face into a threat and playfully punched his arm.

"I'm so scared!" David said in a girly voice.

Dani laughed. "It's so good to see you, Davey."

"You, too."

Dani picked up the suitcase that Micah had left in the hallway, but he heard her struggling with it and insisted on carrying it to her bedroom.

"Thanks so much, Mikey. I'm going to clean up some before Mom and Dad get home."

"Good idea." Micah held his nose. "Pe-eww."

Dani gave him a playful shove. "Out, you."

"I'm going, I'm going," he said, still holding his nose.

Just as Dani was about to close her door, she heard her parents' voices in the kitchen.

"I wonder whose red car that is?" her dad asked in an exaggerated voice. "I don't think we're expecting anyone."

"I have no idea, Cameron," her mother responded in an equal volume. "Maybe it's my Avon lady."

Dani grinned at their attempt at humor knowing she could hear every word in their compact little house.

"You know, Lindy, it might be Dani's car."

"Oh, I don't think it's hers. It's too early."

Dani hopped into the kitchen. "Okay, okay. You can stop performing now. And . . . you really should consider taking acting lessons."

Cameron and Lindy enveloped Dani in a bear hug.

"Welcome home, honey," they said in unison.

"What's wrong with your foot?" Cameron asked. Lindy drew back from the sour odor emanating from their daughter and took in her disheveled appearance. "What in the world happened—"

Dani burst into tears.

Chapter 14

Anxiety weighs down the heart, but a kind word cheers it up.
Proverbs 12:25

As soon as her sobs subsided, Cameron and Lindy helped Dani remove her jacket and guided her to a chair. Lindy dropped to her knees and removed Dani's soiled shoes, examining her swollen foot.

"Can you tell us what happened, honey," Cameron asked, fearing she had been in an accident. He paced around her chair.

"Oh, Daddy. I have been so utterly stupid." Tears threatened to spill again, but she rubbed them away, ashamed of her foolish behavior.

Lindy stood to her feet. "Stupid is not a word I would associate with our daughter," Lindy said. "Now, take your time and tell us what happened. Were you in an accident?"

"Not exactly."

"Not exactly?" Cameron asked. "Would you like to be a little more specific?"

Dani took a deep breath. I . . . I left campus later than I planned, and hoped to be home much earlier, but I had a lot of last minute things to do."

"So, what happened to you between there and here?" Lindy asked, anxious to find out why Dani had come home looking like she did.

"I forgot to stop and get gas—"

"You ran out of gas?" Cameron asked.

"No."

"Dani, please! Just tell us what happened to you." The crease in Cameron's forehead deepened with concern.

Dani launched into the story and told her parents all the details of her encounter with the attendant at the Pure Oil gas station.

"He attacked you!" Cameron yelled.

Micah came bursting into the room. "What's going on?" he asked, his eyes moving from one to the other.

Lindy rose to her feet and placed a trembling arm around her son. "Micah, honey, we need a few minutes alone with Dani."

"What's wrong with her? She said she got sick."

"She's not sick now, but something has happened, and we need to talk privately with her. Please wait in your room, Okay?"

"All right." Micah turned and headed for his bedroom.

"I'm calling the police!" Cameron said as soon as he got all the details from Dani. He picked up the kitchen phone and dialed zero.

"Dani, I assumed you were driving up with Carter?"

"Oh, I'm sorry, Mom. I should have called you. It didn't work out for us to come together because Carter has to preach on Sunday."

"Preach?"

"Yes, at the little church where he is a student pastor."

"Oh, we didn't know about that," Lindy said. "Is he still planning on being here for Thanksgiving?"

"Yes, he'll leave early tomorrow. He insisted I go on ahead, so I could have more time at home since he still needed to work some on his sermon. Unfortunately, that means he'll be leaving on Saturday afternoon."

"I see. My goodness, I would think he could have found a replacement for Sunday."

Dani's foot throbbed, and she was anxious to get out of her smelly clothing. "I suppose he could have, but he feels like it's his responsibility. He's dedicated to becoming a good pastor. He really loves the Lord, Mom."

"It sounds like it. We're certainly anxious to finally meet him, honey." She turned a questioning look at Cameron as he hung up the telephone.

"They're on their way," Cameron said.

Within ten minutes a police car pulled into the driveway behind Dani's car. Cameron stepped outside to meet the officer.

"Mom, I was never so scared in my whole life. I thought he was going to—"

"But he didn't, sweetheart, that's the important thing. God gave you clear thinking when you needed it most."

"I wasn't thinking too clearly when I neglected to stop and get gas on the interstate."

"God doesn't waste anything, sweetheart, not even the mistakes we make."

The officer entered the room along with Cameron and removed his hat.

"Dani, I'm officer Robert Sheldon."

Cameron pulled a chair close to Dani for the officer who thanked Cameron and eased into the chair. "Dani, how are you doing?"

"I'm okay now, except for my ankle."

"I realize it may be painful to think about what happened, but it's important for you to tell me everything you remember about the event. Okay?"

Dani nodded, and relayed the story again.

The officer made a few notes on a pad he pulled from his pocket. His radio squawked, and he stood and stepped aside to respond.

Dani just wanted a hot shower and to forget this had ever happened.

"Good job," the officer said. He turned to Cameron. "They got him."

"Oh, thank God."

"They got the guy who attacked me?" Dani asked.

"Yeah. From what the dispatch said, he's in bad shape. You must have whacked him pretty good." He smiled at Dani, but the image of Bob's bloody face leaning against her car window made her nauseous again.

"Will I have to pay for the garage door?" she asked.

The officer grinned. "Don't worry about the door. The guy who attacked you will have to pay—in more ways than one. Was your car damaged?"

"Yes, the rear is dented and scratched."

"His insurance should take care of that, too. Hopefully, he *has* insurance. Well, I guess that's it for tonight. You need to come to the station and press charges, Dani. I hope you won't neglect to do that. This character needs to stay locked up."

"Thank you," Dani said. I will, for sure."

Officer Sheldon retrieved his hat, replaced it on his head, and bade the Kriegs goodnight.

"I'm going to get a shower," Dani announced.

"Are you sure you can manage, honey. That foot is awfully swollen," Lindy said. "We should take you to the hospital for an x-ray."

"Let me get cleaned up first, okay?"

"Have you had dinner?" Lindy asked.

"I couldn't eat a thing," Dani said.

Cameron helped her stand and insisted she lean on him as she made her way to her room.

Chapter 15

Teach me to do your will, for you are my God; may your good Spirit lead me on level ground. Psalm 143:10

Lindy and Cameron shared their morning coffee on Thanksgiving morning. "I'm so glad Dani only has a sprained ankle," Lindy said.

"Thank God. She's been through so much these last few years."

They had been fortunate to find the emergency room empty last evening, rare for Meadow Glen Memorial. Consequently, they were in and out of the hospital within an hour, with Dani's ankle wrapped in an Ace bandage.

"What time is Carter supposed to arrive today?" Cameron asked.

"Dani said he was trying to make it by eleven."

Lindy sipped her coffee and looked into Cameron's eyes. "I believe our daughter is falling for Carter."

"Why do you say that? It seems to me she just met this young man."

"A woman knows these things," Lindy said with a grin. "I just hope she takes it slowly."

Cameron swallowed a sip of coffee, set his cup down, and drew his eyebrows together in a frown. The kitchen mood changed immediately.

"What's wrong, honey?"

"Oh, I was just thinking about our sweet Betts." Tears glistened in his eyes.

Lindy laid her hand across his, and he smiled through the tears. "It's been two years since we lost her, but the pain goes on."

"It's times like this—the holidays—when it's especially painful." Cameron wiped his eyes with a napkin, unaware that Dani had entered the kitchen.

"Happy Thanks—" Dani's questioning eyes traveled from Cameron to Lindy.

"Well, look who's up bright and early," Lindy said in a strained voice.

"Mom, Dad, what's going on?"

Cameron turned misty eyes to her. "Good morning, sweetheart. We're just thinking about Betts and how very much we miss her."

Cameron stood and pulled out a chair for her.

"Thanks, Dad," she said as she hugged him.

"Oh, I miss her, too, more than I can tell you, espescially at school."

"I'm sure you do," Lindy said. "I have rehearsed David's words in Psalm 119:76 countless times. '*May your unfailing love be my comfort, according to your promise to your servant.*'"

Cameron nodded in agreement. "Knowing that God loves us unconditionally and has our best interests at heart *is* comforting. We don't know why He chose to take our Betts when he did. This is where our faith comes in, faith to rest in His love that is pure and healing."

"I think we're all trying to do that," Lindy said.

Dani played with the ruffled edge of the placemat in front of her. "Not that long ago, I saw no reason to live and blamed myself for Betts's death, but in time, I came to realize that God knows what He's doing and why He took her home to heaven so soon. It wasn't easy, though, and I still have moments when I'm tempted to blame myself and wallow in guilt."

"It has gotten easier for all of us," Cameron said, "and that's only because we are trying our best to put our faith into action."

"Not to change the subject," Lindy said, "but how is your ankle this morning?"

"Not too bad. I'll probably be fine in a day or two. I'll take the med the ER doctor gave me last night if I need to."

"Coffee, honey?" Cameron asked.

"Sounds good."

"Tomorrow, you'll need to go to the police station and press charges against the guy who attacked you."

"Will you go with me, Dad?"

"Of course. We also need to contact an attorney."

"An attorney! Will there be a trial?" The thought sent shivers through Dani.

"I don't really know. The lawyer can help us with the details. I'll call and arrange an appointment."

Lindy rose as she swallowed the last of her coffee. "Well, I really need to get some things going for our dinner before it gets any later. After all, Carter Matthews will be knocking on our door in a few short hours," she said with a grin.

Dani's face lit up. "I'm excited for you to meet him."

"Seems like you really like this young man, Dani," Cameron said.

"Oh, I do," she said. "I'm praying that God will give me wisdom to know if Carter will be the one for me. He has made it very clear that he's interested in me." Her cheeks dimpled in a smile. "I just don't want to make a big mistake again. After all, I really hurt Kurt."

Kurt was Dani's high school boyfriend she was engaged to for a few months. Because of her depression and guilt over the loss of her sister, she couldn't focus on Kurt. Angry and hurt, he broke off their engagement.

"We'll pray too, honey," Lindy said.

Cameron stood and pushed his chair in. "I'm taking the boys out for breakfast at the Buckeye Diner and then out to the shooting range."

"*Shooting* range?" Dani asked.

"Davy's interested in learning to hunt ever since he went on a hunting weekend with his friend's family. Mike's not really interested, but decided to tag along."

"My little brothers are growing up."

"That's for sure. So, I'll see you lovely ladies in a couple of hours."

"Don't be late, Cam."

"What can I do to help, Mom?"

"Chop the celery and onions for the stuffing?"

"Sure thing. When I'm finished, I think I'll go call Grandma and Grandpa. I'm afraid I'll get busy and forget. They've been so wonderful to me."

"To all of us," Lindy added. "They'll be excited to hear from you. She pulled celery from the refrigerator and handed it to Dani. "We have some good news," she said as a smile lit up her face.

"And what would your good news be?" Dani asked.

"We are adding on a room."

Dani's eyes widened in shock. "What did you say?"

"I said, we're adding on a room, actually two rooms—a bedroom and a bath."

"Oh, my goodness, Mom, that's fantastic."

"The boys are getting bigger and need their own space. Thanks to your dad's pay increase we could swing it."

"When will it be finished?"

"Sometime next spring."

"I'm so happy for you, Mom. That *is* good news."

❊❊❊

Dani spent a half hour on the phone with her grandparents and then decided to call Shannon, her long-time friend.

"Hi, Shannon, it's Dani."

"Dani!" squealed Shannon. "When did you get home?"

"Yesterday."

"We *have* to get together while you're here. You won't believe how big Jamie is."

"Is that him I hear in the background?"

"That's him all right. Nothing wrong with that boy's lungs. So can you come over Friday or Saturday?"

"I plan on it. There's someone I want you to meet."

"Let me guess . . . wouldn't be Carter Matthews, would it?"

"How did you guess?" Dani grinned.

"Maybe it is because his name comes up in every conversation we've had these last few months."

"Funny girl. He's actually arriving this morning."

"I'm anxious to meet him."

"Shannon, something happened to me on the way home." A chill passed through Dani at the thought of her nightmare at the gas station.

"What? What happened? Did you have an accident?"

"No, but it's a long story, so why don't I call you back and fill you in? It sounds like Jamie needs his mama."

"Okay. Sounds good. I've missed you terribly. So glad you're home."

"Missed you, too. Bye, Shannon."

❊❊❊

Dani saw Carter's car pull in behind hers probably because she had been glancing out the window every five minutes. "It's him!" she shouted and limped out the door, as her heart bubbled wildly.

Carter stood with suitcase in hand and dropped it on seeing Dani. She threw herself into his arms.

He kissed her long and passionately, shocking them both. At school, they had been restricted to hand-holding, and even that was frowned upon. When Carter finally drew back, Dani's knees threatened to collapse. "Wow!" she said finally.

"Wow!" he repeated. He ran his hands through his mass of dark curls, and laughed.

"You're *laughing*?" she asked, her arms akimbo. "Maybe, I just won't do that again." She feigned a snub.

"Come here, you," he said, as he attempted to pull her into his arms again.

"It's cold out here, Carter, and I think we better head inside, before my mom wonders what happened to me."

"Okay. Hey, what happened to your car? I didn't notice it being dented before."

"A long story. Let's go inside, and I'll explain later."

"And your foot? What's up with the bandage?"

"That's part of the story."

Chapter 16

Give thanks to the Lord for he is good, his love endures forever.
Psalm 107:1

Lindy met Carter at the kitchen door. "Well, well, we finally get to meet Carter Matthews," Lindy said as he entered the cheery kitchen.

Dani grinned and introduced Carter just as Cameron stepped into the room.

Cameron smiled and greeted Carter with a handshake. "It's nice to meet you, Carter. Welcome to our home."

"Thank you. It's a pleasure to meet both of you. Something sure smells good in here."

Lindy smiled. "Hope you like turkey. We're pretty traditional here."

"I sure do. Those wouldn't be pumpkin pies I see on the counter, would they?"

"Indeed they are."

"Yum. Have I already died and gone to heaven?"

"How was the target shooting?" Lindy asked Cameron.

"A hit with Dave, for sure."

"Did you remind the boys to straighten up their room?"

"They're doing it now."

"Follow me, Carter, and I'll show you where you'll be sleeping," Cameron said. "Wish I could offer you a guest room, but no can do."

Carter chuckled. "I'm used to dorm life," he said as he picked up his bag, winked at Dani, and followed Cameron.

"I'm afraid you'll have to bunk with David and Micah.

"That's not a problem. It will give me a chance to get to know them."

❅❅❅

"He seems really nice, honey," Lindy said after Carter and Cameron had left the room.

"He *is* nice. And handsome."

Lindy caught the gleam in her daughter's eyes and caressed her arm. "I can't argue with that, Dani, but please don't rush things."

"I've been praying that God would help me with that."

"You've only just gotten to know him. It takes time to really know someone."

"I really am trying, Mom."

Lindy patted Dani's back. "I know you are, honey."

"I need to tell him about what happened to me on the way home," she said as she glanced at her foot. "Actually, I think it's gone down quite a bit since last night."

❅❅❅

"David and Micah, this is Carter Matthews."

"Hi," David said. "So, you're Dani's boyfriend, huh?"

Carter laughed. "Yes, I believe I am."

"Nice to meet you."

"You, too. Are you Micah?"

"No, He's Dave," Micah said as he stepped forward and shook Carter's hand.

"Great to meet you both. So . . . you're twins?"

"Yup," David said.

"David, that's rude," Cameron said.

"Oh, sorry."

"You guys sure don't look much alike."

"That's because we're fraternal," David said. "You know what that is, right?"

Cameron rolled his eyes.

"Yes, I'm familiar with that term."

"You can have my bed, Carter," Micah said.

"Where will you sleep?" *He looks so much like Dani.*

"He'll be on the floor in his sleeping bag. The boys often do that when they have a friend over," Cameron said.

"Thank you, Micah."

"You can call me, Mike."

"Good enough. Mike it is."

"Carter, have you eaten breakfast?" Cameron asked.

"I stopped at a little diner on the way, so I'm fine."

"*I'm* hungry, Dad," David said.

"You're always hungry. I think you'll be okay until dinner. You had a big breakfast."

"Carter, make yourself at home. If you need anything, just let us know."

"Will do. Thanks so much."

"You can put your suitcase in my closet," Micah said.

"Okey dokey."

"Wanna shoot some hoops?" David asked.

"Tell you what. How about we do that this afternoon? I don't want to get all sweaty before dinner. Sound okay?"

"Yeah. I got picked for our team this year," David said.

"Terrific! How 'bout you, Mike?"

"Nah. I'm not that good."

"No? Well, we'll see this afternoon."

Carter opened the closet and made room for his bag.

"Me and Mike are playin' Battleship, if you wanna play, too."

"Thanks, but I need to see if I can help with dinner."

Carter found the bathroom, freshened up, and then headed back to the kitchen. The wonderful Thanksgiving smells transported him to childhood Thanksgivings at his grandparents' farm. He couldn't remember the last time his mom had cooked Thanksgiving dinner.

"I'm here to help," he announced as he rolled up the sleeves of his rust-colored shirt.

"Oh, we're fine here, Carter," Lindy said.

Dani put the last of the rolls into the baking pan.

"What happened to your foot, Dani?"

"It's nothing, really. I'll tell you about it, but right now, I bet my dad would love for you to watch the football game with him."

"I see." Carter slumped his shoulders and dropped his head. I guess I know when I'm not wanted."

"Now, don't go away sad," Dani said.

"No, just go away." Lindy added.

All three laughed as Carter straightened and headed to the living room.

"I see Carter has a sense of humor," Lindy said.

"Yes. I think it's one of the reasons he is so popular on campus. And you should see how the people at Bethany Community Church flock to him the minute he arrives." Dani popped a casserole into the oven.

"Mom, did you invite Aunt Becky and Uncle Bill for Thanksgiving?"

"We did, but they couldn't come," Lindy said as she placed the turkey on a platter for carving.

"I'll miss seeing them," Dani said, "but it will be good to see the Porters."

"Yes, they're really like family."

Lindy untied her apron and tossed it onto a stool. "Did I tell you Phoebe lost her mother this year?"

"No. How sad."

"Yeah, it's been really hard on her. Phoebe's dad came to live with them, but he wasn't happy. He wanted to be on his own even though Phoebe tried her best to make him comfortable."

"Did they find him a place?"

"Yes, finally. We invited him to join us today, but he declined. Help me remember to send him a plate, okay?"

"Sure."

Dani sighed and fought back tears as an image of Betts flashed through her mind. "Mom?"

"Yes, honey," she said as she opened the refrigerator.

"Remember that Thanksgiving that Betts and I dressed like Pilgrims?"

"I could never forget that. You looked so cute traipsing off to school that day."

Dani swallowed the lump in her throat.

❄❄❄

"Mind if I join you?" Carter asked as he entered the living room.

"Please do. Are you a football fan?" Cameron asked.

Carter moved a cushion on the faded brown sofa and sat down. "I enjoy a good game, whenever I get a chance."

Cameron lowered the television volume. "So, tell me a little about yourself, Carter. Dani has told us that you're studying for the ministry, and you're currently pastoring a small church?"

"I'm a student interim pastor."

"That will be valuable experience for you."

"I'm learning, for sure."

Carter drew his eyebrows together in a serious expression. "I know without a doubt that God has called me to be a pastor. I fought against it for a long time, but finally surrendered my will to His. Hopefully, by taking summer classes, I'll finish my degree early."

"I see. I'm sure the Lord will bless you for your obedience." Cameron's eyes flitted to the television.

Carter grinned at Cameron's attempt to remain focused on their conversation.

"So . . . you're from Florida?"

"Yes. I grew up in Leesburg. My folks are still there."

"Do you have siblings?"

"One sister. She's younger than I."

"My turn for questions," Carter said with a grin. "Dani said that—"

Action in the game caught Cameron's attention again.

"No!" Cameron yelled at the television. He reached up and angrily switched it off. "Terrible game," he muttered.

"Oh, I'm sorry, Carter. What were you saying?"

"Dani said you're originally from Indiana?"

"That's right. We came here so I could attend Meadow Glen College. When I finished my degree, I found a job right here in the Meadow Glen School system, and have been here ever since. Dani and Betts—I assume Dani told you about our Betts?"

"She did. I'm very sorry for your loss."

Cameron sighed. "A tough time in our lives."

A knock interrupted their conversation, and both men stood to greet the guests.

"Come in!" Cameron held the door open as the Porter family stepped inside.

"Happy Thanksgiving!" Phoebe said as she hugged Cameron and smiled at Carter.

"Same to you!"

Cameron shook hands with Bill who was holding a large casserole dish. "Carter, these are our dearest friends, Bill and Phoebe Porter and their son, Sean."

"A pleasure to meet you," he said as he offered a hand in welcome to each.

"Mr. Krieg, where's Dave and Mike?" Sean asked.

"In their room. You can join them if you like."

Sean scrambled toward the twins' bedroom.

"I'll take your coats," Cameron said. "Make yourselves at home."

Phoebe took the dish from Bill. "I think I'll see if Lindy needs help in the kitchen. Say, how is Dani's ankle? Lindy called last night and said she was having it x-rayed."

"Yes, she sprained her ankle, but she'll be fine."

"Thank God for that."

Carter's neck and shoulders tensed. *Did Dani have a car accident?*

❄❄❄

Nothing else was said about Dani's ankle during dinner. *Her car is damaged, and she has an injured ankle. What could have happened?* Carter thought about simply asking right then but decided against it. He focused on getting to know the Krieg family and their friends as they enjoyed a sumptuous Thanksgiving dinner together.

Afterwards, Cameron and Bill retired to the living room, as the three boys scrambled for their coats and headed outside.

Lindy, Phoebe, and Dani began clearing the table. "I'll gladly wash these dishes," Carter said as he hopped to his feet. "I've had lots of experience. My mom hated doing dishes, so my sister and I usually got the job."

"Thank you, Carter," Lindy said, "but—"

"But Lindy and I will clean up here in no time," Phoebe said. "We seldom get time to talk these days."

"Thanks, Phoebe." Lindy gently bit her lip and tried to think of something Dani and Carter could do, other than watch the game with Bill and Cameron. "Dani, why don't you and Carter go for a drive. You can show Carter around out little town."

"That sounds good to me, Dani. Are you up for it?" Carter asked.

"Sure. Let me grab a jacket."

Chapter 17

This is the confidence we have in approaching God: that if we ask anything according to his will, he hears us. 1 John 5:14

Carter insisted he drive his car and suggested Dani do the navigating. "So, now that we're alone," Carter said as he backed out of the driveway, "I need to find out what happened to you on the way home."

Dani leaned her head back against the headrest and sighed. "Well, it all started because I neglected to stop and get gas on the interstate."

"You ran out of gas?"

"No, but I was afraid I would. The gas gauge read 'empty' before I realized it." Dani glanced at him feeling as if she were a naughty child. She had no intention of telling him that her mind had been completely preoccupied with thoughts of him. "Right after I got off on the Meadow Glen exit, I found a gas station, but as soon as I pulled up to one of the pumps, the station lights went out . . ."

As Dani continued her story, Carter was unable to focus on driving and pulled into the IGA parking lot.

"You could have been killed!" He covered his eyes and shook his head as if he were trying to shake the image of Dani's perpetrator from his mind.

"But I wasn't killed or . . . raped."

"But both *could* have happened." Carter reached for her hand and drew it to his cheek. "It's my fault. I should have been with you."

Dani gazed into his anxious eyes. "No, it's certainly not your fault. I have no one to blame but myself."

"I should have gotten a replacement for Sunday and been with you. Priorities, again."

"What do you mean?"

"My dad was always reminding me to get my priorities straight. 'Carter, you're grounded until those grades come up.' Carter, didn't I tell you to mow before you went to the movies?' I have a way of doing what I want first, and putting more important things last. Apparently, I'm still doing that. Dad was right."

"Carter, you do have your priorities straight. You were doing the right thing by sticking to your commitment. I'm the one who messed up by not stopping for gas. So let's not let it destroy our weekend. Okay?"

"I don't know what I would do if—"

"Nothing's going to happen to me. Yes, I was scared, but like my mom says, 'God doesn't waste anything, even our mistakes.' From now on, I'll check my gas gauge and my oil."

"What about that guy? Did you call the police?"

"Dad called, and the guy's already in jail."

"Thank God for that."

Carter studied her, tenderness filling his face. "I've done a lot of thinking and praying lately, and . . . this much I know. He paused for a moment as he searched her eyes. I love you, Danita Krieg."

Dani's heart thundered in her chest, and she inhaled a shallow breath. "I . . . I—"

"Shh," Carter said as he lightly pressed his finger to her lips. "I don't want to pressure you to say anything you're not absolutely sure of." He pulled her as close to him as possible and gently kissed her.

Dani's heart raced with excitement, and her thoughts ran wild as she continued to show Carter the highlights of their small town. *Do I love him, Lord? Am I being too cautious? I was so cruel to Kurt, and I am so afraid of making another mistake. After all, I thought I loved Kurt and look what happened.*

"Dani?"

"Huh? Oh, sorry. Guess I was lost in thought there for a moment."

"What were you thinking?" He glanced at her, as his eyes crinkled teasingly.

"I was thinking about . . . about the weather," she lied.

"The weather, huh? Well, what about it?"

"Okay, smartie, I was thinking about us. So there." She jutted out her chin, averted his glance, and was grateful he dropped the subject.

Carter drove aimlessly through unfamiliar streets waiting for more direction from Dani.

She directed him around Meadow Glen's town square. Dominating the center of the square were two flag poles positioned on either side of a large rock. The American flag and the Ohio flag wafted in the cold November wind.

"This must be a war memorial, right?" Carter asked.

"Yes," Dani said. "The plaques mounted on the rock have the engraved names of Meadow Glen's fallen heroes."

"In the summer, the square has beds of colorful flowers and shrubs. It's kind of drab right now."

Once around the square, Dani directed Carter to the city park. "I have great memories of this little park," Dani said as Carter swung into a parking spot.

"Feel like walking?" Carter asked. "We could check out that stream over there."

"Maybe not. My ankle is starting to ache."

"I'm sorry, Dani. That was thoughtless of me. Shall we head back to the house?"

"I want to show you our church first."

Dani wished it were summer so Carter could see Meadow Glen decked out in her glory. The stately old trees lining the streets were now bare, and no flowers decorated the town.

When they reached the church, a number of people were streaming from the building.

"Who are these folks?" Carter asked.

Dani recognized several of them from years past. "They are needy people who shared Thanksgiving dinner the church provided."

"That's great. Makes me wonder what they do the rest of the year."

"Uh . . . I think Meadow Glen has a food closet." Dani had never considered that.

Carter cut the engine, and they watched the down and outers for a few more minutes.

"Sure makes me realize how many needs are out there." He pointed to the construction site next to the current building. "Your church is adding on, huh?"

"Yes, they're adding a bigger sanctuary. Dad said the church is really growing."

Carter's face lit up as if an internal light had been switched on. "Oh, man," he said as he leaned forward and studied the traditional brick structure, "I can't wait!"

"Can't wait?"

"To start my ministry."

"Seems to me you've already started your ministry."

"I know, but you know what I mean. Have my own church and reach people for Christ. I am so grateful that someone cared enough about me to do that." Carter gazed at the church steeple as if he were offering thanks to God.

His words warmed Dani's heart. *Carter's not just a Christian. He's a Christian who has a burning desire to share Christ with others! He seems so perfect, Lord, and You know I'm far from perfect. A pastor's wife!* The thought sent a shudder through her. *I need to use my head! Me, a pastor's wife? I don't know if I can do that, be that. Do I love Carter Matthews? Do I?*

Carter turned his eyes from the steeple to Dani. "What's wrong?"

Her eyes flew open. "I . . . I am feeling so many things right now." She shivered.

"Are you cold? I can start the engine, or we could get on back to the house."

"No, I'm fine."

"Would you like to share your thoughts with me?"

"I think . . . I think we should pray—together."

Carter took her hand, and began . . . "

Chapter 18

But you, man of God, flee from all this, and pursue righteousness, godliness, faith, love, endurance and gentleness. 1 Timothy 6:11

Cameron and Lindy were sharing breakfast on Friday morning as the rest of the household were still sleeping.

"So, what do you think, hon?" Cameron asked as he popped a bite of cinnamon roll into his mouth.

"About what?" she asked already knowing the purpose of his question.

"About Carter."

"Shh," she cautioned. "Maybe we should talk later?"

The words were scarcely out of her mouth when Carter strolled into the kitchen. "Good morning," he said as he clicked the heels of his gleaming dress shoes.

"Good morning to you," Cameron and Lindy said.

"You're up bright and early," Cameron said as he noted Carter's creased khakis and a blue shirt that revealed no evidence of having been in a suitcase.

"I'm an early riser, always have been, much to the frustration of my mother as I grew up." A smile brightened his face.

Cameron laughed. "Dani and Micah are usually up by this time, but our David is a sleepyhead."

"Have a seat, Carter," Lindy said. "Would you like some coffee?"

"Yes, thank you. It smells so good."

"So, what do you think of our little town?" Cameron asked.

"It looks like a great place to raise a family. I'm sure it's lovely here in summer."

Cameron nodded. "That it is."

Lindy poured a steaming cup of coffee for Carter and offered cream and sugar that he refused.

"Dani said your church is building a new sanctuary?"

"Yes, we are. It's exciting to see how God is working here in Meadow Glen."

Carter sipped his coffee. "I am so anxious to finish school so I can begin my ministry."

"All in God's time, right?" Cameron said. "How about a homemade cinnamon roll to go with that coffee?"

"If it's okay, I'd like to wait for Dani."

"Of course," Lindy said. "There's fresh fruit, too."

"Sounds wonderful. By the way, that was a fabulous meal yesterday, Mrs. Krieg. I appreciate your inviting me to share it with you folks."

"Why, thank you for the compliment, Carter. It's been a pleasure getting to know you. I love it when we can share a meal with others."

"Well, well, well, look who's finally up," Cameron said as Dani stepped into the kitchen in a faded sweatsuit and floppy slippers.

Dani yawned loudly. "Morning," she said, her eyes mere slits.

"Good morning, Dani," Carter said.

"Wha . . . Oh, my goodness. I didn't see you, Carter." She ran her fingers through her morning hair.

"Have a seat, honey," Cameron said.

"I . . . I think I'll get my shower first," she said feeling color creep into her face as she hurried back to her bedroom. *Way to make an impression, Dani.*

"Well, we usually watch the morning news, if you like to join us in the living room, Carter," Lindy said.

"Sure. I haven't caught the news in ages. Okay to bring my coffee?"

"Absolutely."

The three of them settled in front of the television, and Cameron found their usual station.

An hour later, Dani appeared in the room dressed in an outfit her mother had purchased for her a year ago, but Dani had never worn.

Carter jumped to his feet and whistled softly. "You look lovely, Dani."

Her eyes shone with love that did not go unnoticed by Lindy. "Thank you."

"Honey, that dress looks so nice on you, and it fits perfectly," Lindy said. "I'm so glad you are finally getting some use out of it."

Dani smiled, knowing the dress not only fit, but accented her hair and eyes perfectly. "Thanks, Mom."

"Have you eaten breakfast, Carter?" Dani asked.

"No, I was waiting for you."

"How nice. Well, let's go see what we can find."

"Mom made rolls, Dani," Cameron said.

"Yum." She reached for Carter's hand and led him back to the kitchen.

"You're not limping," Carter said.

"It doesn't hurt, even though it's still a bit swollen."

"Oh, I'm so glad to hear that."

Once inside the kitchen, Carter swung Dani into his arms and kissed her. "I love you, Dani Krieg."

Dani backed away from him, her heart tumbling about her chest. "I think . . . you better have a seat and I'll—"

Again he drew her to himself. This time he gently kissed her forehead. "I've never felt like this before," he whispered.

She pressed her lips lightly to his. "I haven't either."

"Not even with Kurt?"

"I thought I loved him, but now . . . "

"That's all I need to know," he said as he kissed her again. "Now, how about some of those cinnamon rolls?"

❊❊❊

The morning passed in a whirl. Cameron took Dani to the police station to file charges against the man who attacked her, while Carter played Monopoly with Micah and David. After lunch was over, Dani called Shannon and arranged a time to visit.

❊❊❊

Shannon met them at the door with Jamie balanced on her hip. "Come in!"

"Oh, Shannon, he's sooo cute!" Dani caressed Jamie's blond curls.

"You must be Carter," Shannon said. She stepped aside so they could enter.

"Oh, I'm sorry. Shannon, I'd like you to meet Carter Matthews."

Shannon extended her hand in welcome. "It's nice to finally meet you, Carter."

"And you, as well."

Shannon led them into the small living room. "Make yourselves comfortable. How about something to drink?"

"Nothing for me, thanks," Carter said.

"You, Dani?"

"No thanks."

"May I hold your son?" Carter asked.

"Absolutely." She placed Jamie in his arms.

For the next twenty minutes, Shannon and Dani caught each other up on their lives while Carter played with the baby. When Jamie tired of peek-a-boo, Carter bounced him on his lap. "Ride a little horsey, down to town, better be careful so you don't fall down!" Carter opened his legs and pretended to drop Jamie on the word 'down.'" Peals of laughter filled the living room.

"It looks like you're a natural with children, Carter," Shannon said.

"I had lots of practice. I used to work in the church nursery when I was a teenager."

"How nice," Dani said.

"It was a way for me to escape long boring sermons."

"Tsk, tsk, Carter Matthews." Dani poked his arm.

"I know, I was a bad boy, wasn't I, Jamie?" He lifted Jamie high and pretended to drop him. "I was a bad boy!" he said as he lifted him up again.

Jamie squealed with delight.

"I think you'd spoil my son if you were around him for long," Shannon said.

"Why not? Right, Jamie?"

"Well, I think we better be going," Dani said as she rose from the sofa a few minutes later.

Shannon hugged her. "I'm happy you came. I miss you so much."

"I miss you, too. Please give my love to Jared. I'm sorry we didn't get to see him."

Carter stood and tried to hand Jamie to his mother, but he whimpered and clung to Carter, wrinkling his shirt. Shannon tugged him from Carter.

"Bye, bye, Jamie," Carter said.

Jamie's whimper exploded into a full-blown wail as Carter and Dani slipped out the door and headed for the car.

Carter laughed as he helped Dani into the car. "Wow, Jamie sure has a powerful set of lungs."

"You obviously enjoyed playing with him," she said as she slipped into the car.

"I did. He's a cute little fellow." Carter shut the passenger door, scooted to the other side, and slid behind the wheel.

"Speaking of babies . . . "

"Yes, I want babies," Carter said with a grin.

Dani poked his arm. "How did you know what I was going to say?"

"Wild guess."

"Smartie."

Chapter 19

I sought the Lord, and he answered me; he delivered me from all my fears. Psalm 34:4

When Carter pulled into the Krieg driveway, Dani saw her parent's car wasn't there. "Mom and Dad must have gone out," she said. *We can have some time alone!* That thought no sooner flashed through Dani's mind than another one followed. *Put on the full armor of God, so that you can take your stand against the devil's schemes.* The verse in Ephesians had been one the Tuesday night Bible study had recently discussed.

"Your folks aren't home, huh?" He pursed his lips and stroked his chin. "Dani, I can't trust myself alone with you. The way I feel about you makes it too risky."

"I know."

"Why don't you go on in? I'll take this time to do a little shopping. How does that sound?"

"Shopping? Why don't I go with you?"

"I need to go by myself. It's kind of personal."

What could possibly be so personal? Deodorant? Toothpaste? Oh, well.

"Oh, sure. No problem. There's a discount store out—"

"Yeah, I remember seeing it when we were out driving around yesterday."

"All right, then."

Carter pulled her to him and kissed her tenderly. "I won't be long."

Dani opened the car door with a trembling hand and headed inside.

❄❄❄

Dani hurried inside, closed the door, and leaned against it. *Dear Lord, You have to help me with these overwhelming feelings!* She headed for her bedroom, grabbed her Bible from her night stand, plopped into her desk chair, and prayed silently. *When Betts died, and I was at the end of my rope, if it wasn't for Your Word, Lord, I don't know if I would have made it. I need You—Your wisdom, Your power. I desperately want my relationship with Carter to remain pure, but it is so hard. I completely melt when he touches me. Is this really love, Lord? Or is it just my flesh?*

With fingers still shaky from Carter's kiss, she tore into her Bible for verses that would sustain her. *I want to live before You in honesty, Lord. In Bible study we all claim the Bible as our guide for living. I really want that to be true in my life. and not just empty words.* Dani found the word 'temptation' in her concordance. *If what I just experienced with Carter isn't temptation, then, I don't know what is!* She looked up I Corinthians 10:13. *No temptation has overtaken you except what is common to mankind. And God is faithful; he will not let you be tempted beyond what you can bear. But when you are tempted, he will also provide a way out so that you can endure it.* He just did that! He made a way out when Carter decided to go shopping alone.

In Mark 14:38, Dani read, *Watch and pray so that you will not fall into temptation. The spirit is willing, but the flesh is weak.*

Dani repeated the words in Mark several times until she knew them by heart. *I need to think when I'm with Carter and not allow myself to be in a compromising situation. How easy it would be to cross that line into sin.* "Watch and pray, watch and pray, watch and pray." Dani repeated the words aloud, unaware that her parents had returned until someone knocked on her door.

"Dani?"

"Come in, Mom."

"We were surprised to see Carter's car gone."

"He had some things to pick up in town."

"And you didn't go with him?" Lindy frowned.

"Honestly, I think he just made up the idea to go shopping."

"What do you mean?"

"He . . . we didn't want to be here alone."

"Seems to me you could still have gone along."

"Yeah, but he said he had to get personal stuff."

Lindy's confusion showed on her face. "Anyway, not being alone together is a good idea." She closed the bedroom door and sat on the edge of Dani's bed.

Dani cleared her throat and fixed her eyes on her mother. "Mom, I'm afraid of what you're going to think about this, but . . . I'm pretty sure Carter and I have fallen in love. There, I've said it." She dropped her eyes to hide her grin.

Lindy smiled, popped up from the bed, and stepped over to the desk chair where Dani sat. She tilted Dani's chin and smiled at her daughter. "I can't say I'm surprised, honey. Dad and I suspected you two were growing closer. You said, 'pretty sure'. Do you still have doubts?"

"I do. I want to be sure it's love and not . . . well, you know—"

"Lust?" Lindy finished.

"Yes, exactly." Dani stood and paced the room.

Lindy took a deep breath and smiled at her daughter. "How well do you know Carter?" Lindy asked.

"Mom, I feel like I *do* know him. Of course, I don't know every little detail about him, but I think I know the big things."

"What do you mean?"

"Well, his love for the Lord for one. Isn't that the most important thing to know?"

"That's a big one, all right."

"I can't tell you how many times our conversations turn to his eagerness to begin ministry."

"What about his family? You met them, right?"

"Yes, I did." Dani plopped back down onto her chair and peered at her mom. "They're nice enough. Carter's mom is . . . well, she seems to be more focused on fashion, her looks, that sort of thing, than on people. Just my opinion, of course."

"And his dad?"

"I liked him. He seems warm and genuine. Funny thing, though. I thought Carter would be closer to his dad than his mom, but it didn't seem so."

"What about his sister?"

"I liked her, too. Her weight seemed to be a big issue for Carter, though."

"Oh?"

"Yeah. That kind of surprised me."

Lindy placed her hands on Dani's shoulders. "Honey, I think the best advice I can give you is to take your time with this relationship until you are absolutely sure Carter's the man God has for you."

"I guess you're right, Mom."

"I am wondering, though . . . " Dani bit her lip.

"Wondering about what?"

"Whether I'm just afraid?"

"Afraid?"

"Afraid to trust myself, to make the right decision. I was just so smart, so confident that I knew what I was doing when I drove during that thunderstorm—"

"Dani Krieg, you must not let that accident color all your decisions."

"I know. I'm trying." She shook her head and sighed. You know something, Mom?"

"What's that?"

"God gave me the best mom ever." Dani popped up and hugged Lindy.

"Thanks, sweetie."

"What are you doing this afternoon?"

"Dad and I are watching a movie . . . or taking a nap, possibly both."

❈❈❈

Dani had changed into a comfortable pair of jeans and a sweater and tied her hair into a pony tail just as Carter pecked on the kitchen door and opened it slightly.

"Hello! Anybody home?"

"Come in," Dani said as she scurried to meet him. Although Dani yearned for him to pull her into his arms, he stayed a few feet away.

"Did you find everything you needed?" she asked as she reined in her emotions.

"Needed?"

"You said you needed some things. That's why you went shopping."

"Oh. Sure, no problem."

"Good."

Carter swept his eyes from Dani's head to her feet, and lifted his eyebrows. "You changed?"

"I kind of like the idea of a walk. You up for it?"

"Sure. A walk will be invigorating. Can you handle a walk with your ankle?"

"I'm fine, just a little swelling. See?" Dani held up her foot and moved it from side to side.

"Wonderful."

Dani pulled a jacket from the coat closet and started to pull it on, but Carter stepped to her side.

"May I assist you, madam?"

"I would be most appreciative," she said as she slid her arm into a sleeve.

Once outside, Carter grasped Dani's hand as they headed down the sidewalk.

"I wish you didn't have to leave so soon," she said. "I wanted to introduce you to more of my friends at church on Sunday."

"I'm sorry. I should have planned better."

"I understand. I guess I'm just being selfish."

"It's not selfish to want to be with the person you . . . love?" Carter squeezed her hand and grinned at her.

"I had a talk with Mom while you were gone."

"That's nice. Anything you want to share with me?"

"To make a long story short, as the old saying goes, I think I have been afraid."

"Afraid? Of me?"

"No, silly. Afraid of trusting myself to make a decision. Afraid I would make another big mistake."

"What decision is that?"

Dani planted her feet on the sidewalk. "The decision to admit that you're the man God has for me, Carter."

"Wow! Hallelujah, praise the Lord!" Carter pulled her into his arms and kissed her.

"What will the neighbors think?" she said as soon as she could draw a breath.

"They'll think, 'There goes a couple in love.'" At that, he lifted her off her feet and twirled her around.

Dani thought that Carter might at any moment jump up and click his heels together. She laughed at his exuberance.

"How would you like to go out to dinner with me tonight? Some place special in honor of your 'decision'."

"I think that sounds wonderful. The Buckeye is a nice place. We could go there."

"Great."

"If we're going out tonight, then I think we had better make this a short walk so I have time to get ready."

All the concern about knowing whether she loved Carter completely dissipated as adrenaline rejuvenated her. How she wished she could whoop with joy.

When Carter and Dani burst back into the house in a few short minutes, the Kriegs exchanged questioning looks.

"Short walk," Cameron said.

"Sure was," Lindy said as she tossed aside the afghan and uncurled from Cameron's arm.

Cameron tuned down the volume on the television as Dani and Carter joined them in the living room.

"You weren't gone long," Lindy said.

"Change of plans, Mom. We're going out to dinner."

"Oh, that's nice, honey."

"So . . . I'm going to get dressed," Dani said as she smiled at Carter.

"And," Carter said, I'd like to use your phone if you don't mind."

"Not at all," Cameron said. "You'll have some privacy if you use the phone in the office."

"Thank you."

Dani pointed to the office door as they turned and headed there. *Hmm . . . wonder who he has to call?*

"Can you believe I totally forgot to call my family? My mom's not going to be too happy about that."

"Oh, no. I thought you probably called before you left the campus."

"I meant to, but I just forgot. Oh, well."

"There you are," Dani said as she opened the office door and pointed to the phone on the desk.

"Great. Thanks, sweetie." He pulled her close and kissed her cheek.

"I'll be ready in about an hour," she said as she left him alone to call his parents.

❄❄❄

After Carter and Dani finished eating dinner, Dani excused herself for a restroom visit. When she returned, a brightly wrapped gift sat where her plate had been.

"Now, what is this, Carter Matthews?" she asked as she slid into her chair.

"Why don't you open it and see?"

Dani hated to spoil the beautiful wrapping, but she was soon looking at a gleaming diamond studded cross necklace. "Oh, Carter, it's lovely." She draped it across her hand and then turned so he could help her put it on.

"Dani, I thought it would be a good symbol of our future life."

"Oh, yes! The cross will be at the center of what we're all about."

"So, you like it?"

"I love it!"

"I bought it at that jewelry store in town."

Dani laughed. "So, that's why you went shopping?"

"Guilty as charged."

Chapter 20

Indeed, if you call out for insight and cry aloud for understanding, and if you look for it as for silver and search for it as for hidden treasure, then you will understand the fear of the Lord and find the knowledge of God. Proverbs 2:3-5

Saturday morning passed in a whirl. After sharing the lunch of turkey sandwiches that Lindy had made, Carter packed his suitcase and prepared to head back to campus.

The whole family had gathered to see Carter off. "It's been a pleasure getting to know you, Carter," Lindy said.

"And all of you," he said smiling.

Lindy handed him a paper bag. "I've packed a few munchies for you to enjoy along the way."

"Thank you. I'll sure enjoy those."

Micah reached for Carter's hand, but Carter drew him into a hug. "Great to meet you, Mike."

"You, too."

"And you, tiger," he said as Carter hugged David.

"Drive safely," Cameron said as he thumped Carter on the back and opened the door for him.

"Will do. Thanks so much for having me." He shook Cameron's hand and stepped outside.

"Here, I'll carry your snack bag," Dani said. Dread gnawed at her as she followed him to the car.

Carter placed his suitcase into the trunk and his snack bag in the passenger seat.

He won't touch those snacks. Dani knew by now that Carter seldom ate between meals.

"Bye, Dani," Carter said as he turned to Dani with his arms outstretched. "I'll see you tomorrow evening."

Dani melted into his arms and kissed him tenderly. "I love you, Carter."

"I love you, too. Drive carefully tomorrow."

"I will. I promise."

Carter kissed her forehead and then opened his door and slid inside. As the car roared to life, he rolled down the window, blew her a kiss, and backed out of the driveway.

Dani returned his kiss, and watched until the car was out of sight.

When she went back inside, only her mother was in the kitchen. "Thanks for making Carter welcome, Mom."

"He seems like a wonderful young man, honey."

"I love him, Mom, so much."

Lindy added detergent to the dishwasher, clicked the door closed, pressed "start" and then turned to face Dani. "Yesterday, you mentioned that you were afraid to say you love him. So, that's obviously changed?"

"It helped sharing my thoughts with you, Mom. I've missed you these last few months."

"I've missed you, too, sweetie."

"Anyway, all I can say is that I finally realized I can't make decisions based on fear."

Lindy hugged Dani. "Your dad and I will be praying for you, honey. You can count on that."

"Thanks, Mom."

Lindy smiled at her. "So what are your plans for the rest of the day?"

"I thought I'd stop by the cemetery and then drop in on Shannon again."

"That's nice. Dad and I would like for all of us to go to dinner tonight, if you can make it."

"Sounds nice. I'll be home in plenty of time."

❊❊❊

As Dani made her way to Betts' grave, thoughts of her sister flooded her mind. God had brought amazing healing to Dani's heart, and she no longer dealt with the grief and guilt that had plagued her in the days following the accident that took Betts' life. Now, she simply missed her. Missed all those sister times when they shared everything, giggled over nothing, and whispered secrets.

She placed the single red rose she had purchased beside the bare rose bush her family had planted. "Love you, Betts. How I wish you could meet Carter. I know you would love him, too. Someday you will. You would not believe how handsome he is, and . . . "

❊❊❊

"Dani!" Shannon said as she held the door open. "Come in! Carter's gone back to school?"

"Yes. I miss him already." Dani stepped inside and smiled at the sight of her friend with a diaper slung over her shoulder. *Can't believe Shannon is a mom.*

"Jamie sleeping?"

"No, he's in the high chair. Have a seat, and I'll get my little guy."

"Sorry, I didn't call ahead. I . . . I have fantastic news I need to share with you."

"Good grief, girl, you don't need to call *me* ahead. Come anytime. Unfortunately, you missed Jared again. He's working overtime today."

Dani peeled off her coat. "Tell him he better be here when I come home for Christmas, or else."

Shannon chuckled. "I certainly will. I'm sorry the place is such a mess, but it's so hard juggling housework and caring for Jamie. Would you like a Coke?"

"Oh, no thanks." Dani made room to sit on the sofa by shoving aside a pacifier, baby blanket, and one shoe that obviously belonged to Jamie.

Shannon returned with a smiling Jamie and plopped him down onto a rug and then sat in the chair that matched the sofa.

Dani held out her arms to Jamie. "Come to Auntie Dani, Jamie."

Jamie babbled delightfully, and scooted over to Dani who swept him up.

"So, what do you think, Shannon?"

"What do I think about what?"

"Don't be coy. You know what."

"Oh," Shannon said, feigning innocence, "you mean what do I think about Carter?"

"Your mommy is so silly, Jamie," Dani said.

"Mum, mum, mum," he said.

"Carter seems wonderful, Dani, and so terribly good looking for sure."

"He is wonderful."

Jamie began to whine, and Dani handed him back to Shannon who placed him back onto the rug with some toys.

"Tell me more," she said.

"Well . . . I'm in love with him, Shannon. I'm in love with Carter Matthews!" Dani felt like she could float away with happiness.

"Oh, Dani, I'm so happy for you."

"I know we haven't known each other long, but . . . "

The two friends visited until Jamie's demand for attention prevented further conversation.

"I'd better put him down for a nap. I'm sorry, Dani."

"That's fine. I need to go anyway."

"Thanks so much for stopping by. You'll always be my best friend, you know."

Dani drew on her coat, planted a kiss on grumpy Jamie's soft neck, and hugged Shannon. "Catch you, later, my friend."

Dani's heart was full of love and gratitude as she drove along the turnpike toward Brady City on Sunday afternoon. *Thank you, Lord, for a beautiful weekend, for my wonderful family and friends, and most of all, for Carter. I can't wait to see him again. How could I have doubted I love him?*

Chapter 21

December 1981

May he give you the desire of your heart and make all your plans succeed. Psalm 20:4

Carter and Dani fell quickly into the routine of studies and work and found little time to be together. When they were able to carve out an hour, their intense desire to be together left them both frustrated. On Wednesday before Christmas break, the couple managed to share a couple of hours and a pizza at The Oasis.

"This is killing me," Carter whispered. "Seeing you, wanting to hold you . . ."

"Shh. I know. I feel the same way." She reached under the table and caressed his hand.

"Carter, your pizza's up!" the fellow manning the order window called.

Carter hopped up to get the pizza.

"Yum, looks great," Dani said.

"So, when are you leaving for Christmas?" Carter asked as he dabbed sauce from his lip.

"My last class is Friday morning. I should probably head out right after that. My dad made an appointment for me to get the dents in my car fixed while I'm home. When are you heading out?"

"I can actually leave Sunday afternoon after church. I had several papers to write for my finals, and I've already done them."

"It's a long drive to Florida."

"Yeah, I dread it. Wish you were going with me."

Carter had found a replacement for the Sundays he would be gone for Christmas break—a married student who was grateful for a chance to make a few extra dollars.

Bethany Church had grown under Carter's leadership. Some former members had returned, and Sunday school had been restarted. Carter was excited at the growth and regretted he had to be gone from them, but he could not disappoint his mother by not coming home for the Christmas holidays.

❄❄❄

The Kriegs' phone rang on Tuesday morning following Christmas day. When Cameron picked up, he wasn't surprised to hear Carter's voice on the other end since he had phoned every day Dani had been home.

"Mr. Krieg, could you do a huge favor for me?"

Cameron chuckled. "I guess that depends on the favor you ask."

"I'm flying in to Dayton next Tuesday. Could you possibly pick me up?"

"Uh . . . you're coming here?"

"Yes. I want to surprise Dani. If you can't do it, I understand. I can always rent a car."

"No, don't do that. I'll gladly pick you up."

"Thanks so much. I'll be on Delta Airlines, flight . . ."

❆❆❆

"Mr. Krieg," Carter said as the two headed home from the airport the following week, "I'm very much in love with your daughter."

Cameron glanced at Carter amused at the catch in his throat. "Lindy and I are aware of that, Carter."

"I want to ask her to marry me, and . . . I'd like your and Mrs. Krieg's blessing."

"Carter, you have our blessing. You seem like a fine Christian young man, and we are confident you will be a good husband for Dani."

Carter sat up straight and drummed his feet on the floor. "Oh, I will. I promise I will. I love her so much."

❆❆❆

Dani had been helping Lindy clean up the lunch dishes when David rushed into the kitchen.

"Where's Dad?" David asked. "He said he'd take me and Mike to the skating rink today."

"He'll be home before long. If Dad said he'd take you, he will."

"Okay," David said as he scooted from the room.

"Did Dad have something he had to do at school?" Dani asked.

"No . . . he had to do a favor for a friend."

"Good old Dad. No wonder everyone likes him."

Dani glanced out the kitchen window. "There he is now, Mom. Who's that with him? Mom, I think it's Carter. Carter is here?" She flew to the door, across the porch, and down the steps into Carter Matthew's arms.

Cameron slipped past them into the house.

"What are you doing here? I am shocked."

"I had to see you. I just couldn't wait until school started again."

"Come on in. So, my folks knew about this, huh?"

"Your dad's my confidant."

"You sneaky people."

❄❄❄

Cameron and the twins piled into the car and headed for the skating rink, and Lindy took advantage of the quiet to read. Carter and Dani thought about going to see Shannon but decided instead to go for a drive.

"I see you got the dents in your car fixed," Carter said as he started to open the passenger door of Dani's car.

"Yeah. A friend of my dad's owns a body shop and he did us a favor."

Dani drove aimlessly around town with one hand on the wheel and one hand in Carter's. "I'm still in shock that you're here with me."

"I had to see you, be with you."

"I'm glad you're here." She squeezed his hand.

"I'd like to take you out to dinner tonight—someplace really nice."

"Sounds great."

"I only have a few days to spend here. I promised Mom I'd take her to the country club New Year's Eve Ball on Saturday night."

"What about your dad?"

"He refused to take her. I don't think she wanted him to go anyway."

"Why not? Your dad seems so nice."

"I think Mom is afraid he wouldn't wear a tux."

Dani chuckled. "Hates tuxedos, huh?"

"My dad can be really stubborn."

"Well, at least you and your mom will get to spend time together."

"Yeah. Now, back to dinner tonight. Is there a good restaurant in Meadow Glen?"

"Well, there's the Coventry. I hear it's pretty fancy since they changed hands and expensive."

"Let's try it."

"We'll probably need a reservation."

"I'll call as soon as we get back."

❈❈❈

Dani had only been at the Coventry once before when the Kriegs and Porters shared a meal there several years ago. To say that the restaurant had been completely renovated was an understatement.

The room they had been seated in featured a huge stone fireplace along one side. Opposite the fireplace a gold ornately-framed mirror centered a black wall, and white satin draperies swept gently back produced an exquisite sight. The glowing embers in the fireplace reflected in the mirror, and the soft concealed lights twinkling star-like all around them created a stunning romantic ambiance. Dani tried not to stare, but the restaurant was so completely changed she couldn't help herself. She felt small sitting in the red velvet high-back chair. She looked at Carter, and the only word she could manage was "Wow!"

"Fantastic, huh?" Carter said. "Perfect room for a perfect night." His smile crinkled his eyes and made Dani's heart race. She reached across the table for his hand as their eyes met. *I love this man, Lord. With all my heart, I love Carter Matthews.*

A waitress approached their table. "Good evening. I am Brittany and I'll be assisting you this evening," she said with a smile....

❈❈❈

The couple dined on black peppercorn-glazed salmon, olive-crusted potatoes, and grilled brussels sprouts. Dani had never experienced fine dining before, and wondered how much this evening cost Carter.

"That was terrific," Dani said as she sipped the last few drops of her cinnamon-infused coffee.

"I'm so happy you liked it. I thought the crème brulée was the best." Carter dabbed his mouth, placed his napkin back on his lap, and reached for Dani's hand. "I love you, Dani, and . . ." Carter released her hand, pulled something from his pocket, eased from his chair, and knelt beside her. "Will you marry me, Danita Krieg?" he asked as he presented a gleaming diamond ring to her.

"Wha—"

"Will you marry me?" he repeated.

"Oh, Carter! Yes, yes, yes! I will marry you."

Carter slipped the ring on her finger, as their lips met.

Dani gazed at the small solitaire amazed that if fit perfectly. "How did you know my size, Carter?"

"I guessed. The clerk said it could be adjusted if it didn't fit."

"I love it, Carter, and I love you. I sure wasn't expecting my day to end like this."

❊❊❊

Dani handed the car keys to Carter and asked him to drive home. "I'm completely shaken, Carter. I woke up this morning thinking how much I missed you, and here we are engaged. Engaged!" She caressed the diamond.

"You've made me one happy man, Dani."

She brushed a piece of lint from her jacket and turned to face Carter. "We have so much to think about."

"That's for sure."

"Our relationship has grown so fast, but I feel at peace about it. You do feel the same way, right?"

"Absolutely. I have complete peace. I have never felt like this about anyone else."

"You've had loads of girlfriends, no doubt?" She lifted her eyebrows in a hope-it-isn't-true answer.

"Well, just like you I have dated some, but it never lasted. There was one girl who I thought I might get serious about, but she broke up with me and got married shortly afterwards. You're the one, Dani. I know it." He tapped the steering wheel to emphasize his words. Otherwise, I wouldn't have told you I love you. I take those words seriously. There are so many divorces today, and I wanted to make sure when I say 'I do' it will be forever."

Tenderness for Carter tugged at her heart.

"Besides, I don't want a marriage like my folks' that's for sure."

"Oh?" Dani sensed from her one meeting with them that there was tension, for sure.

"I love both of them, but I think they stayed together for Margot and me. That's not really a marriage in my book. What about your parents?"

"Well, I must admit, they have a great marriage, although I know they had a rough couple of years in the beginning." *Someday, I'll tell Carter the whole story.* "I wonder how they'll take our news."

"I think they'll be fine with it."

"Oh, you do, huh?"

"Yep. I asked your dad already."

"You did? What did he say?"

"He and your mom think I'm a great catch."

"A great catch, huh?" Dani poked his arm."

"Hey, watch it, lady. I'm driving."

Carter pulled into the Krieg's driveway, cut the engine, and turned to Dani. "I've been praying for God's leading in my life for a long time, and I know He has answered my prayer by sending you to me."

"Oh, that's so sweet, Carter."

"You're beautiful, smart, fun, and . . ."

"And?"

"And you love the Lord."

"How do you know I'm the one for you?"

"Well, I kept stumbling in to you at school when you were dealing with the loss of your sister. I don't believe they were accidents. I felt drawn to you from the first moment I met you. Over the last few months, I know without a doubt God has answered my prayer." He lifted her hand to his lips and gently kissed the ring he had placed on her finger.

Dani's heart overflowed with love for him.

"Let's go break the news, Dani, what do you say?"

Chapter 22

January 1982

To humans belong the plans of the heart, but from the LORD comes the proper answer of the tongue. Proverbs 16:1

Carter glanced out Brady's library window and caught a glimpse of Dani approaching. His heart pounded with excitement to think that this beautiful girl would soon be his wife, at least he hoped it would be soon. Increasingly, marriage had been on his mind as the weeks before his graduation slowly slipped away. The college provided graduating Bible students a list of churches looking for pastors, and he had applied to several. One in particular caught his attention—Grace Community church in Wilburta, Ohio, a small town near Akron.

The ad read: *"We're looking for a committed young man to lead our small congregation on its mission to grow and expand."*

Carter felt it was exactly what God had called him to.

When Dani entered the library, Carter waved her to his table in an area surrounded by stacks of books.

"Hi, beautiful," he whispered as he pulled out a chair for her.

Dani smiled, removed her coat and gloves and slid into the seat.

"I love you," he mouthed.

"Love you, too," her words a bare whisper.

"We need to talk, Dani."

"Okay."

"I mean somewhere private."

"Well, how about the chapel? I go there sometimes to pray, and there's never been anyone there."

"All right, sounds good."

Carter and Dani pulled on their coats, gathered up their books, and headed for the chapel.

As they arrived, Professor Ward was leaving. "Hi Danita," he said as he smiled and continued on.

Dani returned his greeting, and opened the door. *Good, nobody's here.*

His desperation to hold her, to give in to his feelings almost overwhelmed Carter once they were alone. If he did that, and someone saw them, he would risk graduating, so he made sure there were a few feet between them.

Carter leaned forward and tapped his fingers together.

"Carter? Are you okay?"

"I'm fine, but . . . " Carter struggled to find the right words. "As you know, I will graduate in a few months, and—"

"I know. Can you believe it? It's exciting and scary at the same time."

"Why is it scary?"

Dani drew her lips into a pout. "Well, you'll be starting your career, and I'll be here for another year without you. I don't know how I'm going to handle that."

"Maybe you won't have to."

Dani wrinkled her forehead. "Why? Have you changed your plans?"

"I'm hoping *we* can change *our* plans."

"You're sounding awfully mysterious."

Carter took a deep breath. "Let's get married, Dani."

Shock registered on her face. "You mean now? Get married now?"

"Yes, as soon as this term is over."

"But, I won't be finished with my degree for another year or more, Carter."

"I know, but once we're married, you could take part-time classes. It would just take you a bit longer."

"You don't even have a job. How would we support ourselves, let alone the cost of college?"

"*I'll* support us. I already have had a promising telephone interview."

"You have? Where?"

"You won't believe it, but one is in Ohio—Wilburta."

"Wilburta? Never heard of it."

"It's a suburb of Akron. A small church there is looking for a pastor."

Dani shook her head and tried to harness the thoughts swirling through her mind.

"Dani?"

"Wow, I guess I'm in shock. Can this small church afford to *pay* a pastor?" Dani asked.

"I won't know the details until I go for the interview, but I can always get a part time job on the side."

"Oh, Carter, I don't know what to say. She chewed the inside of her cheek, stood and paced around the room. "Where will we live? I can't imagine putting a wedding together on short notice. At the same time, I want so much to be your wife."

Carter reached up and drew her back down near him. "Then, let's do it. We don't have to have a big wedding, and if you really do want one, we can plan it later."

"Okay, let me get this straight," Dani said. "You want to get married as soon as you graduate? That means I won't be coming back to Brady, right?"

"I'm afraid so. But . . . if I don't land that position, we could come back here and live in married student housing until you get your degree. I would just have to find a job around here."

"You would do that?"

Carter's determination to stay arm's length from her vanished as he pulled her close to him and stroked her hair. He gently turned her chin to face him. "Yes, absolutely. I love you, Dani." I can't imagine waiting another year to make you my wife."

Dani struggled against the desire to surrender to his closeness, but reality of the risk they were taking took control, and she shook herself free and stood. "When is your interview at Wilburta?"

"Monday, February first."

Dani stood in silence for a few moments and then turned to face Carter. "I need some time to think about this and discuss it with my parents."

Carter's face reddened as a frown drew his eyebrows together. "We're adults, Dani."

His tone shocked Dani, and she pressed her hands against her chest as if she needed to protect her heart from the stinging words. "Carter!"

"I'm sorry, Dani. I shouldn't have said that. Forgive me, sweetheart. I guess I'm just so anxious for you to say you will marry me."

"I feel the same way, believe me, but I need time to pray and think about this."

"You're right. Absolutely."

"And even if we are adults, the thoughtful thing to do is to discuss it with both our parents."

"I know, and I need to talk to my folks, as well." He glanced at his watch and stood up.

"You have a class?"

"In five minutes. I need to run."

"I have some research to do, so maybe we'll have dinner together?"

"Absolutely." Carter bolted for the door, turned, and blew Dani a kiss.

Chapter 23

The way of fools seems right to them, but the wise listen to advice.
Proverbs 12:15

Lindy picked up the phone on the first ring, and the sound of her voice filled Dani with tenderness. "Hi, Mom."

"Hi sweetheart. Is everything all right?"

"Everything's fine. I . . . uh . . . I need to talk to you and Dad about something."

"Are you sure you're okay? You sound like something is wrong."

Dani took in a deep breath. "Is Dad there?"

"Yes," Lindy said, as a blip of apprehension coursed through her heart.

"Please ask him to pick up the other phone, okay?"

"Sure, honey. He's painting the new addition, so it will take a minute."

Dani could hear her mother's footsteps and muffled words as she spoke with Cameron.

Cameron picked up the phone. "Dani?" Cameron said, "Mom said you want to talk to us?"

"Yes. I have a big decision to make and I want you to help me make the right one."

"Okay," Cameron and Lindy said. "We're listening."

"Carter wants to get married."

"Dani," Lindy said, "he already proposed to you. We are aware he wants to marry you."

Dani twirled the phone cord around her index finger. "He did, I mean, yes, he did propose, but . . . "

"Dani, what's going on?" Cameron asked. "Is something wrong? Have you changed your mind about marrying Carter?"

"Oh, no! Not at all. I love him with all my heart."

"Then, please tell us the reason for this mysterious call," Lindy said.

Silence for a few seconds.

"Dani?" her parents said in unison.

"Carter wants to get married as soon as this semester ends—like in June."

"But, you won't have your degree for at least another year," Cameron said.

"What's the rush?" Lindy asked. "You guys just got engaged a few weeks ago."

"I know. Like I said, I am not sure what to do. I wanted to share this with you before making a decision. I need your prayers and your wisdom."

"Wow! This comes as a shock, sweetheart," Cameron said. "We'll certainly be praying for you."

"How can Carter support the two of you?" Lindy asked. "He doesn't have a job, does he?"

"No, but he has a job interview coming up, and he's praying they'll hire him."

"What kind of job?" Cameron asked.

"Pastor of a small church in a town called Wilburta."

"I've heard of that," Cameron said. "It's near Akron."

"Dani, what do *you* want to do?" Lindy asked.

"I want to marry Carter, for sure, but I also want to finish school. My dream is to teach learning disabled kids."

Silence on the other end, so Dani continued. "Carter said if he doesn't land the job, he will get a job around here and work until I graduate. But, he sure sounds positive about the position. I can always take classes at a school near Wilburta until I finish."

"Dani," Cameron said, "you need to pray about this. Of course, your mom and I will pray, too. That's the first step. The fact that you're seeking counsel from us is important, as well. Here's the thing, lots of decisions we face in life are not between good and bad, but sometimes between good and best. This sounds like what you're facing. If you pray and earnestly seek the Lord, He will lead you to make the best choice."

"Oh, brother, sometimes I wish the Lord used the red light, green light system!"

The three of them chuckled at Dani's words.

"Anyway . . . thanks for listening *and* for praying. I knew I could count on you to give me good advice." A smile filled Dani's face.

"You're strong, smart, and love the Lord," Lindy said, "so, we know you'll not act until you're sure you're making the right choice."

"Thanks, Mom. I better get to class. Give my brothers a hug for me, okay?"

"We love you, Dani," Cameron and Lindy said.

"Love you, too. Bye."

"Bye, bye."

After Cameron and Lindy hung up, they looked at one another with worried expressions.

"This is one of those times I wish Dani was still a little

girl I could simply *tell* her what to do," Cameron said as he pulled out a chair and sat down at the kitchen table.

Lindy sat opposite him, and clasped her hands around his. "I know, Cam, but our Dani is a grown woman."

"That she is. I just remember how difficult it was for us in the beginning, barely able to scrape together money for groceries and rent."

"That's true, but remember our situation was different. Besides, like you said, neither decision is necessarily good or bad."

"Let's pray, okay?"

"Oh, my goodness, just thinking about planning a wedding—"

"Lindy, let's pray."

"Dear Father . . ."

Chapter 24

I call on you, my God, for you will answer me; turn your ear to me and hear my prayer. Psalm 17:6

A week had gone by since Carter's plea to get married in June, and Dani still had no peace about the decision. *I have to know, Lord. Please help me know what to do.*

Between Carter's church demands and his course work, he had little time to spend with Dani. Under the circumstances, both of them felt it was a blessing because the temptation to give in to their feelings had grown even stronger since their engagement. Every time they did share dinner, Dani saw the same unspoken question in his eyes.

Dani was desperate to find time alone to think and pray. Either she had class or Courtney was in their room. While she had grown to love Courtney, she didn't feel it was appropriate to share everything that transpired between Carter and her. So for this week, she decided to skip lunch and eat a snack in her room.

I have to know, Lord. I can't keep on like this.

Dani finished her granola bar, reached for her Bible, and turned to the book of Psalm. She always began her time with the Lord by reading one of the psalms. Today, she chose Chapter 25.

In you, LORD my God, I put my trust. I trust in you; do not let me be put to shame, nor let my enemies triumph over me. No one who hopes in you will ever be put to shame, but shame will come on those who are treacherous without cause. Show me your ways, LORD, teach me your paths. Guide me in your truth and teach me, for you are God my Savior, and my hope is in you all day long. . . .

Dani loved speaking aloud to the Lord as if He were sitting near her. *Father, have I put my trust in You? Or am I trying to figure everything out on my own? I believe You have plans for me, but I'm not sure what they are.* Dani massaged her temples desperate for an easy answer. *Am I to be a teacher of learning disabled children or a pastor's wife? Or both? If so, wouldn't it make sense for me to finish my training before getting married? After all, I could do it in one more year if I really tried. But a whole year without Carter!* Dani shook her head as if she could shake the thought from her mind. *I feel strongly that You led me here for that reason. Was I wrong about that? Why Brady college? There are so many other colleges I could have gone to, but my parents were so set on my coming here to this small Christian school in Tennessee. Was that a coincidence?*

Dani put her Bible aside and flopped back on her bed as she continued her prayer of questions. *Of all people on campus, why was Carter the only one who noticed my tormented state of mind? What was he doing here anyway? Florida certainly must have lots of Christian schools where he could have gotten his degree in Bible! Why did Carter feel compelled to call me at home after barely meeting me? He didn't even know me. What drew him to me? There are loads of beautiful girls who would love to have dated Carter Matthews. I don't get it, Lord. What I need are answers.* Little Mandi's face slipped through her mind, and brought a smile. *Why do I have this intense desire to teach needy children if it isn't in Your plans for me, Lord? If I'm supposed to marry Carter instead of graduating, have I wasted all this time and money? My parents have sacrificed so much. . . .*

Dani sat upright again, lifted her hands in appeal. *Questions, so many questions, Lord.* Dani had never strung all these questions together in her prayers until now. As if she were reading an illustrated children's book, Dani pictured the journey she had been on for the last two years. Slowly, she turned each page until she reached the place where she found herself today. Her eyes flew open and she fully expected to see Jesus sitting in her desk chair. "I'm beginning to see, Lord," she fairly shouted. "I'm getting it, finally!" Dani hopped to her feet and paced the small room.

*You brought me here! Sure, Mom and Dad had a hand in it, but it was You who saw that I enrolled in spite of my apathy. It was You who placed Carter exactly where he would see me and reach out to me when I was at my lowest. It was You who put the love of learning disabled children in me, and grew that into a desire to teach them. None of this has been an accident. They didn't just happen. You meant for me to meet and fall in love with Carter; You meant for me to pursue special education. It's so clear now! Why did it take me so long to see it? Your plan is for me to become a pastor's wife, and very soon! Oh, my, that's a scary thought. My plan was to finish school, and while that may happen someday, that was **my** plan. I believe You've shown me a bend in my path. How You will use my training in special ed someday will be interesting, because I know You will. Like Mom says, "God doesn't waste anything."*

Dani felt like shouting, but instead, she dropped back down on the bed, picked up her Bible and paged through the psalms looking for one to read back to the Lord. Her fingers found Psalm 28:7. *The Lord is my strength and my shield; my heart trusts in him, and he helps me. My heart leaps for joy, and with my song I praise him.* Dani's heart leaped with joy right along with King David's!

I can't wait to tell Carter.

Challenges

Chapter 25

April 1982

Commit your way to the Lord; trust in him and he will do this.
Psalm 37:5

Carter's interview with the Ohio church had gone well, but when he hadn't heard anything from the church in weeks, he sent out several more résumés and landed two interviews. He felt they had gone well, too, but when he heard nothing from them either, he scheduled a session with his advisor.

"Good to see you, Carter," Mr. Wheeler said. "Come on in. Have a seat."

"Thanks," Carter said as he dropped into the chair opposite the old oak teacher's desk.

"What's on your mind, Carter?"

"I am a bit frustrated, confused, and getting a little desperate, you might say." Carter dropped his head and rested his elbows on his knees.

"I see. Shall we pray before we begin?"

"Yes, please, I need prayer."

When Mr. Wheeler finished praying, he leaned forward, tapped his fingertips together, and waited for Carter to speak.

Carter exhaled loudly and then lifted his eyes to meet Mr. Wheeler's. "As you know I will graduate in May."

Wheeler smiled and nodded.

"I have had three interviews with churches looking for a pastor." Carter held up three fingers to reinforce his words. "All three have gone well, actually, I felt they went exceptionally well." He shook his head and frowned. "Don't you think I should have heard something by now? I haven't heard a word. Am I doing something wrong?" The warmth in Mr. Wheeler's smile helped Carter relax.

"One of the things you will learn as you go forward in your life plan for ministry is that church pulpit committees move notoriously slowly. There are several reasons for this. Usually, they meet once a week. If they are considering several candidates, they may be calling references, discussing opinions, and deciding on salaries. Often, this can take weeks, and, unfortunately, many neglect keeping the prospective pastors informed."

"So, do you think I should keep sending out—"

"Of the three interviews you've had, which one interests you the most?"

"Definitely the first one—Wilburta Community Fellowship in Ohio."

"May I ask you why?"

"I feel God has equipped me to lead a congregation to make changes in order to more effectively spread the good news of Jesus."

"And you feel the Wilburta church is in need of the leadership you are capable of providing?"

"I do. I don't mean to sound prideful, but it's like so many struggling churches are on the verge of closing their doors. Why is that? After all, we have the *good news* for crying out loud!"

Wheeler laughed at Carter's expression. "Here's what I suggest, Carter. Take that enthusiasm of yours to the nearest telephone and call the chairman of the pulpit committee at Wilburta Community Fellowship."

"You don't think that would be presumptuous?"

"No. I think at this point it makes sense. If the committee seemed interested in you, they should have gotten back to you."

Carter's relief shone in his eyes that had misted. "Wow, thank you so much! I should have come to you before now."

"Yes, you should have," Mr. Wheeler said. "That's why I'm called your *advisor,*" he teased. "And, by the way, I have heard you are doing an exceptional job as student pastor at Bethany church."

"God is really blessing there. It's experiencing wonderful growth. Attendance has tripled, and they are talking about expanding the auditorium."

"That's fantastic."

Carter stood and extended his hand toward his advisor. "Thank you so much," he said.

"Anytime, Carter. Keep me informed. I'll be praying for you."

Breathless from running across campus to his dorm, Carter forced himself to wait until his breathing slowed before picking up the phone. He pulled his wallet from his back pocket and retrieved the slip of paper with Jacob Hunt's number on it. Carter rehearsed what he would say as he waited for someone to answer. The words he had been waiting weeks to hear sent his heart a-twitter.

"Mr. Matthews! Jacob Hunt here. So glad you called. I'm sorry we haven't gotten back to you. Two of our committee members have been ill, and, we have only recently begun meeting again. We would like you to come to

Wilburta and meet with us again and preach while you're here, if you're still interested."

"Yes, sir. By all means, I am definitely interested."

❄❄❄

"I wish we could offer you more," the committee chairman, Jacob Hunt, said as he ran his hands through his hair that was barely there.

"I understand," Carter said. "As long as we can manage is all I'm concerned with right now."

"And, if the church grows," Hunt added, "your salary will increase."

"I am confident that this is where God wants me. I have to trust if He has called me here, He will provide for my needs."

The two men present, Jacob Hunt and Ryland Tolliver, and the only female, Joanna Bowling, smiled and reached to shake Carter's hand. "Welcome aboard!" Jacob Hunt said, beaming.

"I understand there's a parsonage?" Carter asked.

"Yes. It's small and needs a lot of work," Mr. Tolliver said, "but the church is not in a position financially to do anything about that right now."

"I'm sure the ladies will gladly come out and do some cleaning," Mrs. Bowling said.

Wonder if she's the one who has been ill? Her pale skin appeared to be stretched over the bones in her face, and Carter thought a strong breeze would send her toppling. "Thank you, Mrs. Bowling."

Mr. Tolliver stroked his gray beard and cleared his throat. "Of course, we could probably come up with a small housing allowance, if you choose not to live in the parsonage." He glanced at the other two to assess their opinions.

"Yes, of course," Hunt said. "We'll talk about that and get back to you."

"So, you're getting married soon, Carter?" Ryland Tolliver smiled and asked.

Carter returned his smile. "In June. We were hoping that Wilburta is where we will begin our lives together."

Jacob reached in his pocket, pulled out a key, and handed it to Carter. "Here's the key to the parsonage. It's at 110 Cedar Street."

"Thank you. I saw the Cedar Street sign as I drove here today," Carter said.

The pulpit committee stood and each shook Carter's hand. "We'll be in touch with the specific starting date for you to assume your ministry here, Carter," Jacob Hunt said.

"Fantastic. I'll be waiting to hear from you."

❋❋❋

June 1982

Dani's last days on campus had been difficult as she said goodbye to so many friends she had come to love, especially Courtney and the Tuesday night Bible study pals. Her last shift at the daycare center, when she knew she'd probably never see Mandi again, was the hardest. Mandi had grown so much over the last few months, and it thrilled Dani to see her walking and talking so much better.

After their whirlwind wedding and weekend honeymoon, Carter and Dani stayed with the Kriegs until Carter got the final call from Wilburta.

❋❋❋

The front door of the parsonage squeaked in protest as Carter pushed it open. "After you, m'lady."

Dani curtsied and stepped inside.

The couple stood transfixed as they took in the sight. The tiny living room had been wallpapered, Dani guessed, sometime in the 1940s. She smiled and imagined the faded cabbage roses, now faded with time, were once bright and loved by some happy housewife.

"Oh, brother," Carter groaned.

"Let's check out the kitchen," Dani said.

"Can't be any worse than this."

He's wrong about that, Dani thought as they surveyed the small, dark kitchen.

"Mr. Hunt warned me that the house needed some work—" Carter said. "an understatement for sure!"

Dani ignored the comment as she explored the dreary room with scarred bead-board paneling painted a dreadful green. "Look at that stove, Carter. Do you think it works?"

"Who knows? It doesn't matter. We can't live here."

The ancient sink had a small counter on either side and two rusting metal cabinets above them. The cabinets framed the kitchen's only window on which someone had hung a once-white curtain. Dani pulled the curtain aside. "An apple tree!"

"O..kaaay," Carter said as he rolled his eyes and remained glued to one spot. "This isn't going to work, dear sweet wife."

"Well, let's face it, my loving husband, it's all we can afford right now. So, let's check out the bedrooms." She tugged on his arm.

The two small bedrooms both had access to the tiny bathroom. "I love a claw-foot tub," Dani said.

"Do you also love a sink with no vanity?"

Dani smiled at Carter and playfully shoved his arm. "Come on. It's not all that bad."

"You're right. It's worse than bad."

Dani scanned the living room they had returned to. "I think it's adorable."

"Well, I think *you're* adorable, and this house is hideous."

Chapter 26

July 1982

Therefore, as God's chosen people, holy and dearly loved, clothe yourselves with compassion, kindness, humility, gentleness and patience. Colossians 3:12

Dani and Carter had enough money from their wedding gifts to purchase an inexpensive living room suit, a kitchen table, and four chairs. The bedroom suit from Dani's old room that the Kriegs gave them would work fine until they could afford a better one.

Cameron drove a U-haul truck with Dani's car in tow and followed the newlyweds to Wilburta. Mark Porter came along to help. Both the truck and Dani's car were filled to capacity.

As the little caravan neared Wilburta, Carter said, "I can only imagine what your dad's going to think of the dreary parsonage."

"Knowing Dad, he won't even notice."

"He'd have to be blind."

"Let's try to keep a positive attitude about it, shall we?" She reached over to him and stroked his arm. "It's our first home, Carter." *What's up with his attitude?*

"You're right. I'm sorry, sweetheart."

His smile warmed her all the way to her toes.

Carter drummed on the steering wheel. "If only Jacob Hunt could have offered another $50, we could have swung a nice apartment."

"I know, darling, but you'll be surprised how nice it will be when I get my hands on it! I'm so excited."

As they neared the parsonage, the couple saw several cars parked in the yard leaving the driveway empty. Carter pulled in and drove around to the back so Cameron would have space to park and unload the truck.

Dani hopped out of the car to meet the lady who was waving at them and heading their way.

"You must be Danita," she said. I'm Alice Tolliver." She swiped her hand on her baggy jeans before extending it to Dani.

Dani smiled and shook her hand. "You can call me Dani. This is my husband, Carter," she said as she motioned to him.

"Hello Mrs. Tolliver. It's lovely meeting you."

"And you, as well," she said.

"Ryland Tolliver was one of the men who interviewed me. Would he be related to you?"

"Ryland is my husband."

"I see," Carter said as he smiled at Alice.

As the ladies headed inside, Carter directed Cameron as he backed the U-Haul as closely as possible to the front door of the parsonage.

Alice took Dani by the elbow and guided her inside. "We have been a lot of work on the place this week— painting and cleaning. Lord knows it should have been done before now. Come on in and see what you think."

The two ladies climbed the shaky wooden steps side by side.

"Oh, my!" Dani said as she stepped inside the living room. "You painted the wallpaper. It's lovely."

"We actually scraped it off first because it was peeling in places," Alice said.

"And you hung curtains? I am totally shocked." Tears pooled in Dani's eyes, and she blinked them away.

"You're here," a young woman with thick copper hair amassed atop her head bounced into the room. "Hi, I'm Mavis Moore" she said, "and this character behind me is Nick Edwards."

Dani chuckled and willed her attention from Mavis' warm brown eyes, the color of her dad's favorite cup of Columbia coffee. "Dani Matthews. It's nice to meet both of you."

"Hi, Dani," Nick said. "Welcome to Wilburta."

"Thank you. Looks like you're the one responsible for painting this room."

"Guilty as charged," he said. A smile appeared amid the paint splatters on his ruggedly handsome face.

"Well, I love it. It's exactly the color I would have chosen, and it will go perfectly with our sofa."

Mavis took her hand. "Come see the kitchen."

"I'll finish up the bathroom curtains," Alice said.

Dani allowed Mavis to tug her into the kitchen as Carter stepped inside the living room and propped open the front door. "Right along that wall will be fine," he said.

Cameron and Mark lugged the sofa to the spot Carter indicated and headed back to the truck for the rest of the furniture. In thirty minutes they had everything unloaded and set in place.

"Mavis, I can't believe all the work you've done here," Dani said, "it looks like a different house."

"We just couldn't imagine your moving in here with the place looking like it did," Mavis said. "Nick and a few others from church made some repairs, refinished the floors, and painted the walls. They even installed a vanity in the bathroom."

"You're kidding?"

"It's true. Mavis has been ordering me around like a slave driver." Nick leaned over the gleaming sink to wash the paint from his hands.

"Somebody has to keep you out of trouble," Mavis said as she thumped his back.

A fresh coat of white paint now covered the ugly bead-board, and the polished appliances, though ancient, shone like new. "Oh, my, you even washed the windows and hung curtains! Amazing. I love that apple tree," Dani said, as she pulled the curtain aside for another glimpse.

"Alice made the curtains this morning," Mavis said. "Like them?"

"I more than like everything." Dani hugged Mavis. "Thank you so much. You'll never know how much we appreciate this."

Mavis swept escaping locks and tucked them back into the mound of her hair. "No problem." Her smile relocated the small mole at the corner of her mouth.

"Well, I'm heading home," Nick said. "I'll come back and fix that broken step out back. Just watch it if you go out that way."

"Oh, Nick, do you think you can work on the front steps, as well?"

"See what I mean, Dani? She's a slave driver." Nick winked at her.

"Oh, shush, or you'll never see another one of my chocolate chip cookies."

"You wouldn't do that to your favorite cousin, now would you?"

"Your *only* cousin. And didn't you just say that you were leaving?"

"I'm going, I'm going."

"Thanks for all your hard work," Dani said.

"I'm glad I could do it. See you girls later," he said as he started for the door. "By the way, check out the new cabinets." Nick pointed to a bank of cabinets.

Dani had been so surprised by everything, she had not noticed them. "You're kidding! How can I ever thank you—all of you?"

"No need. I enjoyed doing it." He turned and headed to the living room.

"Oh, hey," Carter said almost colliding with Nick. "Looks like it's *you* I need to thank for the paint job," he said as he shook Nick's hand. "I'm Carter."

"Nick Edwards. You're very welcome. I had some time and thought I'd help out some."

"Well, we're grateful, believe me."

Carter introduced Nick to Cameron and Mark who had plopped down onto the sofa to rest and cool off from the hot July weather.

"Nice to meet all of you. I'll be seeing you at church, Reverend Matthews."

"Oh, please. Call me Carter."

"Carter, it is." Nick touched his finger in a mini salute and headed out the door.

As soon as Nick drove away, another car pulled into the driveway, and Carter stepped outside to greet whoever had arrived.

Jacob Hunt climbed from his car and waved.

Carter dashed to meet him. "Mr. Hunt, it's good to see you again."

"And you, as well. My wife and I have some things for you in the trunk." Jacob held the car door open for his wife and offered her a hand.

Jacob filled Carter's arms with bags of groceries.

"Groceries? You bought groceries?"

"We knew you'd be coming home to empty cabinets."

"Unbelievable. How thoughtful," Carter said.

"This is my wife, Sarah," Jacob said smiling at the tiny gray-haired lady.

"A pleasure to meet you, Mrs. Hunt. I'd shake your hand, but as you can see, they are full of groceries."

Mrs. Hunt smiled at him. "It's nice to meet you, too, Pastor Matthews."

Carter decided to let her title for him remain.

Jacob Hunt offered his wife his arm and the two followed Carter to the house.

"Watch your step." Carter said. "We'll have to get those steps fixed."

"I'll see if Nick can do that," Mr. Hunt said.

Mr. Hunt pulled open the living room door and held it wide for Carter.

"Mr. and Mrs. Hunt, I'd like you to meet my father-in-law, Cameron Krieg, and his friend, Mark Porter," Carter said as they entered the small living room.

Cameron and Mark stood to greet and shake hands with the Hunts.

"I'll just take these groceries to the kitchen if you'll excuse me for a moment," Carter said.

"Please have a seat," Cameron said.

"Oh, we can't stay," Jacob said. "We just wanted to drop off a few things and meet Carter's wife. How nice that we can meet you, as well."

"Carter and Dani are so excited to begin their ministry here in Wilburta."

"And we are equally excited that he accepted our call."

Carter placed the groceries on the table, glanced at Mavis busily scouring the paint splatters from the sink. "Come meet the Hunts, sweetheart," he said as he placed an arm around Dani.

"It's a pleasure to meet you both," Dani said, as Carter introduced her. "I'm so excited to get to know everyone."

"All in God's time," Sarah said.

Dani gazed at Sarah Hunt's eyes as blue as the July sky

and liked her immediately.

"Well, it was nice meeting all of you," Jacob said, as he steered his wife toward the door.

"Thanks so much for stopping by, Jacob," Carter said.

"And for the groceries!" Dani added.

Sarah Hunt turned around, grasped Dani's hand and said, "I would love for you to stop over some afternoon for tea, dear."

"I'd love that, Mrs. Hunt."

The couple watched as the Hunts navigated the front steps and headed for their car.

Dani surveyed the living room again and smiled. "Oh, Dad, can you believe all they have done?"

"I think it's wonderful," he said.

Mark nodded in agreement.

Alice and Mavis appeared in the living room with their hands full of supplies.

"I don't believe we've met," Carter said, as he smiled at Mavis.

"I'm Mavis, Pastor, and I'd love to shake hands, but at the moment, no free hand." She chuckled.

"Nice to meet you," Cameron said.

Dani introduced the ladies to Cameron and Mark.

"My goodness," Carter said, "you ladies have been pretty busy. Thank you so much for everything."

"We're glad we could do it," Alice said.

"Oh, Carter, they have transformed this place!"

"Dani, shall I put those groceries away before I go?" Mavis asked.

"Oh, I can do that. You two have done enough."

"Let us know if you need anything." She smiled at Dani. "Maybe we can have coffee one morning?"

"I'd love that."

Carter held the door open as the two ladies headed outside to their cars.

"Take care, now," Carter said.

Cameron looked from Dani to Carter. "You couldn't have asked for a warmer welcome than these folks have given you."

"That's for sure," Carter said.

Dani's heart was about to burst with joy at the love the small church had showered on them.

Cameron drew Dani into his arms. "I'm so happy for you. For both of you," he said, as he squeezed Carter's arm.

"How about we have prayer before we hit the road?" Mark suggested.

"Please do," Carter said.

The four of them joined hands, as Mark lifted his voice in prayer.

Chapter 27

August 1982

A wife of noble character who can find?
She is worth far more than rubies. Proverbs 31:10

Dani delighted in being a wife. Every morning after she had made breakfast for Carter and herself, she couldn't wait to spend a few minutes with the Lord thanking Him for His blessings. *I'm married to the most wonderful man I've ever met! Thank You, Lord. Thank You for giving him a heart to reach others. Help me be the best wife that I can be.*

Since the folks at church had done so much of the work on the house that she thought would fall on Carter and her, Dani planned to focus on other areas. On this hot August morning, she grabbed a pen and tablet and slipped out the back door. The air was heavy with humidity, and she wished she had taken time to pull on her shorts rather than remain in her nylon robe that clung to her body.

I'm glad we don't have close neighbors. Carter would probably think I'm terrible for coming out like this and barefooted too, for Pete's sake.

Debris from Carter's last mowing covered the step that Nick had recently repaired, and she brushed it aside with her foot. *I need something to sit on out here. I wonder what's in that shed?* Dani knew Carter stored the mower in there, but other than a cursory peek inside, she had never bothered to check it out.

Things I Need to Do, she wrote at the top of a page.

    1. Learn to cook

While Dani knew how to prepare a few simple dishes, she really didn't know much about menu planning and meal preparation.

    2. Check out colleges in the area

I am definitely going to finish my degree. Surely, there's a college close by.

    3. Talk to Carter about buying a washer and dryer.

I know money is tight, Lord, but we need these. The money I'm spending at the laundromat should pay for them in no time.

"Hellooo?"

Dani gathered her flimsy robe tightly to her body. "Who's there?" she called, chiding herself for not dressing.

"It's me, Nick," he said as he tramped around the side of the house. "I rang—" He turned his head slightly when he saw she was in her robe. "Oh, sorry, I should have phoned first."

Dani stood and checked to see if she was at least covered. "No, it's all right, Nick. I. . . I should have gotten dressed long before now. What can I——"

"I have an hour or so before another job, and I thought I'd take a look at that front step."

Dani was grateful he kept his eyes averted from her. "Okay, no problem." She turned and headed back inside. "Let me know if you need anything," she said.

Once inside, she dropped the tablet on the table and headed for the shower. *Another lesson learned, Dani.*

After she had showered and dressed, Dani headed outside to explore the shed. The pounding of Nick's hammer out front reminded her of her embarrassment, and her face flushed at the thought.

The heavy door creaked as Dani slid it open. *This is more like a barn than a shed.*

Carter had shoved the mower barely inside, and she pushed it out of her way. Sun streamed through a small window on the opposite side, and Dani stood agape at the amazing sight.

As she looked around, the condition of the barn stunned her. *My goodness, this barn is in better condition than the house was. That doesn't make sense. Obviously, it hasn't been used as a barn for a long time. No signs of animals anywhere. Almost like somebody lived in here.*

A rake, shovel, and a few other garden tools had been hung neatly along one wall, and an old Indian blanket was draped over the side of a stall. Dani pushed open the first stall door. *A cot?* Beside the cot a crate was upside down and a kerosene lamp atop it. *I need to ask Carter about this.*

Beside the stall was an enclosed area with a door secured with a padlock. *Obviously, this isn't part of the original barn. Hmm . . . Why would this room be locked, yet the outside door left open?*

At the far end of the barn a tarp had been thrown over something as if to protect it. Dani pulled up the tarp and caught her breath. *A bench!* She flung aside the tarp and examined the beautiful old bench. *It's lovely.* She pulled it away from the wall to get a better look. The iron filigree back was shaped like a butterfly. *Somebody loved this bench. I wonder . . .*

"Hello again." Nick Edwards stood in the doorway.

She hadn't heard him approach and his voice startled her for a moment. "Hi, Nick."

"I see you've found Miss Ellie's bench."

"Miss Ellie?"

Nick stepped inside and stood with his back in front of the stall where Dani had seen the cot.

I should ask him about the cot.

"Miss Ellie was the wife of the last pastor who lived in the parsonage, back in the 60s. Word has it she cherished that bench. When her husband died, she was well in her 80s and had no family, so the church allowed her to remain in the parsonage until her death."

"Why is the bench still here?"

"I think the folks who remember her sitting under that apple tree just couldn't get rid of it."

"Do you think anyone would mind if I use it?"

"No, not at all. Here, let me carry it outside for you." Nick picked up the bench and carried it to the apple tree.

Dani folded the tarp and left it where she found it, pushed the door back in place, and followed Nick.

"This where you want it?" he asked.

"Perfect." Dani clasped her hands under her chin and smiled at the bench.

"Dani, I need to hit the road."

"Okay. Well, thanks so much for fixing the steps."

"No problem."

"And helping me with the bench."

"You should wipe it down before you sit on it. It seems like it's still in good shape, though."

"Great. Thanks so much for lugging it out here. See you later."

Nick smiled and strode back around the house.

Oh, I forgot to ask him about the cot.

❋❋❋

Dani raced inside to try and get the phone before it stopped ringing. "Hello?"

"Hi, Dani, it's Mavis."

"Oh, hi, how are you?"

"I'm fine. You too busy to have lunch today?"

"Uh . . ."

"My treat. Up for it?"

"Okay. That sounds really nice, Mavis."

"How about I pick you up around 12:30?"

"I'll be ready."

"Great. See you then."

Dani and Mavis had become friends in the weeks since they arrived in Wilburta. Her warm and bubbly personality made her easy to talk to and confide in.

As Dani munched on her salad, she thought about the barn. She had meant to mention the cot she saw there to Nick, but in the excitement of seeing the bench, it slipped her mind. "Mavis, have you ever been in the barn out back of our house?"

"Yeah. It's been a while, though. Why? Oh, never mind. I know why. You found Nick's cot."

Dani's eyes widened in disbelief. "Nick's cot?"

Mavis put down her fork and met Dani's eyes. "I thought maybe Nick would have told you about it by now or removed it anyway."

"Told me what?"

"Nick has been sleeping in there once in a while."

A frown wrinkled Dani's forehead. "Why on earth would he do that? He's married, isn't he?"

Mavis folded her napkin, turned it over and folded it again. "Well, Nick and his wife are getting a divorce. The only apartment he could find that he could afford is about twenty-five miles from here. He's taking extra work right now in order to keep up the mortgage payments on their house and an apartment which means he works long hours."

"So . . . he sleeps in the barn?"

"Once in a while if he's too tired to drive home. He talked with Jacob Hunt and got permission to stay over at the parsonage. Things changed when he heard you were coming, of course. So, he moved his cot to the barn. It actually came in handy since he worked late several nights getting the parsonage fixed up. Jacob tried to get him to stay with Sarah and him, but he didn't want to impose. I offered to let him crash on my sofa, but he refused that, too. I don't think he's slept there since you guys moved in, but I could be wrong. He needs to get that cot out of there."

"Doesn't Nick have family around here?"

"I'm it. My mom and Nick's dad were brother and sister. My parents both died several years ago, and Nick's dad took off when he was about ten, and he's never heard from him since. His mom died when he was a senior in high school."

"How sad." Dani set her salad bowl aside and leaned on her elbows.

"Yeah, he's had it rough, and now this with Carolyn. I can't imagine why she's calling it quits. Nick is such a great guy."

"He was at the house this morning fixing our steps and helped me drag a bench out of the barn. He didn't mention anything about the cot, and I forgot to ask."

"Did you see his tool room?"

"I saw a locked room. Is that it?"

"Yeah. His equipment is in there. He enclosed a stall and added a lock so that he can keep his tools here in Wilburta. He hopes to buy a place that has a storage area as soon as all this is over. You'll probably see him whenever he needs to get in there."

"Wonder why Nick didn't tell me."

"He's probably embarrassed. Now . . . enough about Nick. I want to hear about your sister, Betts. That was her name, right?"

Chapter 28

October 1982

Let the wise listen and add to their learning, and let the discerning get guidance. Proverbs 1:5

The crib was easier to put together than Carter and Dani thought it would be. When they finished, they flopped down on the new carpet.

Carter rolled over beside Dani and pulled her into his arms. "I love you, Dani Matthews," he said, as he nuzzled her neck with kisses. "Our son is growing right there." He tenderly stroked her abdomen and smiled.

"No, sweet husband of mine, our daughter is —"

"What! That can't be true, a boy it shall be."

"A girl."

"No, I'm pretty sure it's going to be a boy." Carter moved his hand from Dani's abdomen to her side in search of her tickle spot.

"Nooo! Stop, Carter." She wiggled away from him, but Carter caught her leg, and pulled off her shoe.

"I didn't hear you say we're having a girl, did I?" He gripped her ankle and threatened to tickle her toes.

Dani twisted free and scooted away from him. "Girl! Were having a—"

Carter reached her before she got the word out.

"Don't, Carter. Don't tickle me, pleeaseeee. It's okay if we have a boy. I like baby boys."

"You do?" he asked covering her mouth with a kiss.

"Yes, I do." The familiar warmth of his touch started in the toes he had tickled.

"Well," he said, as he cuddled her close to him, "it just so happens that I like baby girls."

"Oh, you!" she said as she shoved him playfully away. "You're terrible."

"Well, you're beautiful, so there."

Carter and Dani had not planned their pregnancy, but now that a baby was on the way both were ecstatic.

"What do you say we call our folks and give them the news," Dani said. "My mom is going to be delirious."

"And my mom probably won't care less."

"Oh, sweetheart, that can't be true."

Carter didn't respond, but rose from the floor and headed from the room.

The atmosphere in the small bedroom suddenly felt oppressive.

❆❆❆

Dani was right about her mom's reaction to the news that Carter and she would be parents, but her dad's tears shocked her.

"Dad, I can't believe you're crying." she had said.

"They're just tears of joy, Dani. It seems impossible that my baby girl's going to be a mommy."

"And you're going to be a grandpa."

"Ouch! I'm getting old." Cameron laughed.

Dani smiled at the memory of his words.

"Where are you going?" Dani asked Carter who had appeared in the kitchen dressed in old work clothes.

"Meeting Nick and some other fellas. We're clearing out the platform area in order to make more room for the worship team."

"Clearing it out? You don't mean you're getting rid of the pulpit, do you?"

"Yep. Old Jacob Hunt was not too happy about that, but the council overruled. If we want to reach young people, we need to meet them where they are."

Dani winced at the reference to Mr. Hunt. She had formed a warm relationship with his wife over the last few months, and she hated Carter's attitude toward Jacob.

"What exactly does that mean, Carter?" She didn't mean to sound critical, but she worried that the changes at church seemed to be happening way too fast.

"It means we have to make the church a place they will want to come to."

"And they won't come if there's a pulpit?"

"Can we talk later, hon? I told the guys I'd be there at two o'clock."

"Okay," she said. "What time will you be home?"

"Not sure," he said, depends on how much we get done. Hopefully, by five or six."

"You need three hours to move a pulpit?"

"For crying out loud, Dani. What's gotten into you? If you must know, after we finish with the platform, we are going to paint the nursery."

Tears smarted Dani's eyes at Carter's harsh words.

"I'm sorry, Dani. Forgive me?" he asked as he lifted her chin and pecked a kiss on her cheek.

Dani buried her face in his shoulder, but didn't reply.

Carter patted her back. "See you later, hon."

After Carter left, Dani wandered into the kitchen, pulled back the curtains, and gazed at Miss Ellie's bench and the leaves still clinging to the apple tree. She liked to think of that space as her private sanctuary where she often spent her quiet time. *Lord, I don't want to argue with Carter, but we seem to be disagreeing on so many things these days. Help me be more patient and understanding.*

Dani dropped the curtain, sighed, and decided to work on her Sunday school lesson. She spread her materials out on the kitchen table and went to work planning for her class of special needs children. *Lord, help me understand these precious ones You have placed in my care. Thank You for showing me how to be more effective as I work with them. Even though my path to this point has wound in unexpected ways, I know without a doubt You have a plan to use what I have learned so far. Give me patience and love for them as You have been patient and loving with me. And, Father, help Carter and me learn to live together in harmony. I want to be the wife Carter needs, but lately I don't understand some of the decisions he's making. Am I wrong to question him? I need Your wisdom, Lord.*

When the Bartrom family visited church for the first time, each parent holding the hand of a Down Syndrome child, God chose that moment to speak to Dani's heart about starting a class. *Finally, I know where I fit in here.* She remembered the scene when she tried to share her idea with Carter over lunch a few weeks ago.

"I want to start a special needs Sunday school class," Dani told Carter.

"Why would you want to do that? They slobber all over . . . oh, sorry. It's just that we need someone to direct the children's choir. You would be so good at that, Dani."

Dani put down the tuna sandwich she was ready to bite into. "You're kidding, right? Me? Direct a choir?"

"It's kids, Dani. There are about a dozen of them."

"I thought Mrs. Walker directed the kids' choir."

Carter took a sip of his tea. "She did for a hundred years." Carter laughed, but the humor was lost on Dani.

"Is that sarcasm I hear?"

"I just meant . . . anyway, Mrs. Walker stepped down."

"Stepped down? Or fired?"

"Why would you say that?"

"Maybe because a lot of people are *stepping* down."

"For instance?" Carter asked.

"Mr. Warren, the worship leader, for one."

"He said he and his wife wanted to be free to travel."

"Why haven't they gone anywhere?"

"Dani, what's wrong? You sound . . . angry."

"Was Mrs. Walker fired, Carter?"

He dabbed the corner of his mouth, folded the napkin, and laid it across his plate. "The council met with her and asked her to pick out more contemporary choruses. That was it. Apparently, she wants to stick with the same old songs she's been doing for decades, and when we insisted she adapt to our new program, she stormed out of the room. So, to answer your question, no, she wasn't fired, she quit."

Dani shook her head and frowned. "What happened to kindness and—"

"Why can't you have a little trust in me, Dani? It seems you oppose every step of progress I've . . . we've made at Wilburta. What's up with that?"

Dani's chin trembled and tears gathered in her eyes at Carter's accusation. *Have I been doing that, Lord?*

Carter dabbed at Dani's tears with a napkin. "Oh, sweetie, don't cry. I'm sorry I hurt you. It's just that you have to realize that I have been trained in church growth techniques. I wish you would believe in me."

Dani swallowed the lump in her throat. "I don't mean to be oppositional, I just have concerns."

"You're entitled to your opinion, honey. Now, about the children's choir . . . "

"Carter, I'm not interested—"

"But, you know music, and you—"

"My *sister* is the one in our family who knew music."

"We need someone who is young and knows how to incorporate some of the new stuff that's out there. It seems a perfect fit for you, sweetheart."

"Except for one thing."

"What's that?"

"I have no interest whatsoever in directing a choir, children or anyone else!" Dani hopped up and scraped the remains of her plate into a trash can.

Carter lifted one eyebrow and stared at her in disbelief. "Okay, Dani, no need to be so . . ."

"So what, Carter? Honest?"

"I just wonder if you're feeling emotional because of the pregnancy? Is that what's bothering you?"

Dani laughed in spite of her anger. "No, I'm not 'emotional,' Carter. I'm frustrated that you aren't hearing me. I want to start a special needs class, not direct a choir!"

Carter pushed his chair back, stood, and held out his arms to his wife. "Okay. I hear you, sweetheart. You go right ahead and start that class. I'm sorry." He drew her into his arms.

Dani shoved Carter. "Get away from me you big lug."

❉❉❉

The phone rang before Dani could finish her lesson.

"Hi, Dani."

"Mavis? Hey, what's going on?"

"Have time to grab a coffee?"

"Uh . . . sure. Here?"

"How about we meet at the diner?"

"No can do. My car is in the shop."

"Oh, sorry. I'll be there in ten minutes."

Ten minutes later, Mavis knocked on Dani's door.

"I have the coffee pot on," Dani said.

"Great," Mavis said as she slipped out of her jacket and slid onto a kitchen chair.

"Cream?"

"Black."

Dani poured two cups of the steaming coffee, replaced the pot on the stove, and sat opposite her friend. "So, what's new?"

"I got a new job!"

"Tell me about it, girl."

"I'm going to be the new church secretary."

"At our church?"

"Of course."

A frown troubled Dani's forehead. "Are we growing fast enough for a second secretary?"

Mavis took a sip of her coffee. "My dear friend, have you looked around lately? The place is booming. Ramona can't keep up."

"I realize the church is growing. Well, I'm sure you'll be a big help to her. You've had lots of experience. Congratulations."

"Thank you, Dani."

Dani stirred her coffee and placed the spoon on a napkin. "Every Sunday there are so many new people. It's hard to believe."

"That's because God has sent us a wonderful pastor who understands what has to be done for us to grow."

Dani smiled. "I think he's pretty wonderful, too."

Mavis chuckled. "By the way, Nick thinks the divorce will be final any day now."

"Oh, really?"

"He's taking it pretty hard. Nick didn't want a divorce. So pray for him. Okay?"

"Absolutely. Divorce is a horrible thing. It's crazy how two people start out so much in love and end up divorced."

"I know, but sadly, it happens to a lot of people. I'm just so sorry it had to happen to Nick."

"I'll be praying for sure."

"Say, did he ever get his cot out of your shed?"

"Oh, sure. Quite a while ago."

"Good. Now, what about you? Are you feeling okay?"

"Except for morning sickness."

"Oh, yuck."

The two friends continued to chat until they finished their coffee.

"Hey, I gotta go. I didn't mean to stay so long. I just wanted to share my news."

"Congratulations, again."

"Thanks, Dani," she said as she carried her cup to the sink. "And thanks for the coffee."

Mavis pulled on her jacket and headed for the door.

"Talk to you later, Mavis."

"Ta ta."

Chapter 29

Be on your guard; stand firm in the faith; be courageous; be strong. Do everything in love. 1 Corinthians 16:13

Dani could hear the tap tap of Sarah's cane as she made her way to the door.

"Come in, Dani. It's so good to see you."

Dani had been visiting Sarah Hunt one afternoon a week since their arrival in Wilburta, and it had become a highlight of her week. An unlikely friendship had grown between the two women, separated in age by many years.

"Please, have a seat, Dani. I hope you like chocolate chip cookies."

"As a matter of fact, I do," Dani said, as she removed her jacket and took her usual seat on the Hunt's sofa.

Sarah had the tea already set up on the coffee table along with a tray of the freshly baked cookies.

"Would you mind pouring, dearie?" Sarah asked. "I'm a bit shaky today."

"Not at all."

"How have you been?" Sarah asked as she lifted a cup to her lips.

Dani noticed the tremors in Sarah's hands had worsened over the last couple of weeks. "Well, other that some morning sickness, I'm fine." Dani added a spoon of sugar to a cup and poured tea for herself.

"I know you must be excited."

Dani smiled and nodded. "Yes, we're very happy about the baby even though we hadn't planned on having a family this soon."

"I'm very happy for you."

"Thank you. I hope you will keep us in your prayers."

"I pray for you and your young man every day."

Dani sampled her tea and returned the cup to the table. She turned worried eyes to Sarah.

"What's troubling you, my young friend?"

Dani sighed. "I don't know if I can put it into words."

"Take your time."

"I'm concerned about Carter. He seems to be . . . I don't know . . . changing somehow."

"Changing?"

"Yes. He was so excited to become a pastor and reach people for the Lord. It's all he talked about in school."

"And now you feel that he is no longer interested in doing that?"

"Well, yes and no." Dani picked up one of Sarah's lace napkins and dabbed her lips. "Maybe it's just that the church has grown so fast, but he seems more concerned with how many people are there rather than . . . I don't know. I can't even describe what I mean."

"Something is obviously troubling you, Dani," Sarah said with a weaker-than-usual voice. Have you tried sharing your concerns with your husband?"

"I have, but he thinks I don't trust his decisions, and we usually end up saying things we don't mean."

A frown troubled Sarah's time-worn forehead, and she

adjusted her wire-rimmed glasses. "Oh, I am sorry to hear that." She reached for the tray of cookies, but Dani handed it to her. "It's important for you to love and respect your husband, honey. If there are things that are bothering you, prayer is the key. You must pray for Carter. God can change things."

An hour later Dani pulled on her jacket, and prepared for her walk home.

"Thank you for the tea, Sarah . . . and the cookies. They were delicious."

Sarah pushed her frail body from the chair and reached for her cane. "I'm glad you liked them."

"And thanks for listening. I am so thankful God has put you in my life."

Sarah smiled and patted Dani's hand. "You just go on home now, honey, and pray for that husband of yours."

Dani opened the door and headed down the sidewalk with a spring in her step. *Thank you, Lord, for Sarah Hunt.*

❄❄❄

Dani awoke to a knock. She hadn't meant to sleep after her walk to the Hunts, but drowsiness overtook her. *Wow, must be the pregnancy.* She fluffed her hair and hurried to answer the door.

"Oh, hi Nick."

"Hey, Dani. I just want to let you know I'll be doing some work in the barn. Don't want you to think there's a burglar or anything." Nick smiled as the glow of the late October sun created highlights in his sandy hair.

"No problem. Let me know if you need anything."

"You wouldn't happen to have iced tea, would you? I could sure use a glass."

"Uh . . . no, but I can easily make some."

"No, no. Don't bother."

"Don't be silly. It's no bother. I'll bring it out to you."

"Well, if you're sure."

Dani hurried to the kitchen and put a teakettle of water on to boil. She pulled out a gallon pitcher, the only one they owned, and dropped in several teabags. *Forgot to ask Nick if he likes his tea sweet. Oh, well, I'll take the sugar bowl out with me, just in case.*

In a few moments, Dani carried a tall glass of iced tea, a sugar bowl, and spoon out the back door and down the path to the barn.

Nick had left the door open, and she stepped inside. "Here you go, Nick. I brought sugar in case."

"No sugar needed," he said. Nick wiped his hands on the sides of his jeans and reached for the glass. "Thanks!"

Dani watched as he gulped down half the glass. "Wow, you must have been thirsty."

"Yeah, I should have stopped for something." Dani looked around at the saw horses set up in the aisle. "So . . . what are you doing?"

"Sanding cabinet doors for a kitchen I'm redoing."

"You seem to have a pretty good business going."

"I guess folks like my work," he said, as he swallowed another drink of tea. "Lord knows I need it right now."

Should I mention the divorce? "I'm so sorry about . . . about your divorce and all. Mavis told me you're having a rough time right now."

Nick sat the glass on an upturned barrel, leaned against a post, and plunged his hands into his pockets. "My cousin is certainly right." He shook his head and stared at the ceiling. "I don't know what happened to us. Carolyn was the love of my life. I might feel better if I knew why she wanted a divorce."

"God will get you through this. He—"

Nick sent a puff of dry dirt flying with the toe of his boot. "Right now, God seems pretty far off."

"He's not, Nick. You can be sure of that."

"You sound awfully sure of that."

"I am absolutely sure. I learned that the hard way when I lost my sister."

"Well, I'd love to hear about that, but right now, I better get back to these cabinets. Need to paint them this afternoon, so I can hang them tomorrow." He reached for the glass and handed it back to Dani. "The tea was great. Thanks again."

"I'll be praying for you, Nick. I mean that."

"Lord knows I need it."

She turned and headed back to the house, and kept her promise by falling to her knees in the living room and crying out to God for troubled Nick.

Dani rose, and her head swam with dizziness, and she dropped to the sofa. *Oh, my. What was that about?* After resting a few moments, she slowly stood up and headed for the bathroom, something she seemed to be doing an awful lot of since getting pregnant.

"Blood?" Chills raced through Dani, and she hurried to the phone.

Dani tried to calm herself by the time Mavis's welcome voice answered. "Wilburta Community Church, how may I help you?"

"Mavis, please tell me Carter is there? I need to talk to him right away."

"Carter's out of the office, Dani. Are you okay?"

"I . . . I think something's wrong. I passed some blood—"

"Oh! Shall I call an ambulance?"

"I don't need an ambulance, but I should get checked out. When will Carter be back?"

"He's in a meeting in Akron this afternoon, but I can try and call him."

"No, I'm sure it's an important meeting. I'll call the doctor and get a taxi—"

"You'll do no such thing. I'll be right over."

"Hold on a second, Mavis. Nick's working in the barn today and I think he's knocking. Be right back."

Dani laid the phone down, and opened the back door.

"Dani, would it be too much trouble to use your phone for a minute?"

Should I ask Nick to take me to the doctor?

"No, not at all. Come on in."

"Are you okay? You look . . . kind of pale."

Dizziness hit her again, and she steadied herself. "I . . . I'm not sure. I tried to call Carter, but he's out of town."

Nick left the door ajar and stepped inside, took Dani's arm and guided her to a chair.

"Mavis is holding on the phone," she said.

"You stay put. I'll talk to Mavis."

Nick picked up the phone, but the line was dead.

"Oh, no. She's probably on her way over here to take me to the doctor."

"We're not waiting. Where can I find your jacket?"

"I can get it," Dani said, as she tried to get up.

"Stay there, Dani." He pulled an afghan from the sofa, wrapped it around her, and picked her up.

"I can walk, Nick. I'll be fine."

Nick ignored her words as he carried her outside, slammed the door shut with his foot, and carried her down the steps and out to his truck.

"Nick, I'm not helpless."

Silence, again.

"Just hold on to me for a second while I get rid of some of this stuff." Nick jammed some papers into the glove box and tossed an empty Coke can into the back seat. After he swiped the seat free of French fry remains, he assisted Dani into the passenger seat.

"Now, where's your doctor's office?"

Chapter 30

Watch and pray so that you will not fall into temptation. The spirit is willing, but the flesh is weak. Matthew 26:41

Dani was admitted to the hospital but experienced no additional bleeding or dizziness. An ultrasound revealed she was carrying twins.

Carter rushed to Dani's bedside as soon as he learned what had happened. "Oh, sweetheart, I'm so sorry I wasn't here for you."

"You couldn't help it, Carter."

"Well, Mavis should have called me." He eased onto the hospital bed beside her and tenderly caressed her forehead and kissed her cheek.

"Everything worked out, darling. You mustn't blame Mavis." She playfully touched her finger to his lips.

"Twins! I can't believe it. Is the doctor sure?"

Dani laughed. "Of course, he's sure."

"Oh, my goodness. We have to move into a bigger place. How will we ever fit two cribs—"

"Sweetheart, the babies won't be here until June!"

"I know, but June will be here before you know it."

For several days following her hospital stay, Carter showered her with affection, assumed more of the household chores, and insisted she rest frequently.

When it appeared she was out of danger, Carter relaxed and returned to the long hours he had been keeping prior to their scare.

❄❄❄

Dani folded a load of towels she had pulled from their brand new dryer and then squeezed them into their spacious linen closet. *Carter was right about us needing more space, but I miss our little house.*

Dani's words to Carter about God providing came true two weeks after she came home from the hospital. The church council gave Carter a substantial raise, and he floated home as if he were filled with helium.

"I know a couple who is moving!" he sang as he twirled Dani around.

"Moving?"

He kissed her, and danced her around the small living room. "Yes! We're moving, my love. I've had my eye on a house for rent over on Hickory Street. When my raise was confirmed, I wasted no time calling about that house. And, we got it!"

Dani planted her feet. "You already rented it?"

"You'll love it, honey. It has three bedrooms and a fenced-in yard."

"Well . . . it would have been nice for me to at least have *seen* it before—"

"I'm sorry. You're right. I was afraid someone else would get to it first. And just think, the twins will have a safe place to play."

"Carter, it will be years before they will play outside."

Petals Beyond the Bend

"Dani, I can't believe you're not excited to get out of this place. We're cramped here, and it's just the two of us."

"I'm sorry. I just hate to think about leaving our little nest. After all, it's our first home."

"I understand, sweetheart. Just wait till you see the house, though. You'll love it."

"I know. I'm sure I will, but everything is just happening so fast."

Nick Edwards and Sam Wilson, one of the deacons from church, had helped them pack up and move. Carter wouldn't allow Dani to lift anything, and so she busied herself organizing the kitchen, and then decided to bake a batch of brownies.

Carter left for a two o'clock meeting at the church as soon as everything was unloaded.

"Don't you have time for a brownie, hon?" Dani asked.

"I wish, but no can do." He pecked a kiss on her cheek. "See you in a couple of hours. Thanks, guys," he said. "See you Sunday."

Dani poured coffee for Nick and Sam and placed a tray of brownies between them.

"Delicious," Sam said.

Nick downed two and reached for another. "Nah, they're just so-so."

"Better watch it, Nick, or you'll choke on that third so-so brownie!" Sam said as he downed the last of his coffee.

"More coffee, Sam?" Dani asked.

Sam checked his watch and pushed his chair back. "Oh, no thanks. I really need to get over to school and pick up Michael."

"Well, thanks so much for helping us with the move."

"I'm glad I could do it. Working the evening shift has its perks."

"Thanks pal," Nick said as he jumped up and thumped Sam on the back.

"You owe me one," Sam said with a smile.

"I need to hit the road, too," Nick said. "Kidding about the brownies."

"I know, silly. Want another?"

"No thanks." Nick stacked Sam's plate with his and carried them to the sink. As he turned around to get the cups, he bumped into Dani who had picked up the cups. Thankfully, Nick caught one as it flew out of her hand.

"Good catch," she said as she chuckled.

He took the other cup from her, and a spark like static electricity passed between them, and they locked eyes.

Dani's face flamed, and she turned away confused and nervous. She felt the warmth of Nick's hand on her shoulder, but she refused to turn around. "Nick, you had better go now."

"I know. I'm sorry, Dani, I didn't mean to upset you."

She corralled her emotions and faced him. "No, you didn't upset me. Thanks again for all your help today."

"No problem. I'll see you around."

Dani didn't respond as she watched Nick grab his cap from the counter where he had laid it, and plop it on his head. *What was that about, Lord?*

❄❄❄

As Thanksgiving neared, Dani thought she and Carter would be spending the day alone, since Cameron and Lindy were traveling to Indiana to be with Dani's grandparents, and they had heard nothing from Carter's parents.

Dani sidled over beside Carter who was sitting at the kitchen table going over the new visitor cards that had been turned in yesterday. She placed an arm around his shoulders, and studied the names with him. "It seems like we are having new people joining every week," Dani said.

"God is really blessing. He's sending us the right people for sure."

"The 'right' people?"

"You know what I mean. "Take this couple here," he said, as he held up a card for Dani to see. "Marcus is in construction, and his wife is an interior decorator. We're going to need someone with his experience before long. I sure hope they join."

"Hmm." Dani didn't say what she was thinking for fear it would start another argument, something they had been doing too much of lately.

"What does that mean?"

"I didn't say anything, Carter."

"It was how you said it."

Dani removed her arm from around him, pulled out a chair, and sat down. "I guess it bothers me that it's more about what Marcus Stanley can do for us than his . . . his walk with God."

Carter slapped the card on the table. "That's ridiculous, Dani. You know I care about the hearts of people. That's why we're here."

"I'm sorry, sweetheart. I shouldn't have said that."

Carter reached over and kissed the tip of her nose. "I understand. We've all had to adjust to a lot of changes in a short amount of time. Oh, by the way, I have several speaking engagements coming up."

"Carter, how can you hold down the job as pastor of our church and travel all over the state?"

"I don't travel 'all over the state.' Besides, we're looking to take on an associate pastor."

"You're kidding? How can the church afford that?"

"Offerings have been really good, but it's not totally decided yet."

Dani covered Carter's hand with hers and drew close to him. "Honey, when we came here, I thought you wanted more than anything to be a pastor and . . . well, invest your life in the lives of others."

Carter brushed her hand away. "What do you think I have been doing?"

A lump grew in Dani's throat, but she forced her words around it. "It seems to me you've become . . . sort of a traveling salesman."

Carter took a deep breath and struggled to control his emotions. "Dani, my call to be a pastor has not changed. Right now, the Lord is leading me to share some ideas with other pastors—ways to jump-start their churches. A pastor's role can change depending on the needs God lays on his heart."

"I'm trying to understand, sweetheart. I just get concerned. I know this much, though . . . "

"What's that?"

"I love you, Carter Matthews." Dani stood and kissed the mass of dark curls on his head.

"Love you, too."

"Not to change the subject . . . "

"But you're changing it?" Carter said with a smile.

"About Thanksgiving, why don't we invite some folks in to share dinner with us? We have plenty of room now."

"Have anyone in mind?"

"I was thinking of the Bartroms. They don't get invited much, I'm sure."

"Uh . . . how about Nick and Mavis. They don't have family at all."

Dani hesitated. She hadn't seen Nick, except at church since the day they moved in. *Why not? It was just a weird moment.* "Okay, sounds good."

❄❄❄

"Dani, that was a fantastic meal! Where did you learn to cook like that?" Mavis asked as they finished putting away the dishes.

"I'm glad you liked it. I'm learning. I wish I had paid more attention to my mom because she's a great cook."

"Well, it was really good. And warm apple pie with a

dollop of ice cream will be the perfect ending to a very perfect day."

"Thanks, Mavis. Sorry, I forgot the ice cream, but the guys didn't seem to mind going to the 7- Eleven for it."

"No, they're fine."

Dani hung up the wet dishtowels and turned toward her friend. "Mavis, can we talk while they're out?"

"Of course. Is something bothering you?"

"Yes and no." Dani swept her hands through her hair. "It seems like people who have been serving in our church all these years are being shoved aside. I don't know. I'm just confused I suppose."

"Are you talking about Jacob Hunt?"

"No, I was thinking of Mrs. Walker."

Mavis studied her fingernails. "Oh, the choir thing. Yeah, it is sad about Alberta Walker, but she was stuck in her ways and refused to get on board with the new changes. They were forced to let her go."

"I just think it could have been handled differently. It seems cruel. You mentioned Jacob Hunt. What happened?"

"I'm surprised Carter didn't tell you."

"He's been so busy lately. . . ."

"Well, Jacob called a meeting of the new church council with some concerns because he wasn't happy about some of the changes."

"And?"

"And Carter asked him to step back for a few months, focus on his wife who has been very sick, and to pray for the church."

"You're kidding?"

"No. I think Carter was brave to stand up to him like that. Jacob's been running things way too long, and look where it's gotten us."

Dani frowned and rubbed the back of her neck.

Mavis leaned against the sink. "Girlfriend, you do know that Wilburta Community was about to close its doors before Carter came on board, right?"

"I know, but there are so many new people, I can't keep up. Mavis, there are two ladies I've never met teaching Sunday School classes. They're not even church members. What do we know about them?"

"Dani, I think you need to trust Carter. For the council to move ahead with its expansion plans, they can't quibble over every little thing."

"Do you call knowing the spiritual qualification of teachers quibbling?"

"Well, that's probably not the right word, but I believe Carter has at least interviewed them."

"What else is Jacob concerned about?"

"Something to do with financing the new building project. I'm not really sure of the details."

"Do you know if the church body will be able to vote on the plans?"

"I guess . . . I don't know."

"Seems to me the congregation has no say in much of anything these days."

"Dani, if I were you, I'd get on board with what's happening at church. I, for one, am excited to see the pews filled again."

"I know. I feel awful for having these thoughts, but I can't help it."

"Well, all I can say is that Carter is doing a great job and he deserves your support."

Dani sighed. "Will you pray for me, Mavis?"

Mavis patted Dani's hand. "Of course, silly. Now let's get you off your feet."

Moments later, the front door burst open with a gust of cold November air. "Got the ice cream," Carter said, "now let's dig into that luscious apple pie!"

Chapter 31

December 1982

The fear of the Lord is the beginning of wisdom; all who follow his precepts have good understanding. Psalm 111:106

Dani peered out her kitchen window. The smattering of snow that fell yesterday barely covered the brown grass and sent a chill through her. She could not get Jacob and Sarah Hunt off her mind. *This couple has faithfully served the Lord all these years, and now they have just been told they're not needed. Father, I am so confused, so torn. This can't be right, can it? Is it just me? The church is growing by leaps and bounds, and people are getting saved every week. Why can't I be happy? Why can't I do what Mavis suggested—trust Carter? I want to. I want to be the happy supportive wife Carter needs. I need your wisdom, Lord.*

Dani wrapped the gift she had bought for Sarah, grabbed her coat from the closet, and pulled on her boots. She checked her watch. *I think I have time to visit with the Hunts before Adrian gets here.* Dani had volunteered to sit with the Bartrom girls while Adrian attended a progress meeting with the girls' teachers. She had grown to love Lily and Maggie and hoped her Sunday school class was helping them.

"Hello, Dani. Come on in," Jacob Hunt said as he greeted her at the door.

Dani stepped inside. "How are you, Mr. Hunt?"

Jacob smiled at her. "Oh, fine," he said. "I'm afraid Sarah's under the weather today, though."

"Oh, I'm so sorry to hear that."

"I appreciate your prayers for her, dear. She's very weak. I don't think she can handle a visit today. I'm sorry. I should have called you."

Dani's heart sank. "I will definitely be praying." *Don't let her die, Lord.*

"Would you like to rest before heading home? Actually, I can drive you. You have a longer walk now that you've moved."

"Oh, no. It's not even a mile, and the walk is really good for me."

"If you're sure. I certainly don't mind."

Dani turned to go and then remembered the gift she was holding. "I almost forgot. I brought a small gift for Sarah. Will you give it to her when she's feeling better?"

"Of course. She'll be delighted you remembered her."

Dani handed Jacob the small package. "And . . . I'm so sorry for the way things have turned out at church."

"You need not concern yourself, Dani. I'm just fine. God knows my heart, and He knows I have no room for bitterness or anger. You just keep being the sweet person you are."

Dani smiled. "Thank you."

"You have a nice afternoon, and I'll tell Sarah you stopped by."

"Goodbye, Mr. Hunt."

Thoughts of the Hunts troubled her all the way home. *Was I wrong to mention anything to Jacob? Am I being disloyal to Carter? No, I have a right to my own thoughts, don't I? Do I have to agree with everything Carter says and does? Oh, Lord. I don't know what to think anymore.*

As soon as Dani peeled off her coat, she shivered. *Brrr . . . chilly in here.* She checked the thermostat and saw that it read 60. *Hmm . . . I hope Carter's in.* Dani put her coat back on and headed for the phone. The message light flashed "2," and she pressed the button.

"Hey, Dani, it's Courtney. How are you? Long time no see. Call me. You know my number."

Dani smiled at the sound of her dear friend's voice and couldn't wait to return her call.

The second message was from Adrian. "Hi Dani, it's Adrian. I had to cancel my appointment today because both girls are sick. Thanks for offering to sit with them, anyway. Appreciate your prayers."

Oh, dear. I'll have to call Adrian later and see if I can help her. Dani dialed the church number. "Hi Mavis." *I wonder why Ramona never answers anymore? Did they get rid of her, too?*

"Hi, Dani."

Does she sound cold? "Is Carter there, Mavis?"

"He's in a meeting. Can I help you?"

"Our heat's out. Can you get a message to him?"

"He's over at First Baptist."

"Oh, don't bother. Just tell him I called. Okay?"

"Nick might be able to help you. He's here installing shelves in the youth room."

"That's okay, Mavis. I'll curl up with a quilt and wait for Carter to call."

Fifteen minutes later, Dani answered the door and found Nick Edwards standing there. "Nick, what are you doing here?" she said through chattering teeth.

"Came to help a lady in distress," he said as he stepped inside. "Wow . . . it is cold in here." Nick checked the thermostat and then headed for the basement door. "Better get back under that quilt, Dani."

Dani returned to her spot on the sofa.

A few minutes later, she heard Nick's boots stomping back up the basement steps.

"Did you find the problem?"

"Well, I hit the restart button, and the furnace fired up. Carter should probably contact the landlord, though, so he can have the furnace checked out."

"Thanks so much for your help, Nick. I didn't want to disturb you while you're working."

"No problem. We can't have you without heat in this cold weather."

"Can I make you a cup of coffee for your trouble?"

"I'd love one."

Dani tossed the quilt aside and headed for the kitchen. "It's already warming up in here. You're a genius, Nick."

"No, just blessed to have a little know-how." He followed her to the kitchen, and slid into a chair.

Dani started the coffee brewing, removed two cups from the cabinet, and then sat opposite Nick.

"Sorry, Mavis had you come out here. I guess I should have insisted she call Carter out of a meeting."

"It's fine. Don't worry about it. Glad I could do it."

Dani drew her eyebrows together in a frown. "Carter is one busy man these days. Too busy, if you ask me."

"A lot going on at church—big changes."

"I know, and . . . well, I'm not real sure how I feel about all these changes."

"You're not the only one who has mixed feelings. I can tell you that."

"What about you, Nick? Mavis said your divorce is final, huh?"

"Yeah." He drummed his fingers on the table.

Petals Beyond the Bend

"No hope of you two getting back together?"

"I tried everything I could think of to avoid this, but she was set on a divorce. I lay awake at night trying to understand what happened to us, what I could have done differently, but I have no answers. Carolyn's got her freedom. Already left town."

Dani felt the pain in his voice. On impulse she reached for Nick's hand. "I'm so sorry, Nick."

His calloused hand squeezed hers, and as their fingers touched, they locked eyes. "Dani—"

Nick caressed her fingers, and Dani closed her eyes relishing the intimate moment.

"Oh!" Dani said, as she pulled away from Nick's touch. "I . . . I need to check the coffee," she said as she hopped up almost knocking over her chair.

Nick dropped his head. "Oh, man. I'm so sorry, Dani."

Dani stared out the window as she attempted to calm her quivering heart. "I don't know what just happened, Nick, but—"

"You know, I think we should skip the coffee. I really should get back over to the church." Nick stood and scooted the chair back under the table.

Dani turned and faced him. "I'm so embarrassed."

"Hey, let's just say that moment didn't happen. It's my fault anyway." Nick found his coat and pulled it on. "Don't forget to tell Carter to get that furnace checked out, okay?"

As soon as Nick closed the door, Dani shut off the coffee pot, and fell on her knees in front of the sofa. *Oh, God, forgive me. I've been so foolish. I know better than to be alone with a man who isn't my husband, and I totally ignored common sense. Thank you for sparing me from harming Nick and my marriage.*

Dani continued to weep and pray and then fell asleep. That's where Carter found her an hour later. "Dani?"

She raised her head, and wiped her eyes on the edge of the quilt that lay in front of her.

"What's wrong, sweetheart? Have you been crying?" Carter leaned down and offered his hand.

Stiff from the position she fell asleep in, she grasped his hand and pulled herself up.

"Oh, Carter, I'm so glad you're home." She felt tears falling down her cheeks again as she fell into his arms.

Carter stroked her back. "Mavis said our heat went out. Is that what's wrong? I'm worried about you."

"I'm fine," she said as she swiped her tears.

Carter kissed her lightly. "So, Nick was able to help us out, huh?"

At the sound of Nick's name, Dani's face flamed. "Yes. He said you should call the landlord about it."

"I'll take care of that now because we can't risk the heat going out again in this weather. Oh, and I have a meeting tonight."

"Again? You've been out every night this week."

"I know. I'm sorry. The capital funding committee is meeting, and I have to be there."

Of course.

❄❄❄

As soon as Carter left for the church, Dani dialed Courtney's number.

"Hello?"

"Hello, my friend."

"Dani? Oh, my word, it's really you."

At the sound of Courtney's voice, Dani wished that she and her dear roommate were this minute sharing a pizza in The Oasis. "The one and only."

"I have a million questions for you."

"First things first." Dani smiled to herself at the cliché. She and Courtney had such fun exchanging them.

"So, your mom said you and Carter are in Wilburta, Ohio? Is that close to your hometown?"

"It's a small town a few hours north."

"Carter is pastoring a church there, right?"

"Yes, he sure is, and the church has mushroomed in the few short months we've been there."

"Wow, that's amazing. What about you, Dani? What have you been up to?"

"Well . . . I teach a special needs class. I have four amazing kids."

"That's terrific. And married life? How's that going?"

Dani paused before answering. "Good."

"Well, that was weak. What's going on Dani?"

"We're fine. We really are. It's just that Carter has so many demands on him because the church has grown so fast—"

"Let me guess . . . he's never home."

"Something like that."

"I'm sorry, Dani. I'll pray things will get better."

"Did Mom tell you our news?"

"News?"

"We're expecting a baby . . . actually two babies."

"Oh, wow! You're kidding? Twins! When?"

"June."

"Well, congratulations. You're going to be a wonderful mom, Dani."

"I hope so. Anyway, enough about me. What's going on with you?"

"I'm at home for Christmas break right now. Guess who's here with me?"

"Hmm . . . wouldn't be Michael, would it?"

"You're smarter than the average bear, Dani. Yep, Mike in the flesh."

"Getting serious?"

"Very. Mike asked me to marry him right after graduation."

"That's wonderful, Courtney. You're going to graduate first, right?"

"Absolutely."

A tinge of regret that she married Carter before graduating loitered in her mind as the two friends finished getting caught up on campus happenings.

"Thank you so much for calling, Dani. I've missed you terribly. Let's stay in touch, okay?"

"For sure. I'll let you know when the babies arrive."

"Please do. Love you bunches, Dani."

"Ditto. Bye now."

Dani hung up the phone and immediately called her mother. "Mom? It's me. Do you have a minute?"

"Of course, sweetie. Are you okay?"

"I'm fine. Just missing everyone."

Chapter 32

December 1982

Blessed are those who find wisdom, those who gain understanding, for she is more profitable than silver and yields better returns than gold. Proverbs 3:13

Carter piled the beautifully wrapped gifts into the back seat of the car, shut the door, and slid in behind the steering wheel. "When we get back, we need to look into replacing your car," Carter said.

"Can we afford it?"

"It'll cost more to fix it than it's worth. Besides, the council has given me a sizeable raise."

"What! Why didn't you tell me?"

"I saved it for a Christmas surprise." Carter's grin reminded her of their engagement when he surprised her with a ring and proposal.

Carter backed onto the street. "Meadow Glen, Ohio, here we come."

Dani shook her head, amazed at Carter's news.

Dani had not seen her family for months, and she chattered about them for the first twenty miles of their trip. "I wish we could stay longer than three days," she said.

"I know, but there's so much work at the church right now, hon. I can scarcely keep up. We're working on hiring more staff."

"Again? We just hired an associate."

"We need a youth pastor who can work with the teens we have coming."

"What will happen to James?"

"Not sure exactly." Carter glanced at her.

"I know. He'll be asked to retire, right?"

Carter hesitated. "Probably. I know you don't understand, but we need a young man who is trained to work with these kids."

"Well, if so many kids are coming, James must be doing something right."

"How about we not talk about this right now? We disagree and that's that. I don't want to spoil our Christmas by arguing."

Dani studied Carter's profile. *How can one man be so incredibly handsome?* His jaw line, chiseled as finely as a Greek god, gave him the appearance of strength and wisdom, and Dani thought his new closely-cropped hair style made him look older than his twenty-four years. She reached over and traced his jaw down to his lips.

"Ooh, that tickles," Carter said as he kissed her finger.

"Are you happy, Carter? I know this is what you dreamed of, but now that it's happening, I wonder how you're feeling about things. We hardly get time to really talk anymore."

Carter turned a puzzled face to her. "Of course, I'm happy. Wilburta church has done a complete turn-a-round. It's growing by leaps and bounds."

Hmm . . . not exactly the answer I hoped for.

"Great." Dani smiled at him, patted his arm, and turned her thoughts to her family.

Carter pulled into the Krieg's driveway, and Dani's parents rushed out the back door to meet them.

Carter stepped out of the car and shook Cameron's extended hand.

"So glad you're here," Cameron said. "Can I help with your luggage?"

"You sure can," Carter said as he headed for the trunk.

Dani hopped out of the car into her mom's waiting arms. "Oh, Mom, it's good to see you."

Tears filled Lindy's eyes. "And you, too, honey."

Arm in arm, the two of them headed inside. "Are my brothers home?" Dani asked.

"They should be shortly. Phoebe took them Christmas shopping."

Once Dani stepped inside the familiar kitchen, and all the tension and frustrations she had been feeling for weeks peeled away. *Home. I'm home.*

❄❄❄

Lindy sliced the roast into serving size pieces as Dani set the table for the evening meal.

"That smells so good, Mom. I have missed your wonderful cooking."

"And I've missed your help around here," Lindy said with a chuckle. "How have you been feeling, honey?"

"I feel great now that morning sickness is over. Yuck."

"You're really getting big, aren't you?"

Dani caressed her growing belly. "I am. Nothing fits me now. I need to buy some maternity clothes."

Lindy reached and pulled her daughter into a tight hug. "I'm so happy for you and Carter. My little girl is going to be a mom. And twins! Have I ever told you that twins run in my family?"

"Mo-om. You *have* a set of twins."

"Si, but I have cousins who are twins, too."

Dani smiled at Lindy's use of "Si." "I'm sorry I didn't get to know your family, Mom. I'm sure you have really missed them all these years."

Tears glistened in her mother's eyes, and she wiped them with her apron. "I have missed them, but God has been good to me." She grasped Dani's shoulders. "Just look at what an amazing daughter He gave me."

"Two amazing daughters, right?"

"Oh, yes. My sweet Bettina and you."

"Okay, let's get back to the task at hand." Lindy pulled rolls from the oven as Dani finished folding the napkins and placed one by each place at the dining room table.

"Shall I call the guys?" Dani asked.

"Soon as I spoon up the gravy."

"Sure smells good in here," Carter said as he strode into the kitchen.

"Roast beef," Lindy said as she smiled at Carter.

❈❈❈

On Saturday morning, Lindy announced that she had plans to meet Phoebe for coffee. The two friends had been carving out a few hours every Christmas to reflect on their friendship and exchange gifts. Dani hoped that her friendship with Mavis would grow like that, but of late, Mavis seemed different somehow, and Dani hadn't been able to put her finger on the problem.

Dani was glad that Carter volunteered to take Mike and Dave roller skating since she wanted some time alone with her dad. She waved goodbye to her husband and brothers and joined Cameron in the living room. "Dad, can we talk while everyone's out?"

Cameron brought his recliner to an up position.

"If you don't mind, that is."

"Of course, I don't mind, honey."

Dani plopped down on the sofa. "I'm kind of worried. No, that's not the word. Confused is better. I'm confused about some things at our church."

Cameron drew his eyebrows together and leaned forward. "What is bothering you, Dani?"

"I'm sure Carter has shared with you how fast the church is growing."

"Yes, he said you've gone to two services and will soon be building a new sanctuary."

"Well, that's what is bothering me."

"It's bothering you?"

"I feel like I'm not being a supportive wife, Dad. I have these feelings . . . " Dani rubbed her hands together.

"Can you be more specific, honey?"

"I'll try. For one thing, I don't like the way some of the original members were pushed aside with no regard for all their years of service. I don't feel good about the way the church council has done away with the hymns, and—"

"It sounds like Carter is moving the church to a contemporary service."

"That's for sure."

"Dani, a lot of pastors are doing that. They feel that a contemporary style of worship service will reach the young people today."

"I know. I get that. But, how do we know if the people joining are even saved? We just vote them in without knowing anything about them. And sometimes we don't even vote! They just appear as teachers, or song leaders. I can't keep up with what's going on anymore. And I'm the pastor's wife!"

"Perhaps the new people have met with a deacon or the council prior to the vote and you just don't know about it."

"I asked Carter, and . . . well, he doesn't like me to question things at church. If I do, we end up quarreling."

"You're quarreling? Oh, my. I'm really sorry to hear that, Dani."

"I really hate saying this, Dad, but I'm afraid that Carter is losing his zeal to win people to Christ. These days he seems to focus more on building a big church."

Cameron inhaled a deep breath. "Honey, I think the best advice I can give you is to pray for Carter. God can change circumstances that appear hopeless to us."

"I know. He certainly changed me."

Cameron listened intently to Dani for another fifteen minutes. "I'm so sorry you are having these troubling thoughts, Dani. At least I know better how to pray for you."

"Oh, one more thing," she said. "Carter is out of town a lot. Hardly a week goes by that he isn't away."

"Where does he go?"

"Apparently, there are a lot of pastors who have heard about Wilburta church's success, and request Carter come and share his secrets."

"So, you're alone a lot, huh?"

"Yes, and it gets old. Dad, I feel awful telling you all this stuff, but I have nobody I can talk to honestly. I have made friends with Mavis, but she thinks everything at church is wonderful, so I can't be honest with her. I want to be the kind of wife God wants me to be, but I can't deny my concerns. What am I to do?"

"Pray, Dani. Start with prayer and ask God to show you the best way to work out these issues. Are you being faithful to your quiet time?"

Dani admitted that she hasn't been praying like she knew she should. "Would you pray with me now, Dad?"

"Of course." Dani slid down to the floor in front of her father's chair, and grasped his hands.

"Our Father, how blessed we are that you gave your life so that we can have eternal life. Lord, we pray for Carter. He has taken on a huge challenge and is facing many difficult decisions. We pray that You will guide him in the decisions he makes so that they will bring honor and glory to You. We pray for Dani. Bless her, Father, with wisdom beyond her years so that she will know when to speak and when to keep silent. Give her the peace of mind that she needs in the coming months prior to bringing her babies into the world. Watch over and protect this young couple in these early days of their marriage. Grow them together as a couple. We pray in the name of Your Son, Jesus. Amen."

Cameron helped Dani to her feet and hugged her.

"Thank you, Dad. You're the best."

"Anytime, sweetie. Keep me posted on how things are going. Okay?"

❄❄❄

Carter and Dani started for home the day after Christmas. Dani had hoped to drop in on Shannon and Jared, but there simply wasn't time.

"I'm disappointed I didn't get to see Shannon," Dani said. "At least we had a chance to chat on the phone."

"I'm sorry, hon. After we trade in your car, maybe you can come by yourself and stay longer."

"With two babies? I don't think so."

"Well, maybe I can take you, and your dad could bring you home?"

"That sounds good, or maybe we can go together when you get a vacation."

"It'll be another few months before I get one. Even so, I need to plan a trip to see my folks."

"Oh, absolutely. I'm sure they miss you terribly."

"I've been thinking, honey, that we need to buy some new clothes."

"Well, I know *I* do. In another week, I won't have one thing that fits me."

"Well, I want you to pick out some really nice things."

"What do you mean?"

"I mean buy some quality clothes, not just off the rack at K-Mart."

Is Carter embarrassed by the way I dress?

Carter kept glancing at Dani as if to check her reactions. "Maybe Mavis could take you into Akron. She said there are some great dress shops there."

"You discussed my clothing with Mavis?"

"No, not exactly. Just in passing, honey." Carter patted her knee.

"Do you have any idea how that makes me feel?" Dani said as she slapped the seat with both hands.

"What do you mean?"

"You had to ask another woman how to fix up your poor little frumpy wife. *That's* what I mean."

Carter sighed, rolled his eyes, and took a deep breath. "Dani, you know I love you. What I'm trying to say is that you are the pastor's wife of a large church."

"If there's one thing I know, believe me, that's it."

"Anyway, just listen, okay? People expect you to dress in a way that fits your position—someone they can point to and say with pride, 'That's our pastor's wife.'"

"Or my husband could say, 'That's my wife,' right, Carter?"

"Let's drop it, Dani. Forget I mentioned it."

Dani sank back into the seat, pulled her coat tightly around her, and refused to sniff as tears streamed down her face and dripped onto her coat.

Chapter 33

April 1983

Do not be quickly provoked in your spirit, for anger resides in the lap of fools. Ecclesiastes 7:8

Dani plowed through the next few days feeling as if a black cloud hung over her head. If it weren't for her babies, she might very well have given in to the beckoning gloom.

"What do you say we go car shopping today, hon?" Carter asked one morning in late April. He had been aware of her worsening sadness, and thought a new car might cheer her up, and she did need a dependable vehicle.

"Okay," she said with little enthusiasm. Thoughts of her grandfather Krieg skimmed through her mind. He had given Dani the money for the car with only one promise and that was to send him a picture of her with the car. *Oh, Grandpa, I never sent that photo. I'm so sorry.* Tears misted her eyes.

"Do you like it, Dani?" Carter asked as she pulled the silver Honda Accord into their garage.

"Yes. It's great. It's perfect, really."

As Carter pointed out some of the car's features, Dani tried to focus on his words, but her heart wasn't in it.

❄❄❄

The friendship that began so hopefully between Mavis and herself had cooled to non-existent, and Dani didn't know the reason. She wracked her brain trying to remember if she had said or done something to offend Mavis to no avail. What she did know was that she missed the camaraderie they once shared.

I miss Shannon so much. And how fun it would be to spend one afternoon with Courtney.

A few days after they purchased the Honda, Dani studied her image in their floor-length mirror. Carter's hints about her appearance on their way home from Meadow Glen ate at her. Her thick and naturally curly hair had always been a breeze to care for, and she usually just washed it and let it dry. With only a few strokes of her hairbrush, she was set to go. She had always enjoyed compliments on her hair. *Hmm . . . I guess I could experiment with a new style and maybe some highlights.*

She hated to admit it, but she realized Carter was right about her clothing. She at least needed nice maternity clothes. *Apparently, as a pastor's wife, I have to dress a cut above K-Mart and Penney's. If Carter thinks I'm asking Mavis Moore to take me clothes shopping in Akron, he's got another think coming.*

To prove herself a capable young woman to her husband, Dani drove her new car to Akron where she purchased expensive, top-of-the-line maternity clothes and charged them to their credit card. She relished the exhilaration of shopping with abandon as she tried on dozens of outfits and refused to give in to the fatigue that hit her mid-afternoon. *Money seems to be no object these days, so I'll find matching shoes and some nice pieces of jewelry.*

❄︎❄︎❄︎

"Dani?" Carter asked as he arrived home that evening to find dozens of boxes and bags strewn about the living room, but no sign of his wife. He picked up some of the packages and saw the price tags. *Oh, good. She bought some nice things.* "Dani, where are you?" he said as he strode down the hall to their bedroom.

Dani lay in the fetal position, her arm protectively draped over her belly.

Carter slipped into bed beside her. "Honey," he said as he gently shook her.

Dani opened her eyes and stirred. "Huh?" She rolled to her back and rubbed her eyes. "What time is it?"

"It's six-thirty. Are you okay?"

Dani sat up and swung her feet to the floor.

"Your feet are swollen. Lie back down, and I'll rub them for you."

"I need to fix dinner."

"I'll fix dinner."

Her head throbbed, and she needed the bathroom more than she needed a foot rub. "I'll be right back," she said.

When she returned, she stretched out on the bed again.

"So, you went shopping, huh?" Carter asked as he massaged Dani's swollen feet and ankles.

Dani nodded. She prepared herself for his verbal assault, but it didn't come.

"Did you find some things you like?" he asked.

"As much as you can like maternity clothes."

"Good. Who went with you?"

"I went by myself, Carter. I am perfectly capable of shopping by myself."

Carter ignored her words.

The longer he worked on her legs, the heavier Dani's guilt grew.

"You look really tired, honey. How about I go pick up Chinese for dinner? You need to stay off your feet the rest of the evening."

The concern in his voice triggered her tears. "Oh, Carter . . . I bought all—"

"I know, honey. I saw them. Don't worry about it."

"But how will we pay for all that stuff?"

Carter grabbed a tissue from a night stand and handed it to Dani. "I'll handle it. Don't worry about it."

"I can take everything back."

"No, you're going to wear them, and not give it another thought."

"Now, just relax while I go pick up dinner. Okay?"

"Okay."

Carter kissed her tenderly. "Be back in a few minutes."

As soon as Dani heard the door close, she scrambled out of bed and scooted to the living room. In minutes, she had all her purchases gathered up and tossed on the bed in the guest room. *I have been a foolish woman today, Lord.*

Before Carter returned with dinner, the phone rang.

"Dani, it's Jacob Hunt."

"Hello, Mr. Hunt. How are you?"

"Shaken at the moment, I'm sorry to say."

Dani's heart fluttered. "What's wrong, Mr. Hunt?"

"I'm afraid Sarah has passed, Dani."

"Oh, no. I'm so sorry." Dani blinked away tears.

"She was ready to go, dear. She was tired of fighting."

"I know, but I will really miss her."

"Everyone who knew Sarah will miss her."

"Carter went out to pick up dinner. Shall I have him call when he gets back?"

"It's not necessary. I need some time alone. Just let him know about Sarah, and tell him I'll call tomorrow."

"I sure will. You're in my prayers, Mr. Hunt."

"Thank you, Dani. Goodnight."

When Carter returned with their dinner, Dani broke the news to him about Sarah. "Jacob said not to bother calling back tonight, and he'll call you tomorrow."

Carter placed the food he purchased on the counter and went directly to the phone. "How would that look for his pastor not showing up to offer condolences? I can just imagine how tongues would wag."

"I don't think it's a matter of how it looks, Carter. Jacob sounded like he wants some time alone."

Carter paged through the church directory they kept beside the phone and found Jacob Hunt's number. "Jacob's going to have a lot of time alone now that Sarah's gone," he said as he dialed Jacob's number.

Carter's words stunned Dani. *Who is this man I married? One minute he's kind and tender and the next, cold as ice.*

The words Carter used as he spoke with Jacob fell off his tongue as if coated with the smoothest silk. As soon as he hung up, he headed back outside to the car, all interest in Dani's swollen feet and legs completely forgotten.

What is happening to us, Lord?

Dani ignored the pungent smell of the Chinese food having lost her appetite and plopped down on the sofa. She pulled the afghan her grandmother had crocheted for her up to her chin, closed her eyes, and prayed. *Father, forgive my behavior today. I was spiteful and angry, and I spent money we don't really have. I don't know what's happening to me, to Carter. Please be with Jacob during this painful time . . .*

❄❄❄

As the final days of April neared, the new maternity clothes she had splurged on barely fit. She stared at her profile in the mirror. *I am humungous. Six more weeks.* The babies chose that moment to tumble—at least it felt like tumbling— as Dani watched in fascination at the show in the mirror. "You're as anxious as Mommy is to be out of there, aren't you?"

"I hear Daddy," she said as she heard Carter coming in the back door.

"Hi, honey," Dani said as she met him with a kiss.

"Hello sweetheart," he said. "How was your day?" He removed his coat and hung it in the coat closet.

"Laundry day. Yours?"

"Counseling and sermon preparation all day," he said.

"Dinner's ready, if you want to wash up."

"Great. I'm famished. Be right back."

Carter returned in a few moments. "Looks great, hon."

"Thank you," she said as she placed a bowl of steaming mashed potatoes on the table, and took the chair opposite him.

After he had prayed, Carter helped himself to a healthy size slice of meat loaf.

"Guess what?" Dani asked. "My mom is coming for my birthday."

"By herself?" Carter said.

"Dad has to work, and Mom doesn't want to take the boys out of school."

"That's wonderful. It'll be a good chance for the two of you to have some one-on-one time."

"I've really missed her."

"It would be nice for her to stay long enough for the ground-breaking ceremony."

"So, I guess they finally got all the financing worked out, huh?" Dani said as she poured a glass of tea for Carter.

"We did. It's amazing how God provided. I think the naysayers who opposed us every step of the way will change their tune when they see the new building."

Dani winced at his words and dribbled a bit of the tea on their new white tablecloth. "I haven't seen the plans."

"We posted the architectural drawings weeks ago. Maybe you should take more of an interest in what is happening at church rather than spend so much time in your little Sunday school class."

Dani's face flamed in anger. "My 'little Sunday school class'? What exactly do you mean by that?"

"I meant what I said. I know you're going to get mad, but the truth is that class seems to be the only thing at church that matters to you."

"That's ridiculous." Dani stroked her abdomen when she felt her babies move as if they were responding to the threatening words in the room.

Carter sipped his tea and studied his wife. "It's ridiculous, huh? Have you joined a small group? No. Have you volunteered to participate in the ladies' mission outreach? No. Did you volunteer to bake cookies for the shut-ins? No. I'm sure people wonder why their pastor's wife doesn't support his ministry. All your free time goes to those . . . "

"Special needs children." Dani completed the sentence he couldn't bring himself to say.

"Either them or Sarah Hunt," he muttered.

At the mention of Sarah's name, Dani's eyes pooled.

"Dani, you don't even try to get to know the new people. You use the side entrance to the classrooms, spend an hour there, then you come late to worship and sit in the back of the sanctuary."

"Now that we're pointing out shortcomings, husband dear, where were you when I asked you to go to birthing classes with me? You were way too busy. Why is it only Mavis seems to know where you are these days? If I need to talk to you, she acts like she is in charge of your every move. Why is that, Carter?"

"She merely tries to keep me from being stuck on the phone with—"

"Oh, I get it. With a 'naysayer.'"

"That's not what I was going to say."

Dani paused in her ranting and turned worried eyes on her husband. "Carter, what happened to the young zealous man I married—the one whose dream was to be a master builder of *people* and not a builder of buildings?"

Carter dropped his fork, tossed his napkin on the table, and stood up. "I'm going out."

Dani didn't respond, but gathered the dishes, put the uneaten food away, and collapsed onto the sofa sobbing.

Chapter 34

Is anyone among you in trouble? Let them pray. Is anyone happy? Let them sing songs of praise. James 5:13

Dani had cleaned the house, prepared a casserole for dinner, and peeked out the window every few minutes hoping to see her mother's grey Ford Fairlane. *Where can she be? She said she'd be here by five and it's almost six. Maybe I should call Dad. I'll wait a few more minutes.*

Dani flipped on the television and stretched out on the sofa, and in minutes she was sound asleep.

It took a few seconds for her to realize someone was knocking. *It's Mom!* Dani pushed herself to her feet and lumbered to the door.

"Oh, Mom, I've been worried. Come in."

Lindy dropped her suitcase and held her arms out for her daughter. "I'm sorry, honey. The traffic was horrible."

"I'm so glad you're here." Dani bent to pick up Lindy's bag.

"I'll get that, honey. You just show me to my room."

By the time Lindy had unpacked her suitcase and freshened up, she could hear voices in the kitchen and assumed Carter had arrived home from the church. She took a moment to admire the way her daughter had decorated the room. Dani had never been one for frills and lace growing up, but Lindy could see her taste had certainly changed evidenced by the Victorian style of the room.

Lindy slid her feet into slippers, happy to be free of her panty hose and dress shoes and headed to the kitchen.

"Oh, hello, Carter. I didn't know you were home."

Carter smiled and hugged Lindy. "So good to see you. I trust you had a good trip."

"Other than being delayed by heavy traffic, no problems at all."

"Dinner will be ready in five minutes," Dani said as she carried the hot casserole to the dining room table.

"Can I help, Dani?"

"Would you like to put ice in our glasses?" Dani asked as she pulled rolls from the oven and a tossed salad from the refrigerator.

Carter loosened his tie, removed his suit jacket, and dropped into a chair with a sigh.

"Hard day, hon?" Dani asked as she filled the glasses with water and carried them to the table.

"Meeting of the council this afternoon to hammer out some details of the new building."

"I'm sure there are a lot of details to work out, Carter," Lindy said as she and Dani took their places.

"You know how it goes. Everybody thinks their idea is the best. Let's return thanks, shall we?" he said.

❅❅❅

Dani and Lindy cleaned up the kitchen and found Carter had fallen asleep in his recliner, the newspaper covering his face. Dani quietly removed the paper and motioned for her mother to follow her. "I want you to see the nursery," Dani whispered.

"Oh, that reminds me," Lindy said, I have some packages in the back seat."

"We can get them when Carter wakes up," Dani said as she swung the nursery door open.

"Oh, Dani, it's lovely. You have become quite the little decorator."

"Thanks, Mom." Dani pulled open the dresser drawers to show her mother the stacks of tiny garments waiting to be worn by her precious babies.

"I have forgotten how small newborns are," Lindy said as she held up a miniature onesie.

"The doctor said the babies will most likely be small."

"Believe it or not, your brothers were tiny babies."

Dani laughed. "They are sure big boys now."

"Have you picked names yet?"

"Sort of. We're considering 'Grace and Grady' if they're a boy and girl. That's all we've agreed on so far."

"I like those names."

"Dani!" Carter yelled from the living room.

Dani popped her head out of the nursery. "Do you want something, Carter?"

"I told you I have a meeting tonight," he said as he pulled his suit jacket back on and fixed his tie.

"No, you did not mention any meeting to me, Carter."

"I'm sure I did. Now I'm late. Thanks a lot." Carter shoved his arms into his coat, and slammed out the door.

Humiliated and stunned, Dani stared after Carter.

Lindy hugged Dani and steered her to the sofa and handed her a tissue.

"Oh, Mom, I...I don't know what's happening to us." She sobbed in her mother's arms.

When Dani's tears subsided, she pulled several tissues from a box on the coffee table and blew her nose.

"Hmm . . . why don't I make us a cup of tea?" Lindy said. "We need to talk."

"I can get the tea, Mom."

"You just rest a moment."

"Okay."

Lindy put the teakettle on to boil and opened three cabinets before finding Dani's supply of tea. In a few minutes, she had two steaming cups ready and on the table with sugar and honey.

"Dani, the tea's ready. Come, let's talk."

Dani pulled out a chair and sat across from Lindy as she poured out her heart to her mother.

"Oh, honey, I'm so sorry to hear all this. Many couples have a tough time during their first year of marriage as they work toward growing together as a family."

"I know, Mom. But it takes two people working on it. Carter's never home. He's always in some meeting or out of town or counseling or . . . whatever. He's not the man I married. Mom, he was so excited to reach people for the Lord. You remember, don't you? He wanted to be a pastor who would make a difference in people's lives. All he cares about now is a bigger building, more people, and making a big impression. At least that's what it seems like to me."

"The strife between you and Carter isn't good for you or for your babies," Lindy said. "That concerns me."

"I know. I have tried. I really have."

"What are your arguments about?"

"Mostly about me not agreeing with the way decisions are made at church."

"What do you mean?"

Dani shared how Jacob Hunt and other leaders had been asked to step down and were replaced although they had served the Lord faithfully for years, how decisions were being made without sanction from the church body, and how the council appears to have exclusive power. Dani continued, "Oh, and people are joining the church without the church body knowing anything about them. Every time I try to share my opinion with Carter . . . well to make a long story short . . . we end up arguing."

The more Lindy heard, the more concerned she grew about Dani's health and her developing babies, not to mention her marriage.

"Dani, through the years, God has taught me so much about the power of prayer."

"I *do* pray, Mom, all the time."

"I'm sure you do, honey, but you and Carter need specific and concentrated prayer. You need to pray for your husband. I *do* remember Carter's zeal. Satan is the enemy of his soul and would like nothing better than to distract Carter from his call."

"I get so confused," Dani said. She smacked the table almost upsetting her teacup.

"What do you mean?"

"I mean people are joining our church right and left. If the church is growing under Carter's leadership, am I just being judgmental and critical? Mavis told me I just need to trust my husband."

"Mavis? Who is Mavis?"

"She's Carter's administrative assistant."

"Carter wants me to be excited about what's happening at church, and honestly, I try, but . . . I don't know. See what I mean? I'm confused."

"Where's your Bible, Dani?"

"In the bedroom."

"Let's go."

"To the bedroom?"

"Yes, we're going to fight back."

"Fight back?"

"Absolutely."

"The devil's been busy in this home, Dani. He's trying

to come between you and your husband, and it sounds like he's been pretty successful. Your battle is won in prayer, sweetie."

Lindy paged through Dani's Bible as she read passage after passage on prayer. "Dani, you must pray . . . pray for Carter, for your babies, and for yourself. Ask God to reveal attitudes in *your* heart that need to be changed. Plead with God for your husband . . . every single day."

It amazed Dani to hear these desperate words pouring out of her mother.

"Satan would like nothing better than to turn you against Carter. Look at this verse," Lindy said, as she turned the Bible so Dani could read with her. "It's Matthew 26:41. *Watch and pray so that you will not fall into temptation. The spirit is willing, but the flesh is weak.*"

The few tempting moments she shared with Nick flashed through her mind, and her face flamed, and she hoped her mother hadn't noticed.

Lindy tipped Dani's chin so that they made eye contact. "Remember this, my daughter; *The prayer of a righteous person is powerful.* Now, let's pray."

Chapter 35

Do not be quick with your mouth, do not be hasty in your heart to utter anything before God. God is in heaven and you are on earth, so let your words be few. Ecclesiastes 5:2

Lindy lay awake almost all night as she prayed for Carter and Dani. As dawn neared, she finally fell asleep and slept until she heard voices and Carter's car starting.

She pushed back the sheet, and sat on the side of the bed as a headache assaulted her. She tiptoed to the bathroom. *Coffee. I need coffee.* Lindy pulled on the robe that Dani had laid out for her and slid her feet into slippers.

The aroma of fresh brewed coffee drew her to the kitchen, but there was no sign of Dani. *Hmm . . . must have gone back to bed.* Lindy glanced at the clock. *Nine. I hope she's okay.*

Lindy decided to pad back down the hall and check on her daughter. She quietly opened Dani's bedroom door and found her sound asleep.

Returning to the kitchen, Lindy found the bread and made toast that she enjoyed with her coffee. *Wish this headache would go away.*

Back in the guest room, Lindy showered and dressed in slacks and a top. After she applied her scant make-up and pulled her hair into a bun on top of her head, she plopped down on the bed. Every time she moved her head, shocks of pain shot through her. *I haven't had a headache like this in months.*

Lindy rehearsed some of the things Dani shared with her last night—Carter's rudeness, his lack of respect for Dani's opinions, and especially being gone every night. *And his young wife pregnant with twins!* The longer she thought about it, the angrier she became. Lindy forgot that with fatigue, her usual wise and patient personality warps from kind to critical and from concern to correction. She massaged her temples. *Dear Father, I know I shouldn't be angry, but Carter Matthews needs a wake-up call, and I think I'm just the one to give it!*

Lindy opened the coat closet and retrieved her coat, grabbed her purse and car keys, and headed out the door.

"Mom?" Dani asked just as Lindy was about to close the door. "Where are you going?"

"I'll be right back, sweetie. The coffee's still hot."

❈ ❈ ❈

Lindy had no idea where Wilburta Community Church was located. As she drove up and down the streets of the small town, thoughts of what she would say to Carter raced through her head causing it to throb even more. Finally, she spied the church sign and pulled in beside Carter's car.

Each step Lindy took toward the front entrance sent a stab of pain to her head. She swung open the heavy door and stepped into the quiet foyer. Not knowing which way she should go to find the offices, she opted to go left.

As soon as she had taken a few steps, she heard voices and recognized one was Carter's.

Lindy took a deep breath and winced at the pain the breath created. She rapped softly on the office door.

"Mrs. Krieg!" Carter said. He was impeccably dressed as usual, and smiled at Lindy revealing his stunningly white teeth. "How nice of you to come down. Is Dani with you?"

"No, I came alone. Dani is resting. May I speak with you privately, Carter?"

"Of course. Mavis, please hold my calls."

Lindy glanced at the young woman behind the desk. *Hmm . . . so that's Mavis.*

Carter closed the office door and led Lindy down the hall to a classroom where he pulled out a chair for his mother-in-law and then sat opposite her. "So, what's on your mind, Mrs. Krieg?"

Lindy studied her handsome son-in-law for a moment as fatigue extinguished her anger. *What on earth was I thinking by coming here?*

"Lindy . . er Mrs. Krieg, are you okay?"

"I do have a horrible headache, but I . . . I wanted to see the church." *God, forgive my lie.*

"That's wonderful. I guess I'm a little surprised Dani didn't come with you."

"She slept in, and I thought I could run over here and get back before she woke up."

"I see. Well, I'm pleased you've come."

Excuses for her impromptu visit whirled through her mind, but her brain stalled. "Uh . . . Dani tells me how the work here has grown."

Carter crossed his legs and smiled at Lindy. "Yes, God is growing this church, and growing it fast. Would you like to look around?"

"Sure, I'd love to."

Lindy trailed Carter as he showed her their updated classrooms and where their new addition would be.

"So, what do you think?" Carter asked.

"There's a lot going on here, Carter. It's fantastic." Lindy glanced at her watch. "I really need to get back before Dani starts to worry about me."

"Thanks so much for coming, Mrs. Krieg."

"You could call me 'mom' if you'd like."

"I'd love to, but it might take some getting used to."

"I want you to know that Cameron and I pray for you and Dani every day."

"I can't thank you enough for that."

"Soon you'll have two babies! How exciting is that? Two little ones."

Carter chuckled. "Then you can pray for us even more fervently. I'll be home early today. I'm taking you and the birthday girl out to dinner."

"Thanks for the tour."

"Happy to do it. Thanks again for stopping by."

Lindy slid behind the wheel of her car and headed for a donut shop she had passed on the way to the church.

Father, forgive my foolish behavior. I urged Dani to pray and trust God for her marriage, and I jump in and try to help You out. Oh, my.

"You went to get donuts!"

"I also dropped by the church."

"You did? But you didn't know where it is."

"Wilburta is a small town," Lindy said as she peeled off her coat. "Happy birthday, my dear daughter."

"Thanks, Mom. Was Carter at the church?"

"He sure was, and he took me for a tour."

"Wow, I guess I'm kind of shocked."

"Why? He *is* my son-in-law after all. Now, how about another cup of coffee and a donut?"

"Sounds great. Thanks for getting donuts."

"Dani, do you have any aspirin?"

Chapter 36

Jesus said, "Let the little children come to me, and do not hinder them, for the kingdom of heaven belongs to such as these."
Matthew 19:14

Dani took her mother's advice to heart and began dedicating an hour each day to praying for her husband. No matter how frustrated she got with his long hours and attitudes that were anything but Christ-honoring, she continued to pray and trust God with their future. *Lord, I know the young man I married is in there somewhere. He had an amazing burden for lost people, and knew in his heart that God had called him to be a light to them. Father, I pray that you would rekindle that flame.*

"Dani, how about I pick you up for lunch today?"

In all these months, he has never once asked me to go to lunch, and here I am as big as a house. "Oh, Carter, look at me. I'm so fat."

"You look fine. You could wear that yellow dress."

Dani laughed. "No way."

"I'd really like you to go. It'll be a kind of celebration before our twins come. We won't be going anywhere for a while once they arrive."

"All right. I'll see what I can find. What time?"

"Two."

"Two?" Kind of late for lunch isn't it?"

"I have some things I need to take care of this morning, so two is the first I can get away."

"Two it is."

❄❄❄

Carter arrived shortly before two o'clock. He took the steps two at a time and burst in the back door, a rare smile lighting his face.

What's going on? Something's up.

"You look nice, Dani," he said as he kissed her cheek.

Dani was pleased with her new hair style that perfectly suited her and was a cinch to care for. She found that the green and gold maternity dress worked better than anything else she had. *If only my feet weren't swollen, I could wear my brown pumps, but not today.* She shoved her feet into the widest pair of flats she owned. "I'm ready."

Carter held the door open for her, assisted her down the steps, and then held out his arm for her.

"Well, well, aren't you the gentleman today?"

"My dear wife, I'm always a gentleman." Carter said as he opened the car door for Dani.

"So, where are we going?"

"It's a surprise."

"A surprise, huh? Well, I hope it includes food because the babies and I are hungry."

"Oh, yes, there will be food."

He's heading for the church. What on earth?

"We're going to church, Carter? I thought you were taking me to a celebration lunch?"

"I am," he said as he swung into the full parking lot.

"What are all these cars here for? Is there some kind of church meeting? I didn't hear about one."

"Sometimes you ask too many questions, sweetheart," he said as he pulled into his parking place. "Now, come with me, okay?"

"What have you done, Carter Matthews?"

"Nothing. I have done nothing."

Carter held the fellowship hall door open for his wife, and as soon as she stepped over the threshold, a burst of "Surprise" echoed through the room.

Dani gasped and fell into Carter's arms. "How . . . when . . . you stinker." Speechless, she scanned the crowd that filled the hall. "I am so shocked!"

Adrian Bartrom stepped forward as her girls each took one of Dani's hands and led her to the guest of honor chair.

Carter followed her, pulled out her chair, and kissed her. Enjoy your surprise, honey."

❆❆❆

As the next few hours wore on, and Dani opened what seemed to her to be a hundred packages of tiny little outfits, she began to realize that Carter was right about her lack of involvement in their church. *Why have I avoided their friendships? What was I thinking?*

Cynthia Miller, a young woman with golden blond hair cascading down her back approached her. "Dani, I will gladly drive you home and help you put your gifts away."

Her smile warmed Dani's heart. "Cynthia, that would be wonderful. Are you sure?"

"Absolutely. I've been hoping for a chance to get to know you better."

When Sally Cotton suggested the ladies form a circle

around Dani and pray for her, tears smarted her eyes. *I have missed so much!*

"Ladies, I can't thank you enough. What a lovely surprise. I love all the gifts, and we'll put them to good use for sure."

"Dani," Mavis said, "I'll tell Carter that Cynthia is taking you home, okay?"

"Oh, thanks so much, Mavis. I'm sure he would appreciate that."

Several ladies picked up armloads of gifts and carried them to Cynthia's car, and Sally held the passenger door open for Dani.

"Sally, thank you so much. I had such a good time."

Sally hugged Dani. "It was a joint effort, hon."

"Well, it was wonderful, and we won't have to buy anything for quite a while."

❈❈❈

May 1983

"Mom, I think I might be going into labor."

"Have you called your doctor, sweetie?"

"No, not yet."

"Well, what's going on?"

"I'm leaking water."

"Dani, hang up the phone and call your doctor. I will pack a bag and be on my way within the hour."

"Do you think the babies will come today? They're not due for three and a half weeks."

"I don't know, Dani, but it's not unusual for twins to come early. So, I'll see you in a few hours. Now, hang up and call your doctor. Okay?"

❈❈❈

Grady Aaron and Grace Anna Matthews were born Friday, May 6th at 11:30 pm. Grace was a few ounces heavier than Grady, but both babies were healthy.

"Congratulations, Dani." Nick Edwards popped his head into her room the day after the babies arrived.

Dani fluffed her hair. "Nick, how nice to see you."

"You, too. How are you feeling?"

"Not too bad considering. Did you see the twins?"

"I did. They're beautiful babies."

"Thank you. I haven't seen much of you lately, Nick. How are you?"

"I'm fine, Dani. I have news, though. I'm going to be leaving Wilburta."

"Leaving? What do you mean?"

"Landed a job in Arizona, so I'll be heading west in a few days."

"Really?"

"Yeah. I need a brand new start away from here . . . away from memories." Nick twisted the cap he had taken off on entering the room.

Sadness crept into Dani, and she reached for his hand. "Nick, I will miss you, but I . . . I know it's for the best."

Nick squeezed her hand, and then bent over and kissed her cheek. "Goodbye Dani." At that, Nick whirled and headed from the room.

The babies went home with Carter and Dani a few days later.

❉❉❉

"Mom, thank you so much for coming. I don't know what we would have done without you," Dani said two weeks following the twins' birth.

"I'm glad I could do it, sweetie. Now, I need to get home to *my* twins," she said with a chuckle. "Your friend, Cynthia, said she is planning to come and help out."

"I know. Isn't she nice, Mom? And several others offered as well."

"That's wonderful, honey."

"Carter's mother called and is trying to work out a time to visit. They are eager to see the babies."

"I'm sure they are."

❄❄❄

Carter picked up his parents and sister at the airport a week after Lindy left for home.

Unfortunately, with only one guest room, Margo was relegated to the sofa.

"I'm sorry, Margo, we should have at least bought a sleeper sofa."

"No problem, Dani. I wasn't planning on coming, but at the last minute, I didn't want to miss seeing my niece and nephew while they're little. Who knows when I'll have a chance to get back."

"You know you're welcome anytime."

"Thanks."

Dani found it interesting that Mr. Matthews and Margo never tired of rocking the babies. Each of them had a baby in arms every chance they got. After her nap one afternoon, Dani tripped into the living room to find Mr. Matthews singing a hymn to Gracie, and Margo patting Grady's back hoping for a burp. Dani smiled at the scene.

"Where's Mom Matthews?" Dani asked.

"She heard about a dress shop in Akron she wanted to check out. I don't think she'll be gone much longer," Hugh Matthews whispered.

"I hope not. I want us to have at least one dinner together before you leave. Carter promised he'd come home on time."

"He's gone a lot, huh?" Mr. Matthews said.

"Unfortunately, yes. I do miss him when he's gone."

"Tea, anyone?"

"I'd love a cup, Dani," Margo said.

"Nothing for me, honey." Mr. Matthews stood and placed Gracie in her seat. "Think I'll take a quick nap."

"Why don't you put Grady in his seat, Margo, and we'll share a cup in the kitchen?"

"Sounds good."

"I'm really going to miss you two," Dani said. "What a huge help you've been."

"Glad we could do it," Mr. Matthew mouthed.

Dani paused before heading to the kitchen as she admired the wonder of her twin babies in their side-by-side baby seats. *Thank you Lord, for this miracle.* "Come, sister," Dani said as she put her arm around Margot and smiled, "Let's make that tea."

Two hours later, the front door burst open and Sheila Matthews stumbled inside. She kicked the door closed with her stylishly clad foot.

"Shh," Mr. Matthews said, "the babies are sleeping."

"Oh, sorry," she whispered.

"Well, it looks like you have found some things from the looks of all those bags."

"Oh, I did!" she said as she dropped the bags, kicked off her shoes, and plopped down on the sofa. "Where's Margo? I bought some new tops for her."

"She's out back with Dani. Hon, you know how Margot hates for you to pick out her clothing. Why do you insist on doing that?"

"Why?" Sheila whispered, "because she goes around in ridiculous outfits."

"Sheila, stop it," Hugh Matthews warned. "Be thankful you have a daughter who—"

"I am thankful. I just wish . . . oh, well, who knows, maybe she will actually like what I bought."

"I hope you can fit all that stuff in your suitcase."

"If not, I'll get Carter to ship it to me."

"Wanna see what I bought?"

"Actually, I was about to take a little nap."

Sheila gathered up her purchases and took them to the guest room.

❉❉❉

Dani bit her tongue to keep from saying something she knew would lead to an argument when Carter arrived home at nine.

"Hi, hon," he said as he kissed Dani's cheek. Sorry, I'm late, but I had a—"

"Your folks are leaving tomorrow, Carter," she said. "I'll warm your dinner while you visit with them." She tried to sound cheerful, but she was in no mood to listen to another one of his excuses.

Chapter 37

June 16, 1983

Let love and faithfulness never leave you; bind them around your neck, write them on the tablet of your heart. Proverbs 3:3

D ani awoke with a start. "Carter, what time is it?"
Carter opened one eye and peeked at the clock. "Six."

Dani tossed the covers aside and bounded out of bed. "The babies!"

"What about the ba—?"

Dani flew down the hall to the nursery her heart pounding in her chest. *Oh, dear God.*

The sight of two sleeping infants filled her with relief, and she dropped down onto the soft carpet. *You little stinkers. You scared your mommy.*

Carter staggered into the room as he rubbed the sleep from his eyes. "What's going on?"

"Shh!" she whispered as she stood up and shooed him from the room. "They slept all night."

"Yeah?"

Dani threw her arms around him. "Did you hear me? I said they slept all night!"

"Oh . . . well, that's great, hon," he said.

"It *is* great," she said as she noted his lack of enthusiasm in the hug.

"Let's get the coffeepot on, okay?" Carter said.

❄❄❄

Dani loved being a mom and had become quite capable at bathing, feeding, and dressing the two wiggly babies. Gracie was more of a challenge since she wasn't as content as Grady, but Dani found if she sang to her while she was busy with her brother, it helped.

She put the babies in their carriers and set them on the kitchen table and then filled the baby tub with warm water.

"Okay, you two, who wants to go first? She tickled Grady's little toes.

Grady cooed.

She peeled off his diaper and slipped him into the warm water.

"And what shall we sing, beautiful baby?" Dani said.

Gracie's tiny mouth broke into a grin that warmed Dani's heart. "You charmer, you."

❄❄❄

Dani had just finished the babies' two o'clock feeding and put them down for naps when someone rang the doorbell, and she hurried to the door.

"Mavis! Hey, how are you?"

"I'm good. I have something for you," she said.

"A stroller?" Dani asked with a puzzled look.

"I was hoping you didn't already have one."

"I'm shocked, Mavis. You actually bought us a stroller for twins! Well, we definitely need to pay you for that."

"Okay, you can pay me by making me a cup of tea."

"Well come on in." Dani held the door open as Mavis pushed the stroller into the room.

"Oh, Mavis, I love it. The other day I was thinking how nice it would be to take the babies for a walk."

"Well, now you can."

Mavis followed her into the kitchen and leaned against the counter watching Dani put the teakettle on. "How are you feeling by now?"

"Great. It's been a challenge, though, I have to admit."

"I can't believe you've already lost your baby weight."

Dani swept her eyes down her body and laughed. "I guess I don't have much time to eat these days. I've missed you, Mavis. I hope we can spend more time together."

"Ah, yeah, that would be great." Mavis looked around the pleasant kitchen. "Looks like you've done a lot of work in here."

"Just paint and curtains," Dani said as she pulled two cups and teabags from the cabinet. The teakettle whistled. "Still like Red Zinger?"

"Sure do." Mavis pulled out a chair and sat at the table.

"So, how's the job going by now?" Dani asked as she poured the boiling water into the two cups.

"Now that Ramona's gone, busier than ever."

Dani put the teakettle back on the stove and sat opposite Mavis. "Honey?" she asked, glad she remembered Mavis took honey in her tea.

"Oh, no thanks. Trying to cut out a few calories."

"Surely they'll hire a replacement for Ramona, right?"

"I hope so."

Dani had trouble keeping the conversation going and couldn't wait for the strained visit to end. "More tea?" Dani asked. "Sorry, I should have offered you cookies or—"

"Oh, no thanks. Tea is fine."

Mavis is different. She's not the same girl I first met and became friends with. What is going on?

"Dani, do you think I could have a peek at the babies? I'll be really quiet."

"Of course. Don't be silly. They're sound sleepers."

Mavis tiptoed to each crib, but when she reached Grady's bed, she reached down and stroked the baby's soft dark curls. "Oh," she whispered, "he's so adorable. Has Carter's hair, huh?"

Mavis' expression confused Dani, and even disturbed her. "Psst," Dani said as she motioned Mavis away from the crib. "I want to show you what we've done out back."

Mavis nodded, glanced at Grady again, and followed Dani out to the patio.

"So, what do you think?" Dani asked as she pointed out their new patio furniture.

"Nice. You'll enjoy that grill this summer."

"Yeah, I can't wait to grill a nice steak for Carter. I just have to learn how to use it," she said with a chuckle.

"Oh, I thought Carter wasn't eating that much red meat these days."

What else does she know about Carter? "Well, that's news to me."

Mavis glanced at her watch. "Oh, my, I have to get back to work. Carter will wonder where I am."

Finally. "Well, thank you so much for the stroller. I can't wait to try it out."

"You're very welcome."

Chapter 38

June 17, 1983

The LORD is close to the brokenhearted and saves those who are crushed in spirit. Psalm 34:18

Dani was enjoying a second cup of coffee relishing the silence of the house on Friday morning before the babies woke. Her Bible lay open on the table, and as her custom has been of late, she had read a Psalm and would follow it with a Proverb. After that, if time permitted, she would dig into the book of Colossians. She read these words in Psalm 28:7 again: *The Lord is my strength and my shield; my heart trusts in him, and he helps me. My heart leaps for joy, and with my song I praise him.*

Immediately, Dani fell into prayer.

Oh, Father, I do have so much to thank you for. When I think of the darkness you saved me from when dear Betts died, words cannot express my gratitude. Now, here I am a pastor's wife with a husband and two children. Like the Psalmist, my heart leaps for joy, too!

Dani flipped to Proverbs and read Chapter 31. When she came to verse 28, she read the words several times. *Her children arise and call her blessed; her husband also, and he praises her.*

Hmm . . . This Proverbs 31 lady must have been something. I want that, Lord, but You'll have to help me. I feel like I have failed Carter. He seems so . . . distracted, so far from me. Show me what I need to do Lord.

The cries of two hungry babies ended her quiet time, and she hurried to the nursery.

By ten o'clock nap time, besides caring for the babies, Dani had tidied the house, washed two loads of clothes, and planned dinner. She called Mr. Hunt just to say hello, and then checked in with Adrian to see how the girls were doing with the substitute Sunday school teacher. She missed her class and hoped to return soon.

When she hung up, she checked the calendar for the date of the babies' checkup. *Oh my goodness, our wedding anniversary is on Monday! How could I have forgotten?* She tapped her finger on the calendar as thoughts whirled through her mind. *I want to do something special for him today . . . I wonder . . . I'm going to call Sally Cotton and see if she could come by and sit with the twins for an hour.*

Dani looked up Sally's number and dialed. *Please, let her be home. Let her say yes.*

❄❄❄

Dani pulled into the space beside Carter's car and cut the engine. She peeked in the rearview mirror to check her lipstick and fluffed her hair. She was glad she had taken the time to spritz some of the cologne Carter had given her for her birthday. She paused outside his office, inhaled deeply, and smiled as she eased the door open. Her brain switched to slow motion as it attempted to process the scene. *Mavis and Carter?* Truth reeled through her, and she dropped the basket filled with Carter's surprise early anniversary lunch, unaware of glass that splintered around her feet. Tears blurred her vision as she stumbled down the hall of the church. She pawed through her purse for the keys as her heart bubbled oddly. *Oh, God! Oh, God!* Her hands shook violently and made it difficult to insert the key into the ignition, but finally, the car roared to life.

"Dani, wait!" Carter yelled as he tore from the church toward her.

Dani jammed the door lock and squealed from the parking lot.

❅❅❅

Dani's head pounded with each beat of her hammering heart as she pressed the gas pedal and sped out of town. *How could he? Oh God, how could Carter do this?* Images of Mavis in Carter's arms shot waves of pure jealousy through her body almost blinding her, but she fed more gas to the engine anyway as if she were fleeing a menacing ogre. When jealous anger submitted to tears, Dani pulled into the parking lot of a Kroger store, cut the engine, and grabbed a tissue from her purse. *Carter, why? I believed you when you said you loved me. How could you do this?* She pounded the steering wheel. "Why, why why!"

Dani sobbed until she had no strength left and then rummaged in her purse for another tissue. Finding none, she pulled open the glove box for anything she could use as a tissue. A spare box of baby wipes shocked her back to reality. *My babies! Oh, no. How long have I been gone? She pulled a baby wipe from the box and mopped her face, started the car, and pulled back onto the highway.*

Hatred for Mavis seethed in her. *So, now I know why*

our friendship cooled. You went after my husband!

The vision of Carter and Mavis together flew into her mind, and she fought the urge to vomit. *What am I to do now, Lord? What will I do?*

❇︎❇︎❇︎

Dani raced from the car and stumbled in the front door. "Sally, I'm so sorry. I . . I'm late. The babies . . . are they okay? I'm so sorry, so sorry."

"The babies are fine, honey. They're sleeping. Are you okay?" Sally rose from the sofa and embraced Dani.

"Am I okay?" Dani didn't mean to laugh. "Am I okay? Sally, I'll never be okay again." Dani couldn't stop her tears, and sobbed in Sally's arms.

Sally led Dani to a chair. "Can I get you something, honey? Some tea? Maybe you'd like to talk?"

"No amount of talking will fix this, Sally. I . . I—" Dani bolted from the chair to her bedroom, slammed the door, oblivious of the sleeping babies, and threw herself onto her bed, sobbing and wailing.

Unsure of what to do, Sally stood in shock. *What on earth has Dani so upset? I think Carter needs to know about this.*

Sally picked up the phone and dialed the church, but got the answering machine. She found the church directory tucked under the phone and paged through it for Cynthia Miller's number. She could hear Gracie's cries from the nursery, and prayed she wouldn't wake Grady. *Answer Cynthia, please.*

"Hello?"

"Cynthia, it's Sally.

"Hey, Sally."

"Are you busy right now?"

"Just catching up on laundry. Why?"

"Can you come over to the Matthews'?"

"Uh, I guess so. What's up?"
"Something's wrong with Dani and I need—"
"Say no more. I'll be there in fifteen minutes."

❇︎❇︎❇︎

By the time Cynthia arrived, both babies were crying. Sally was holding both of them, rocking and trying her best to comfort them.

"Here, I'll take Grace," Cynthia said as she swept the infant up into her arms. "Are they hungry, Sally?"

"No, I don't think so. They didn't get their nap out. They're just grumpy."

Grady found his thumb and soon settled back into Sally's arms while Cynthia walked the floor patting baby Grace until she fell asleep again.

After Dani's friends returned the babies to their cribs, Sally motioned for Cynthia to follow her to the kitchen.

"What's going on here, Sally?"

"I have no idea. What I do know is that Dani Matthews is one very upset young lady. She came home just before I called you, sobbing hysterically. I tried to call the church, but got the machine."

"Oh, dear. What can we do?"

"We can pray, and then I'll try the church again. Carter needs to come home."

After Sally and Cynthia had prayed, Sally said, "I think I'll check on Dani."

She tapped on Dani's bedroom door and entered. "Dani?" she whispered.

No answer.

She eased onto the bed and stroked Dani's back. "Honey, I tried to call Carter."

The mention of Carter's name triggered another barrage of weeping.

"I'm sorry, honey. I wish I knew how to help you."

Sally remained with Dani until her cries subsided and then tiptoed from the bedroom.

Moments later Carter burst through the back door and finding Sally and Cynthia asked, "Where's my wife?"

Chapter 39

My days are over. My hopes have disappeared. My heart's desires are broken. Job 17:11

Carter didn't wait until the ladies responded, but headed down the hallway.

"Pastor, your wife is very upset about something," Sally called after him.

Carter suddenly remembered he couldn't risk a rumor starting, turned and smiled at them. "Yes, I know, but she'll be fine. We just had a misunderstanding, and she's been very emotional lately. I guess Dani asked you to sit with the babies, huh?"

"Yes," Sally said. "She was headed to the church to surprise you with lunch."

Carter stepped back into the room. "Well, thanks so much for helping out, but I can take it from here." Carter tried his best to form the words using his best pastor voice.

"We're willing to stay and help out if you need us," Cynthia said.

"No, that won't be necessary."

"Well, if you're sure," Sally said as she gathered her things. "We're only a phone call away."

The two ladies then headed for the door.

"Thanks again," Carter said.

When the door clicked in place, Carter eased open the bedroom door and found a sleeping Dani.

"Dani? Sweetheart?" Carter caressed her hair.

Dani twisted to her back and swung her feet to the floor as reality slammed into her mind. She smoothed her tousled hair as if she were removing the touch of his hand. She grabbed a tissue from the box on her night stand and wiped her bloodshot eyes. "Get out!" she shouted. "Get out of here and never come back!"

"Please, Dani, I—"

"Don't 'Please, Dani,' me. I saw you with Mavis, Carter. You broke our marriage vows, now get out! Now! I never want to see you again!"

"I can't leave you here alone with the babies, Dani. You have to be reasonable."

"Be reasonable! Is it reasonable for a pastor to have an affair with his secretary? And, by the way, I'm alone with the babies almost every night anyway."

The babies had awakened and demanded attention.

"Dani, honest, I don't—"

"Get out of my way, Carter," she said as she shoved him. "I have no interest in hearing your excuses. Now, move so I can get my babies."

Carter stepped aside. "They're my babies, too."

"Oh, yeah, well you haven't been acting like it. I guess you didn't have time with all your meetings, not to mention time with your girlfriend."

"She's not my girlfriend. You have to listen to me."

"No, you have to listen to me. The suitcases are in the guest room closet. Pack and get out, Carter."

"Where will I go?"

"That's your problem."

Dani carried both babies to the living room, and placed them in their seats as Carter went about packing a suitcase.

Dani took bottles from the refrigerator to warm as Carter shuffled into the kitchen with suitcase in hand, his pleading eyes trained on Dani.

When she refused to look at him, he opened the door and left.

Dani changed and fed the babies, trying not to give in to the darkness that threatened to consume her. When she heard Carter's car door shut, the sound pierced her heart like a surgeon's scalpel.

Grady cooed from his seat as Dani held Gracie close to her heart and wept.

❄❄❄

Dani tossed and turned all night, and when the babies' squirming turned to squalling, she dragged her exhausted body from the bed. *Oh, dear Lord, I need You more than I ever have.*

By mid-morning, she knew she had to call her parents. The babies sensed her anxiety and fussed continuously. Dani paced the floor with Gracie and when she quieted, Grady fussed. Her emotions swung like a pendulum and her head felt like it was filled with lead.

When she finally got the babies down for their morning naps, Dani dialed her parent's number.

"Hello?"

"Mom?"

"Dani! How are you?"

Silence. *How do I tell my mother my marriage is over?*

"Sweetie? Is something wrong? Is it the babies?"

Dani took a deep breath. "No, the babies are fine."

"Good. What's going on, Dani. Are you okay?"

"No, Mom. I guess I'm not okay."

"Honey, tell me. I'm listening."

"Our marriage is over."

Now there was silence on the other end as Lindy tried to absorb her daughter's words.

"Did you hear me? Carter and I are finished."

"What on earth are you talking about?"

"Mom, Carter has been having an affair. I never want to see him again."

"Oh, Dani. I'm so sorry. Is he there with you?"

"No, he left. I'm alone with the babies." Dani's voice broke, and tears gushed down her face.

"Is there someone who can come and help you?"

Dani blew her nose. "Mom, can you and Dad come and get me?"

"Are you sure about what happened, honey?"

"I saw them, Mom!" Dani fairly shrieked into the phone. "I saw them together."

"Oh, my. I'll call your dad, and we'll make arangements to be there tomorrow. I'm concerned about you being alone right now. Please call someone, Dani. Now promise me."

Dani wiped her face on a tissue. "Okay. I'll call Sally."

"Mom?"

"Yes, honey."

"I'm sorry."

"You have nothing to be sorry for."

"Seems like I always have some big problem."

"Dani, I want you to hang up and call Sally."

"I will. Thanks, Mom. I love you."

"Love you, too. I'll call you later after I talk to Dad."

Chapter 40

In your anger do not sin. Do not let the sun go down while you are still angry, and do not give the devil a foothold.
Ephesians 3:26-27

Dani hung up the phone and headed down the hall to peek in on the babies. The sight of her precious twins slumbering in the security and warmth of their cribs gripped her heart with despair. *Oh dear God, they are so tiny, so innocent. Why, Carter? How could you do this to them? To us?* She pushed a hand over her mouth and smothered the sobs that demanded release and backed out of the room.

She tried to focus on what she had to do to be ready to leave the minute her parents arrived tomorrow but could only manage her normal routine. Images of Carter with Mavis stalked her as she showered and dressed, made her bed, washed baby bottles, and made formula. Dani jumped when the phone rang, and she dropped a bottle of formula. The milk oozed over the black tiled floor navigating among the shards of glass. "Broken . . . it's broken. Oh, dear God, it's . . . it's broken." A shudder rippled through Dani, and she sagged against a cabinet and sank to the floor oblivious of the broken glass scattered around her. She didn't hear the back door open, but recognized Adrian Bartrom's voice.

"Girls, it's not polite to just walk into somebody's house. You must knock fir—"

"Mommy, what's wrong wiff Mith Dani?"

"Oh, my goodness," Adrian said, as she shooed her girls into the living room. She stepped carefully through the glass, and helped Dani to her feet. "Are you hurt, honey?" she asked as she reached for paper towels to clean up the mess on the floor.

"I . . . I dropped a—"

"A bottle. I see that. Are you sure you're okay? Shall I call the pastor?"

Dani recovered her wits and assured Adrian she wasn't hurt. "I'm sorry, Adrian, the place is a mess."

"How about you lie down for a few minutes while I get this glass cleaned up?"

"Oh, I . . . I'm fine. I'm just tired . . . not sleeping."

"I insist," Adrian said and led Dani to the sofa, fluffed the sofa pillow and helped her lie down. "I remember how it is with little ones. How about I fix you a nice cup of tea? The babies are napping, huh?"

With all the energy she could muster, Dani nodded.

❄❄❄

Maggie always headed for the rocking chair whenever Adrian brought the girls for a visit, and today was no different. Back and forth she rocked exuberantly while Lily marched around the coffee table in her sturdy orthopedic shoes counting aloud each time she circled. Ready for a change, she stopped beside Dani and tugged on her arm.

"Can we thee the babyth?" Lily pleaded.

"Lily, don't bother Miss Dani right now. She's not feeling good," Adrian said as she stepped back into the living room.

"Oh, thorry, Mith Dani."

Dani managed a weak smile and tried to lift her head that felt as if a sandbag had been placed on it crushing her against the sofa pillow.

A few minutes later, Adrian had tea ready and had found cookies for the girls, but when she approached Dani, she found her sound asleep.

"Would you like a cookie?" Adrian whispered to Maggie and Lily.

The girls followed their mother back to the kitchen where Adrian handed them a chocolate chip cookie. She dumped the freshly made tea, rinsed out the cups, and motioned the girls toward the door.

"No babyth?" Lily asked.

"We need to let Miss Dani rest while the babies are sleeping, honey."

❈❈❈

Dani wasn't sure if the phone woke her or the babies' cries, but she lurched up from the sofa and threw off the afghan that Adrian must have placed on her. She reached the phone just as it ceased ringing, and then staggered down the hall toward the nursery.

Before Dani had finished changing the babies' diapers, Carter bolted through the kitchen door, and raced down the hall. He found a wailing Grady in the middle of their bed, his blue pacifier beside him. Carter scooped him up. "Shh, shh," he said as he soothed his son with the pacifier.

Carter stepped out of the bedroom and met Dani with a grumpy Gracie resting on her shoulder.

"Wha—"

"You didn't answer the phone, Dani. I was worried."

"I told you to get out."

"I know what you said, but you obviously need help."

"I've been handling things since they were born, if you recall." Dani felt as if Gracie weighed a hundred pounds, and her hunger cries tugged at Dani's heart. Tears pooled in her eyes. "Hand Grady to me," she instructed.

"No, you feed Gracie, and I'll feed Grady."

"Whatever." Dani swiped the tears that began slipping down her face.

With a free hand, Carter gently nudged Dani toward the kitchen. "The babies are hungry, Dani."

While Dani heated two bottles, Carter rocked Grady and replaced the pacifier each time he squalled in protest when no milk flowed into his mouth.

Finally, Dani handed Carter a bottle. "Burp him after three ounces," she ordered.

"I remember."

I'm surprised you remembered.

No words passed between Carter and Dani while they fed the babies. When Gracie had finished her bottle, Dani placed her in the playpen, and then held out her arms to Carter. "I'll take Grady, now," she said.

Carter ignored her, stood, kissed Grady's soft cheek, and placed him beside his sister. "You two, be good for Mommy, you hear?"

That was more than Dani could bear to witness. She whisked up the empty bottles, and escaped to the kitchen where she melted in tears over the sink as she rinsed out the two bottles.

When she felt his hand on her back, she brushed it off as if she had been stung. "Get out . . . Carter. Please, go."

"Dani, I—"

"Please, Carter, I'm very tired. I need you to go."

"I know you're tired and hurt, and I'm so sorry, but we need to talk."

She turned from the sink to face him, her eyes red and swollen, as heat flamed her face. "What exactly are you sorry for, Carter Matthews? Sorry you got caught? Sorry you didn't marry a model like Mavis? Sorry you're straddled with two kids? Yeah, Carter, just what *are* you sorry for?"

The mist forming in Carter's eyes shocked Dani momentarily, but she continued. "Oh, that's right," she said, feigning a surprised expression, "you must be sorry that you married a woman whose choice of clothing doesn't match your elevated position as pastor."

"Dani, please can't we talk this out?"

Dani turned her eyes to the ceiling, frowned, and tapped her finger against her cheek. "Hmm . . . let's see, how does one 'talk out' adultery? Oh, I know. The adulterer says, 'I'm sorry, hon, I cheated on you, and then the innocent person says, 'That's okay. I forgive you.' If that's what you're expecting, forget it, Carter. And, I'd really like for you to go now. I need to get packed."

"Packed?"

"My parents are coming tomorrow. I'm going home."

Carter swiped at his eyes. "*This* is your home, Dani."

"No, it *was* my home. You destroyed that."

Carter tried to pull her into his arms, but she twisted free. "Dani, you and the babies are everything to me. I see that now. I've been so foolish." He dropped his head into his hands and sobbed.

"Carter, I can't handle this" she said as she handed him a paper towel.

"I know. I'm sorry, Dani." Carter sniffed and wiped his face. Without a word, he returned to the living room picked up the babies one at a time, and kissed them.

Neither baby woke up which shocked Dani, and his tenderness with them gripped her heart. For one split second, she was tempted to forgive him, but the mental image of him with Mavis prevented that.

Dani watched the scene as if she were viewing a sad movie and then turned away, so she wouldn't see Carter shuffling to the door. "Staying at the parsonage," he said as he closed the door behind him."

Choices

Chapter 41

Many are the plans in a person's heart, but it is the Lord's purpose that prevails. Proverbs 19:21

By the time Cameron and Lindy arrived in Wilburta, Dani's anger had turned to despair.

For two days, Lindy watched her plod through the process of packing while caring for Grady and Gracie. Finally, Lindy caught her daughter by both shoulders and gently shook her as if she were a rag doll. "Dani, listen to me. I know you are hurting, but you must not give in to this. You have two little babies who desperately need you."

Dani blinked and willed herself to focus on her mother. "Oh, Mom, I can't believe this has happened. Why?"

"I don't know why Carter did this, but what I do know is that we are all capable of sin." The thought of how she and Cameron had given in to their passion before their wedding flashed through her mind.

"Are you excusing what Carter did, Mom?"

"No, I'm saying there are no perfect people."

"I know that, but Carter is a pastor, for crying out loud. A pastor! That should count for something." Dani flopped down onto the sofa.

Lindy sat down beside her and took her hand. "Listen, honey, pastors are people, too. Just people. They are tempted to sin like everybody. It *is* especially sad when they fall into sin, because it affects so many people and causes people to criticize the church."

"Well, right now, it's affecting him the most."

Lindy frowned at Dani's tone. "Why do you say that?"

"He's lost his children, will probably lose his job when word gets out what he's done, and he's stuck living in the parsonage, the parsonage he hated, I might add."

"Oh, Dani, we should never rejoice when bad things happen to people."

"I'm not rejoicing. Just stating facts."

"Carter's at the parsonage?"

"That's what he said, anyway. A few months ago, the church began keeping it ready for visiting missionaries or special speakers. I don't know how he'll explain living there if people find out. Doesn't matter anyway. He'll come here as soon as we leave for Meadow Glen."

In a complete change of attitude, a furrow appeared in Dani's forehead, and she looked questioningly in her mother's eyes. "Mom?"

"Yes, sweetie?"

"Did I do this?"

"Do what?"

"Cause Carter to turn to another woman." Dani shook free of Lindy's hand, rose to her feet, and paced the room.

Lindy listened.

"I mean . . . look at me, Mom." Dani halted her pacing and swept her hands down her body. "I'm a wreck."

"You're beautiful."

"Some days I don't have time to do more than brush my teeth and comb my hair. A shower is a luxury."

"Dani Matthews, you are a lovely young woman. You gave birth to twin babies a few weeks ago, and they need a lot of care right now."

"Then why did Carter—"

"I think it's best if we don't keep talking about the sin. The Bible tells us to think on good things."

"A little hard to do, Mom, when I just found out two days ago that my husband . . . well, you know."

"Come over here and let's talk while the babies are sleeping, and your dad is out," Lindy said as she patted the spot beside her.

Dani sat back down. "Mom, I'm going to need help with babysitting when I get home. Will you and Dad be able to help until I find a job and a place of my own?"

"You know we'll help, Dani."

"It's overwhelming to think about it."

Lindy smoothed Dani's hair. "Honey, have you considered that you and Carter could go for counseling?"

Dani smacked her lips and smirked. "I am *married* to the man people in our church *go to* for counseling. Ironic, isn't it?"

Lindy didn't respond.

"What would counseling do for us anyway? It won't change what Carter has done, and I could never trust him again. Never." Dani shook her head as if she were flinging off a stinging insect.

"Dani, the Bible says that a person who listens to advice is wise. It doesn't mean you have to *take* the advice, but at least listen to it."

The conversation ended when they heard Cameron coming in the back door.

"I'm back," Cameron called. "Anybody want some butter pecan ice cream?"

"Sounds great, Dad. So that's where you went, huh?"

"Well, I did stop and have a talk with Carter.

"You did what?" Dani asked."

✲✲✲

On the pretense of going for ice cream, Cameron had headed the car toward Wilburta Community Fellowship. He and Lindy had arrived late yesterday afternoon and found that Dani needed both of them not only to help with the babies, but to listen and encourage their wounded daughter.

As Cameron pulled into the church parking lot, he didn't see Carter's car, but wanted to be sure he wasn't inside in case he had a new car.

Once inside the building, the sound of hammering echoed through the building, but Cameron didn't see anyone. A small sign, "Offices" with an arrow under it pointed left, and Cameron turned down that hall.

As he neared an office, he peeked through the small window and immediately recognized Mavis, having met her when she helped fix up the parsonage for Carter and Dani. *Dear Father, help me to remember that "All have sinned and come short of your glory."*

Cameron tapped on the door and entered the office. "Good afternoon," Cameron said. "Mavis, isn't it?"

Mavis' face blanched as white as the paper she was holding. "Why, yes," she managed. "And you're Dani's father." Mavis stood and offered her hand to Cameron.

After the two had shaken hands, Mavis asked, "What can I do for you, Mr. Krieg?"

"Well, I'm looking for Carter, and I was hoping to catch him here."

"Oh, I'm sorry you missed him. Pastor Carter isn't in. I actually haven't seen him today. Can I take a message for him or have him call?"

Cameron stepped to Mavis' desk. He leaned his six foot muscular frame close enough to Mavis. "Listen to me, young lady. I'm well aware of what has been going on here, and unless you want everyone to know, I suggest you tell me right now where I can find my son-in-law."

Mavis' hands trembled as she scratched information on a note pad, ripped it off, and handed it to Cameron.

Cameron studied the note. "Isn't this the address of the church parsonage?"

"Yes, Mr. Krieg, Carter's staying at the parsonage, at least for now." Mavis' confident voice failed her as she appeared to struggle to simply breathe.

"Thank you," he said cordially as he headed for the door.

❊❊❊

Cameron remembered the parsonage was only a few blocks from the church and he had no trouble finding the small house.

He pulled into the driveway, cut the engine, and rested his arms on the steering wheel. The memory of the day Carter and Dani moved into the parsonage filled him with a mix of frustration, sadness, and disbelief. He recalled Dani's excitement as she and Carter were moving into their first home. *The joy of that special day has been marred, Carter, and you don't know the pain you've caused your wife and yourself. You will always regret the day you gave in to temptation. I know, believe me. I know.*

Cameron dropped his head and cried out to God for Carter and his daughter. *Oh, Father, I'm sitting here asking You to give me the right words to say to my son-in-law. Thank You for Your forgiving love that never fails. Carter has done a terrible thing. He has hurt Dani deeply, he has sinned against Mavis, but most importantly, he has sinned against You. Use me, Father, to speak Your words to Carter. Amen.*

Chapter 42

If we confess our sins, he is faithful and just and will forgive us our sins and purify us from all unrighteousness. 1 John 1:9

Cameron ascended the sturdy front steps remembering their need for repair on moving day.

Carter must have been watching Cameron's car pull in since the door opened before he could knock.

"Hello, Carter." Cameron barely recognized him—the always impeccably-groomed man his daughter married.

Barefoot and wearing pajama bottoms and a coffee-dribbled tee shirt, the unshaven Carter forced his eyes to meet Cameron's, and then ran his hand through his tangled mass of hair.

"May I come in, Carter?"

Carter stood aside as Cameron entered the small living room and eased into a chair.

Carter closed the door and turned to his father-in-law. "If you came here to tell me what a horrible person I am, don't bother. I've already done that a hundred times."

Carter clenched his fists and smacked the sides of his head. "I have been so stupid." Carter dropped his head into his hands and sobbed.

Cameron stood and embraced the broken man until his sobs subsided and then pulled a handkerchief from his pocket and handed it to Carter.

"I love Dani, Dad. I love her with all my heart." Carter blew his nose. "I don't know why I let this happen. I'm such a fool. I've lost the most precious things in my life—Dani and my babies. Oh, God, Oh, God!"

"I think we need to talk, Carter." With a half-laugh, Cameron pointed to Carter's shirt. "From the looks of that tee shirt, I'm sure you have coffee. Mind fixing a cup?"

"Oh, sure. It's instant, though."

"That's fine," Cameron said, as he followed Carter to the kitchen.

While Carter made the coffee, Cameron prayed silently for wisdom and for God to use him to speak truth and wise counsel to Carter.

"Sorry, no sugar or cream," Carter said as he carried the two steaming mugs to the table.

Cameron smiled. "Black is fine," he said as he sipped the hot coffee.

"They only keep the bare minimum here for guests."

"A great use of the parsonage."

Carter picked up his cup and scanned the small kitchen as his eyes pooled again. "I have been wrong about so many things, and this house was one. Dani loved our first home and she did so much to make it warm and . . . " He grabbed a napkin and wiped his eyes. "What did I do? Complain about it." His eyes met Cameron's. "I have hurt her deeply. She will never forgive me, and I don't blame her one bit."

Cameron listened to the agony of his son-in-law without comment until he was certain he had vented the torture of his broken heart.

"I don't know what to do, Dad. I can't preach anymore." He ran his hands through his hair. "My preaching days are over. My marriage is finished after barely one year, and I've lost my children. I deserve everything that's happened to me after what I've done." Carter slumped over his cup.

"Carter, I came here today not knowing what I would find, and I wasn't even sure if you would be willing to talk with me."

Carter frowned and looked up at his father-in-law. "Of course, I would talk with you. I have respected you from the moment I first met you."

"In that case, I'd like to speak honestly to you."

"Absolutely. If ever I needed counsel it is now."

"You committed adultery, Carter, right? You're admitting that is true?"

Carter worked his wedding ring back and forth with downcast eyes. "I did. I didn't mean for it to happen, oh, dear God, Dad, I didn't mean, didn't plan for this to happen. Even though it was one time, I did it. I cheated on my precious Dani." He pressed his fingertips against his temples. "How could I?"

Cameron sipped his cooled bitter coffee. "Carter, you're an intelligent man who knows the Word of God and preaches it. How did this affair with Mavis get started?"

Hearing the name "Mavis" delivered a stab of shame to Carter's heart. He chewed his lip and frowned as he appeared to study the ceiling. "I noticed that Mavis started dressing up for work more than usual. She *is* a beautiful woman. There's no denying that. I don't know, Dad, how it started really. Wait, yes I do know. She handed me my messages one day, and our hands touched, and our eyes met. Then when Ramona quit—"

"Ramona?"

"The other secretary."

"That meant you and Mavis had time alone, right?"

"Exactly. I'm not saying that is an excuse for my behavior, though." Carter closed his eyes and shook his head. "I'm so ashamed to tell you this, but it began with a hug and then . . . well, you can guess the rest."

Cameron nodded.

"Why do you think you didn't heed the warning signs and flee like Joseph fled Potiphar's wife?"

"I keep asking myself that question. It had been drilled into us who were studying for the ministry not to ever be alone with a woman other than our wife. When Ramona left, I put myself at risk."

"How about you and Dani? How was your marriage?"

Carter sighed. "Honestly, we were arguing quite a bit. She didn't like that I had to be gone so many evenings, but I couldn't help it."

"Hmm . . ."

"It really bothered me, too, that she disagreed with many of the decisions the council made. I wanted us to work as a team, but she really wasn't happy."

Cameron spoke slowly and deliberately. "So . . . you were lacking harmony in your marriage; a beautiful woman you saw every day thought you were amazing and loved your ideas; and the opportunity to give into temptation was available when Ramona left and the two of you were alone. Is that right?"

"Exactly right."

"When you and Mavis became intimate, did you plan when and where that would happen?"

"Uh . . . yes. She invited me to her place."

"How did you react to the invitation?"

"I wish I could say, I prayed about it and asked God to help me, but I didn't. I actually couldn't wait for that day to end so I could make love to Mavis. Just saying this out loud makes me want to throw up."

"And when it was over, that night, how did you feel?"

"Embarrassed, awkward, sorry, dirty. I left there and

drove around for hours trying to rid myself of the shame of my behavior. When I climbed into bed beside Dani, the horror of my actions filled me with grief. I wanted to tell her what I'd done. I wanted her to know I loved her more than anything, that I didn't love Mavis, but how could I do that? It would break her heart."

"I'm confused, Carter. Dani said she caught you and Mavis together. If that's true, then the affair must have continued after that night, right?"

"No, it didn't. When we were finally alone the next day, I told Mavis we had made a mistake, and it wouldn't happen again. What Dani saw was Mavis clinging to me as I tried to convince her there would be nothing more than a professional relationship between us."

"Hmm . . . I see."

Carter rubbed his stubbled chin. "Dad, I really mean it when I say I don't know what to do. Should I confess to the church and resign?"

"I believe the first thing you need to do is confess your sin to God. You know very well what the Scripture says to do when you know you've sinned. Why don't you do that now? It's one thing to *know* you sinned and feel bad about it, it's another to confess your sin to God and ask Him for forgiveness. Carter, you sinned against several people when you committed adultery. Are you aware of that?"

"What do you mean?"

"Not only did you sin against Dani, but you sinned against Mavis, your children, and also your congregation. Ultimately, you sinned against the God who called you to serve Him. Remember the story of David's sin with Bathsheba? That horrible act had far-reaching and tragic results for many people, too."

"Oh, man."

"After you pray, you need to try and convince Dani to go to marriage counseling with you."

Carter popped up and began pacing. "Dad, she won't

even talk to me. She wants nothing else to do with me. And I don't blame her."

"Sit back down, Carter. I have a few more things to say to you."

Carter dropped back down into his chair.

"Even if you and Dani don't get back together, you both need to know what went wrong in your marriage, and how each of you contributed to its breakdown."

"Honestly, Dani did nothing wrong. It's all my fault."

"I realize you sinned, and sinned greatly, Carter, but most of the time, a divorce occurs because both spouses contributed to it."

"Dani is so hurt and angry. I can't imagine she would agree to go to marriage counseling."

"Another thing to pray about." Cameron glanced at his watch. "I really need to get back to the house," he said as he stood and shoved his chair back under the table.

Carter stood and offered Cameron his hand. "Thank you so much for coming. I will take your advice, for sure. If I lose Dani, I'll be losing a family I've grown to love. I'm sorry I haven't been a very good son-in-law."

Cameron hugged Carter. "I'll be praying for you," he said as he headed for the door.

When the door closed behind Cameron, Carter fell face down onto the carpet and cried out to God.

Chapter 43

Whoever heeds life-giving correction will be at home among the wise. Proverbs 15:31

Dani popped to her feet on hearing that her father had gone to see Carter. "How did you know where he is?" she asked.

Cameron paused and looked at his daughter. "Mavis."

"That figures." Dani rolled her eyes and watched her dad spoon ice cream into three bowls.

Lindy overheard their brief exchange and feared what would ensue as she stepped into the kitchen.

"Shall we?" Cameron said as he handed one bowl to Dani and carried the other two to the table. "How about we sit and enjoy the ice cream before it melts and the babies wake up?"

"I can just imagine what Carter told you, Dad," Dani said as she slid into a chair opposite him.

"Oh?"

"Probably denied everything."

Cameron lifted a spoonful of ice cream to his mouth. "Actually, quite the opposite."

"You mean he owned up to it?"

Cameron put his spoon down and reached for Dani's hand. "Yes, he admitted he committed adultery, honey."

Dani tried her best to maintain her anger because it helped prevent the tears that were always at the ready. At her dad's words, though, they dripped from her eyes.

"Cam, hon, what else did Carter say?" Lindy asked as she handed Dani a tissue and squeezed her hand.

"Carter Matthews is a broken man."

Dani wiped her face. "What does that mean?"

Cameron spent the next thirty minutes trying to convince Dani that Carter deeply regretted what he had done and has asked God to forgive him.

Dani stood up, shoved her chair in, and dumped her melted ice cream in the sink. "Dad, it really doesn't matter what Carter told you. He violated our marriage vows, and I can never trust him again. It's over. Our marriage is over. Why are you taking his side?"

"There are no sides, Dani."

Lindy trailed after her and gently massaged her shoulders. "Oh, sweetie, I'm so sorry you're going through this. Why don't you lie down for a little while? I'll take care of the babies if they wake."

Dani turned and fell into her mother's arms and sobbed uncontrollably.

When her tears subsided, Dani headed for her bedroom, but Cameron reached out, took her hand, and asked her to sit back down for a moment.

Dani sighed and sat into a chair.

"Carter is willing to go to marriage counsel—"

"No way, Dad. If Carter was so unhappy, he could have suggested marriage counseling instead of turning to another woman. Now, I just want to move on."

"Honey, a marriage isn't something to just toss—"

Dani's face flamed. "*I'm* not the one who tossed our marriage out, remember?" Dani regretted her tone the moment the words escaped her mouth. "I'm sorry, Dad, but that's the way I feel. It's over. My marriage is over."

❄❄❄

No amount of pleading convinced Dani to remain in Wilburta and agree to marriage counseling. Reluctantly, Cameron had rented a small U-Haul trailer and loaded it with Dani's personal belongings, two cribs, and an assortment of baby items.

Cameron would not hear of Dani driving her car to Meadow Glen in her emotional state of mind, so they all crammed into the Krieg's station wagon—Dani seated between two car seats in the back.

As Cameron pulled out of the driveway, Dani kept her teary eyes on the home she had decided to leave until it was no longer in view. *Oh, Father, my heart feels like it's broken in tiny pieces with no hope of it ever being put together again. How has my life come to this?* Dani removed a tissue from her purse and wiped the tears flowing now in earnest.

Lindy could hear Dani's soft crying and uttered a silent prayer for her daughter. "Are you okay, honey?" Lindy asked when she finished praying.

"I'm fine, Mom. I don't want you worrying about me."

"That's what moms do, sweetheart. You've already had a taste of that."

Dani smiled. "Yes, I have. That's for sure."

❄❄❄

David and Micah agreed to bunk together again so that Dani would have a separate room for a nursery.

"I'm so sorry, guys. Hopefully, I can get my own place

before too long."

Dani slept fitfully the first night back in her old bedroom. About midnight, she turned and reached for the warmth of Carter's body only to find emptiness. Dani stared into the darkness of the room. "Oh, Carter, how could you do this?" she whispered as if he were present. A chill raced through her body, and she pulled the blanket up to her chin and then decided to check on the babies.

She slipped from her bed and tiptoed across the hall to the nursery and found them sleeping peacefully. Wide awake now, she padded down the hall to the kitchen for a cup of tea.

Dani forgot to catch the teakettle before it whistled, and in a few moments, Lindy joined her daughter.

Lindy hugged Dani. "Can't sleep, honey?"

Dani shook her head. "Can't seem to turn off my brain. Cup of tea, Mom?"

"Sure," she said as she slid onto a kitchen stool.

Dani brought both cups to the counter and set one in front of Lindy.

Dani tested the tea, and then massaged her temples.

Lindy studied Dani. "Headache?"

"Yeah."

"There's Tylenol in the bathroom medicine cabinet."

"Thanks, Mom." Dani sighed.

"What's troubling you, honey?"

"What's troubling me? I can't believe this has happened. Here I am married only one year and already separated with two babies to raise alone. How could this have happened to me? I . . . we were so happy, so in love. Actually, I should have known this would happen."

"What do you mean?"

Dani sipped her tea. "All the girls at college practically swooned over him, Mom. And I see how they are at church. They're always trying to get his attention. What did he ever see in me? I'm certainly no Mavis. Besides, half of our marriage, I'm as big as a house with the twins."

"Oh, Dani, you are beautiful inside and outside, and I'm sure Carter thinks so, too."

"It's too late now, anyway. I have to focus on making a life here for my children."

"Well, tonight you need your rest. So why don't we pray and ask God to give you peace in your heart and a restful sleep."

"You're right, Mom."

Lindy covered Dani's hands with her own and prayed for her wounded and troubled daughter.

❊❊❊

Carter called the Krieg home every day for three straight days, but each time Dani refused to talk to him. On Friday morning, a week later, Dani awoke to two fussy babies. Gracie was running a temp, and Grady wanted to be held. When the phone rang as Dani paced the kitchen floor with Gracie, she reached for it without thinking. "Hello?"

"Dani?"

"I don't have anything to say to you, Carter."

"How are the babies?"

Dani forced herself to ignore the catch in Carter's voice. "Gracie is sick."

"What's wrong?"

"I don't know. She's running a temp. I guess I'll have to take her to the doctor."

"Do you have money?"

"Some, I guess."

"I'll send you a check. In the meantime, you can go to an ATM machine and draw out a hundred dollars. That's all they'll let you get at one time."

"Okay."

"Dani?"

"I'm listening."

"I'm begging you to please consider going to marriage counseling with me."

Gracie wailed and Grady took up the chorus.

"I . . . I gotta go, Carter."

"Dani, I—"

"Carter, I have to —"

"I know. I love you, Dani."

"You *love* me? You've had an odd way of showing it this past year. Goodbye, Carter."

Chapter 44

July 1983

But if you do not forgive others their sins, your Father will not forgive your sins. Matthew 6:15

The Krieg household had to completely readjust with the addition of Dani and the babies. The reality of what she was facing weighed heavily on Dani especially when she heard her brothers quarreling in their room and her mom constantly reminding them to be quiet and not wake the babies. It had been a little over two weeks since she had moved in, and the stress on everyone had been something Dani hadn't counted on when she asked to come back home.

Every day there was laundry either in the washer or in the dryer or both. Coupled with the constant stream of mixing formula and feeding two hungry babies left no time for Dani to just sit and relax. Even if she did get a few moments to herself, her mind raced with concerns. And one was money. *I can't keep living here and expecting my parents to support the babies and me. I need to get a job, but I can't ask Mom to keep Gracie and Grady. She deserves a life of her own. Oh, Dear Father, please show me what to do.*

Dani had not prayed for Carter since she found out about Mavis and him even though Cameron had advised her to do that several times. She had not kept her quiet time as often as she knew she should have either, and even when she did, she was so tired she usually fell asleep while she was praying.

Dani put the babies to bed on Saturday night, took a shower, and slipped into her pajamas. She stretched out on her bed and her mind turned to Wilburta, something that had been happening often lately. *I wonder how Lily and Maggie are doing? They loved Gracie and Grady. I can't imagine what kind of story Carter came up with to explain my absence. Could he have told the truth? I doubt it since it would probably mean his job.*

A knock interrupted Dani's thoughts. Lindy poked her head inside. "How would you like to share popcorn and a TV show with me since your dad is out with the boys?"

"Oh, Mom, I'm really tired."

"You sure?"

"Well . . . okay," she said as she scooted out of bed and trailed her mother to the living room.

"What's on?" she asked as she piled on the sofa and pulled the afghan over her.

"*Love Boat.*"

"Carter and I have watched that a few times—when he managed to be home on Saturday night."

Lindy turned the television channel to ABC. "Dani, how about you go with us to church tomorrow?"

Dani frowned. "I don't know, Mom, it's so embarrassing. I feel like such a failure."

"You have nothing to be embarrassed about, honey."

"How in the world will I ever get the twins and myself ready in time? It takes me forever to bathe and feed them. I only took them to church once while we were in Wilburta, and I wouldn't have made it if Carter hadn't helped me."

"I'll help you—be happy to."

"All of us won't even fit in the car, Mom."

"Dad will drive the boys separately. He won't mind it."

"All right, if you're sure. Now, how about we get on with *Love Boat*."

❄❄❄

The Krieg's made it to church during the first hymn, but by the time Dani and Lindy dropped the babies off in the nursery, the hymn had ended.

The two slid into the pew beside Cameron and the boys, grateful he had found a seat near the back.

Dani looked around and spotted several of her old friends. *It seems like a lifetime ago that Betts and I hung out with them.* The thought of her beloved sister stung her heart for a moment. *Oh, Betts, how I wish you were here. I've made a mess of my life.* That thought jolted her and she immediately corrected her thinking. *Actually, it was Carter Matthews who made a mess of my life.*

Dani could not focus on the service. Her thoughts rocketed back and forth from worry over her plight to anger at Carter.

When Pastor Anderson announced the title of his sermon, "It Comes Naturally," Dani flipped to the enclosed outline included in her bulletin, pulled a pen from her purse, and prepared to take notes.

The July sun streamed through the stained glass window at the end of their pew as if highlighting Mary and the baby Jesus. Again her mind switched to her own little babies in the church nursery. *Oh, dear God, help me raise them to know You.*

"Yes, beloved, sin comes naturally to all of us. No one had to teach us to do wrong. The Bible says everyone has sinned. Even though some sins such as murder have more serious consequences than others, they're all sin. Committing even one, makes us a sinner . . . "

That's certainly true. What Carter has done has destroyed a family and robbed his children of a loving mother and father.

"What hope would we have this morning had Christ not taken our sins upon himself and forgiven us? Romans 6:23 says *For the wages of sin is death, but the gift of God is eternal life in Christ Jesus our Lord.* We deserve to die for the sins we have committed even if our sins don't seem as bad as someone else's."

He's right. I've been taught that all my life, but how is that fair, Lord? I have always been truthful, I've done my share of things I regret, but . . . The vision of Mavis in Carter's arms sent her heart racing.

"Our flesh doesn't like to think of ourselves on the same level as, say a thief, or a murderer, does it? No, we pride ourselves on living upright lives, don't we? Have you gossiped this week? Have you cheated your employer because you didn't work as hard as you know you should have? Did you call in sick when you just wanted a day off?" A ripple of laughter spread through the sanctuary. "If so, you sinned, and your sin was paid for because Jesus died for it. He died for the sin of a thief, a murderer, and an adulterer as well. All sin, big or small, is a transgression of God's law and separates us from a holy God."

Lindy peeked at Dani and saw that the sermon outline had slipped from her lap and dropped to the floor, and she was wringing her hands. Lindy patted Dani's knee, and mouthed, "You okay?"

Dani met her mother's worried eyes and nodded.

"If you're here this morning and you are a child of God, you have been forgiven of your sin. Because you're forgiven, the Bible says you have a responsibility to forgive what others have done to you. Mark 11:25 says, *And when you stand praying, if you hold anything against anyone, forgive him, so that your Father in heaven may forgive you your sins.* How dare we accept God's forgiveness and not forgive others? But how can I possibly forgive someone who has hurt me, abused me you ask? You can because the Holy Spirit lives in you. Forgiveness is normal for Christians, at least it should be. As we go through life, you and I will invariably encounter those who wrong us. God's grace given us through His indwelling Spirit enables us to keep harmony in relationships by exercising genuine forgiveness.

Are you finding forgiveness impossible because you can't get over your hurt or anger? The Lord knows that forgiveness is important not just for you but for the person who has hurt you. Is it even possible for us to forgive? Yes, for the Believer, it *is* possible, but only because Christ lives in you. How else could we possibly do all the things we're challenged to do in Scripture? Things like loving your enemies, praying for those who persecute you, going the second mile, for example? These don't even make sense to a non-Christian.

Something wonderful happens when there is true forgiveness between two people. There is a sweetness that is healing and freeing to both."

Pastor Anderson continued his sermon on forgiveness, but Dani Matthews again retreated into her dark thoughts.

"In conclusion, if unforgiveness has plagued you, there is a remedy. Won't you face it honestly and depend on the grace given to you that truly enables you to forgive."

The pastor stepped from the platform and asked the congregation to stand and turn to page 87 in their hymnals.

"If you would like prayer today for any reason, you're invited to come forward and someone will pray with you," the Pastor announced as the pianist began the hymn.

Dani left the auditorium as the singing began and stormed toward the nursery, forgetting she needed her mother to help her with the babies. *Mom had to know what the sermon would be about! Thanks, Mom.*

As soon as she reached the nursery door, Lindy was beside her. "Dani, what's the matter?"

Dani glared at her mother. "Did you know that was the subject of today's sermon, Mother?"

"No, Dani, I did not. Even if I did, Pastor spoke only the truth."

Chapter 45

Where there is strife, there is pride, but wisdom is found in those who take advice. Proverbs 13:10

David and Micah went home with the Porters to spend the afternoon with their son, Sean. Dani was secretly glad, since her brothers had a way of getting on her nerves lately.

On the way home, Lindy again assured Dani that she had no idea the topic of Pastor Anderson's message.

"I'm sorry, Mom. It sounded like he was talking directly to me."

"Maybe he was, Dani," Lindy said.

"Mom, I'm trying to work on forgiveness, but that doesn't mean Carter and I will get back together."

"What does 'working on forgiveness' mean?"

Dani sighed. "It means I'm thinking about it. Now, could we please just drop it?"

Lindy forced to herself not to respond.

❄❄❄

As soon as Dani had the babies down for their afternoon nap, she checked her purse to see how much of the money Carter had sent was left. *Oh, man. I'm out of formula, and there's barely enough here for a case. Should I call Carter?* Dani bit her lip. *I can't ask Mom and Dad to buy formula again. Oh, well, the babies belong to Carter, and he simply has to send money for their care.*

"Mom, I need to run to the drugstore for formula. May I use your car?"

"Of course, honey. Do you have enough money?"

"Just enough. I'm going to call Carter when I get back. He has to send money for his children."

Lindy nodded in agreement and handed Dani the keys.

"Thanks, Mom. The babies should sleep for at least an hour, probably two."

"No problem. I'll listen for them."

❄❄❄

Dani pulled into the parking lot of Eckerd Pharmacy, and headed inside. Her dad had bought the formula for her as soon as they had arrived, and Carter had been the one buying it when she was at home, so she wasn't even sure where to find it. She retrieved a small cart and waved to Lisa Wilson, a girl working checkout that she remembered from high school and then headed toward the back of the store. *There are so many things I'm going to need for Grady and Gracie before long. They're growing like weeds.* She looked down each aisle and finally spotted a display of baby toys at the end of an aisle. Just as she turned into the aisle a man bumped into her cart.

"Oh, I'm so *sorry*," they said at the same time.

"Dani? Dani Krieg?"

"Bill? Oh, my goodness. It's you! How *are* you?"

"I'm fine. It's so good to see you."

"How's your family?"

"Good. Angie and Lindsey are wonderful."

His familiar voice filled Dani with warmth.

Bill Weber had been her physical therapist after the auto accident that left her with a broken leg and claimed her sister's life. He had become so much more than that over the succeeding months as his patient and truthful counsel helped her sort out her mixed-up feelings.

"You won't believe our daughter is walking all over the place," Bill said. "She keeps us hopping."

"Oh, that's wonderful, Bill. I'd love to see her."

"You in town visiting your folks?"

Dani chewed her lip and averted Bill's eyes. "Well, yes, and no."

"That sounds mysterious."

"Carter and I are separated."

"Oh, no. I'm so sorry to hear that."

"It's certainly not what I planned."

"Why don't you come over one evening, Dani? Angie would love to see you again. You can meet little Lindsey and we can talk. How does that sound?"

"Sounds great. Did you hear Carter and I had twins?"

"Twins! You're kidding. I can't imagine two babies to keep up with."

"I guess I could drop over one evening," Dani said.

"Great. How does Tuesday sound?"

"Good. It'll be after the babies are asleep."

"Perfect. See you Tuesday!"

❄❄❄

When Dani returned home, she recognized Carter's car in the driveway. *Oh, no.* Dani considered driving right on by the house hoping his car would be gone if she drove around for a while. She pulled in beside him, turned off the

Eva C. Maddox

ignition, and slid out of the car. By the time she had popped the trunk to get the case of formula, Carter was beside her.

"Hi Dani. I'll get that."

"What are you doing here, Carter?" She tried her best to ignore her heart doing strange things in her chest.

"I'm here to see my beautiful wife and babies."

"Well, you've seen us. Now you can be on your way."

"The babies are sleeping. I need to hold them. They need to remember their dad."

"Didn't you preach today? It *is* Sunday," she said as she folded her arms and stood stiffly by the open trunk.

"The Associate is filling in for me for a few Sundays."

"It must have been interesting explaining your wife and children's absence to your congregation." Dani knew her words sounded spiteful, but truthfully, she had been wondering about that lately.

"I told them you and the babies are visiting your parents for a while. And, Dani, I'm going for personal counseling to try and—"

"Well, good for you, but I really need to get inside." She slung her purse over her shoulder and headed for her parents' back door. "Thanks for bringing in the formula."

"Wait, Dani, please!"

Dani halted without turning to him. Her longing for him stirred strongly in her, but she refused to give in to her the familiar feelings.

Carter approached her from behind and placed a hand on her shoulder, but she shook it away ignoring the warmth his hand created. "Please," he pleaded "can't we talk?"

"What's to talk about, Carter? Except that I need money for Grady and Grace."

"I know. I'm not a dead-beat dad, Dani. I brought you a check. We need to talk about us."

"There is no *us* anymore, Carter."

"Yes, there is, and we need to discuss that. We can't go on like this not talking."

Hot anger flooded Dani, and she turned to face him. "When you chose Mavis Moore over me it ended us. That should make you happy. It's what you wanted obviously." She hurried inside before her anger melted into tears.

Carter lifted the case of formula from the trunk, shut the door, and followed her inside.

❄❄❄

Carter stayed for quite a while, holding and talking to the babies, but Dani remained in her bedroom.

When he was ready to leave, he pecked on her door. "Yes?"

"I have a check for you, Dani," he said as he neared her bed. where she lay with a book pretending to read. "It's upside down."

Dani glared at him refusing to acknowledge her longing for him. "What?"

"Your book is upside down."

Embarrassed, she slammed the book shut. "Just go, Carter. This is *my* room."

"I'm going, but I'm staying in town for a few days in case you change your mind and decide to talk to me."

"Give it up, Carter. We're through." Dani rolled over and turned her back to him.

"I'm at the Best Western. I love you."

No reply.

❄❄❄

"Dani, it's so nice to see you again," Angie Weber said as she held the door open for her. "Welcome to our home."

"It's good to see you, as well."

"Please, have a seat," she said.

"Mum, mum, mum," a little blond cherub babbled as she toddled into the living room.

"Well, hello there, Lindsey," Dani said as she held out her arms for the baby girl.

Lindsey obviously didn't know a stranger as she climbed onto Dani's lap.

"You are adorable," Dani said as she jiggled the toddler on her knees.

"Well, I see you've met our Lindsey," Bill said as he entered the room.

Lindsey slipped down and headed for her daddy. "Da-da-da," she said.

Bill bent and swooped her up, kissed her chubby cheek and then handed her to Angie. "Bedtime for you little one," he said. "Night, night."

"Excuse us, Dani," Angie said with a smile."

"Of course."

"Bill told me you have twins. How old are they?"

"They're two months old this week."

"We'd love to meet them."

"I'll see if I can work that out," Dani said. "Bye, bye, Lindsey. I'm so glad I met you."

Lindsey hid her face in Angie's shoulder.

"It is good to see you again, Dani," Bill said as he settled into a recliner. "But I am sorry to hear about you and Carter."

"I'm sorry to have to tell you about it, but it looks like I'm going to be a single mom."

"Do you mind sharing with me what happened?"

Dani toyed with a loose thread on a buttonhole. "Carter had an affair with his secretary."

Bill closed his eyes briefly. "I'm so sorry to hear that. I'm sure you're devastated."

Tears gathered in Dani's eyes, and she reached for her purse for a tissue.

"So, how do things stand, now?" Bill asked.

Dani sniffed. "Carter's actually in town."

"He's at your folks?"

"No, he's at a local motel. He keeps begging me to talk to him."

"And you are refusing?"

Dani drew in a long breath and turned her palms up. "What's to talk about, Bill? He admitted he had an affair. I even caught them together."

Bill swept a hand across his face. "I see."

"My parents think I need to agree to go to marriage counseling with Carter."

"And Carter . . . does he want you to go?"

"Oh, yes. Nobody understands that I could never trust Carter again. Every time I see him, I see *her* in his arms." Dani choked the words out over the lump in her throat.

Bill leaned toward Dani and squeezed her hand. "I do understand, Dani. I really do. But you must remember all of us are capable of doing bad things."

Dani turned blood-shot eyes to Bill. "Not you, too? Can't anyone understand how I feel?"

"I do understand. I can just imagine how I would feel if. . if, God forbid, Angie would do that to me. But, listen Dani, as Christians we are admonished in Scripture that we must forgive those who hurt us."

"How in the world can I ever do that?"

"*You* can't by yourself, but the Christ who lives in you can help you do that."

"That's what Pastor Anderson said last Sunday."

"Hmm . . ."

"Oh, Bill, I'm so confused. I don't want to love Carter. I want to keep hating him, but when I saw him Sunday afternoon, I just wanted him to hold me. That's just sick."

"No, that's normal. What Carter has done is terrible. There's no denying that, but that doesn't mean the love that drew you together died the moment he sinned."

"What am I going to do? I can't go back to him and pretend nothing happened. I *won't* do that."

"Pretending it didn't happen isn't the answer."

Dani hit the sofa with both hands. "What *is* the answer, Bill?" Dani began to cry softly.

"Agree to at least meet with Carter. See if he really is repentant of his sin. That's where to start. Ask the Lord to give you wisdom and show you the path to take. "

Dani blew her nose. "So, I should talk with him?"

"Absolutely. Even if you never get together again, you need to understand what happened, how it happened, and what Carter was thinking and feeling. In other words, if he is willing to go to counseling, then you should agree to go."

Dani frowned and bit her lip.

"This is a marriage you're talking about here, not something to be cast aside so easily."

"What if — "

"Why don't you leave the 'What ifs' to God?"

Angie appeared in the doorway. "How about something to drink, Dani? And I made chocolate chip cookies today."

"That's so sweet, Angie, but I had better get back. Thanks so much for lending me your husband's ear for a few minutes."

Angie laughed. "If I know him, he has given you an earful!"

Dani picked up her purse and stood as Angie stepped across the room and hugged her. "Please stop in again, Dani. We'd love to meet your twins."

"I will. I promise."

Dani turned to Bill who had risen from the chair and reached for her hand. "Keep in touch, Dani. Let me know how things go. Okay?"

"Absolutely." She looked from one dear face to the other. "You two are angels."

"Saints, not angels," Bill said with a laugh.

Chapter 46

In him we have redemption through his blood, the forgiveness of sins, in accordance with the riches of God's grace. Ephesians 1:7

On the way back to her parent's house, Dani was overcome with emotion and decided to head toward the church. She pulled into the empty parking lot as memories of the time she spent here with Carter flooded her mind. *Oh, Father, I do still love him. I do. But how can I forgive what he's done? What did pastor say this morning? He said You would enable me to forgive the unforgiveable. Bill said the same thing.*

Dani leaned her head back on the headrest. *What happened to us, Father? We were so excited and happy to begin our life together. Help me understand, Lord. Show me what I'm not seeing. Should I talk to Carter?*

Again, that horrible vision of him with Mavis inched through her mind. *I can't! do it, Lord! It's easy for Bill to say I must forgive Carter. His wife is loyal to him. As for Pastor Anderson, his wife has been by his side for years.*

They have no idea how it feels to be completely betrayed!

"We've all sinned." Pastor Anderson's words slinked into the silence of the car, and Dani began to sob.

"Yes, I've sinned. I know that," she said as she pounded the steering wheel inside the dark car. "But, I haven't done what Carter has done. I've been true to him, to our vows. I've put up with the long nights alone while carrying his babies."

Dani's anger grew the longer she defended herself against the words of her parents, Bill Weber, and her pastor. She started the car, and turned it back toward her parent's home.

Lindy had been lying on the sofa and praying for Dani. Her prayer was that Bill and Angie Weber would finally be the ones to convince Dani that she needed to forgive Carter, for her own peace of mind. Lindy knew that Dani's anger and bitterness against Carter would not only harden her own heart, but would eventually affect her children. When Dani entered the back door as if a wind had blown her inside, she suspected the visit didn't go well.

"Hi, sweetie. How was your visit?" Lindy asked.

Dani dropped onto a chair opposite her mother. "Well, Bill and Angie are doing fine. They are two happily married people, and their Lindsey is adorable."

Lindy didn't miss the slight edge of bitterness in Dani's words. "That's wonderful, honey."

"Did the babies wake up while I was gone?"

"No. I think they're down for the night."

"Thanks for watching them, Mom."

"That's what family is for, honey."

"Well, I'm going to bed. Thanks, again."

Dani's attempts at sleep failed her completely. She rehearsed the year she and Carter dated, recalling how he pledged his love to her over and over. The day he pleaded with her to marry him before she finished school, made her smile in spite of her weariness.

I have to go to sleep! She admonished herself knowing that the twins would be awake and ready to eat in a few short hours. As soon as she tried to focus on relaxing and allowing sleep to happen, another thought filled her mind.

Carter was so excited when he knew we were going to have a baby. He must have been scared knowing that we were no way prepared to have a child. Did he hide his fear from me?

The last time Dani looked at the clock it was four a.m. and finally, she drifted off to sleep.

"Dani?" Lindy's voice broke through to Dani.

"Mom?"

"The babies, honey. They want to be fed."

Dani slapped the covers aside, rubbed the sleep from her eyes, and peered at the clock. "Eight o'clock! Oh, my goodness, I didn't hear them, Mom." She jumped out of bed and padded to the nursery.

"I changed and fed Gracie," Lindy called after her, but I have a doctor's appointment this morning and—"

Dani picked up a sopping wet Grady whose crying didn't bother his sister a bit as she cooed in her crib. "Oh, Grady, Mommy's so sorry." Dani quickly changed his diaper and his wet onesie and cuddled him.

Lindy stood and watched Dani from the doorway. "Your dad would have taken care of him, but he and the boys left on a fishing trip early this morning."

"Thanks, Mom. I can't believe I didn't hear them."

"You probably didn't get much sleep is my guess."

Dani carried Grady to the kitchen where she found her mother had warmed a bottle for him.

"I shouldn't be gone long, honey," Lindy said.

"Are you okay, Mom?" Dani realized she hadn't even asked her mother why she was going to the doctor.

"I'm fine. It's just a follow-up to my physical."

❄❄❄

All day, Bill's words kept playing in Dani's mind, and they were no sooner gone than her pastor's words echoed through her. By mid-afternoon, she was desperate to get away from the house, to be alone so she could think. *I wish I had my car.*

"Mom, I hate to ask, but can I borrow your car for about an hour?"

"Okay."

"Can you listen for the babies? They should sleep while I'm gone."

"No problem. Keys are on the hook."

Dani drove around Meadow Glen for a few minutes and then drove to the beautiful Meadow Glen College campus. She remembered going there through the years for various community events and always loved the beautiful trees that graced the lawns.

Dani bypassed the main parking lot filled with summer school students' cars and drove down the lane that led to the school's arboretum.

As she neared the area, she was struck by the sight of the path reserved for those who enjoyed walking through the arboretum. It was covered with pink petals. Dani whipped into a parking spot, thankful the lot was empty. She cut the engine and eased out from behind the wheel.

Thank you, Father. What an amazing sight.

Dani was stunned by the carpet of soft, pink petals. From where she was standing, she could only see part of the path before it curved to the left. *Wonder if the path is strewn with petals beyond the bend?* Dani remembered a book her mother read to her when she was a little girl, and how her mother made the book come alive for her. Sally goes for a walk down a winding path. Each time she rounds a bend in the path, a surprise awaits her. Dani smiled as she remembered how her mom tried to get her to guess at what the next surprise would be. At the end of the book, Sally is surprised to find her daddy waiting for her with open arms.

Dani turned her eyes to the blue sky. *Did you bring that story to my mind, Lord? After all, I've been on some path these last few years! First, my path led to college, then marriage, a pastor's wife, and now a mom. A single mom—at least for the moment. What will be the next bend in my path? One thing I do know for sure, You'll be there for me with open arms.*

The wind had carried some of the petals near her, and she gathered a few and caressed them. Their silky softness amazed her. *The petals have made this path stunningly beautiful, but only for a time. In a few days, they will fade away. In a couple of months, this path will be covered with leaves, after that, snow. Lord, you have filled my path with many wonderful things, beautiful things. Right now, something ugly has darkened my path . . . something I didn't see coming. Now, I'm looking at a curve, a bend that I can't see around. My parents, my friends, and my pastor all tell me I need to forgive Carter. How can I do that? How will I ever be rid of the image of Mavis Moore in the arms of my husband? I've been taught all my life about forgiveness. When Betts died, and I blamed myself for her death, it took months for me to understand that I had to forgive myself. You're a Believer, Dani Matthews. Do you believe, or is Scripture just so many words to you? The Bible says to forgive as you've been forgiven. Do I need to be forgiven of something I've done that contributed to Carter's cheating?*

Dani continued to think about her own behavior over the past year. Ever so gently, the Spirit of God began convicting Dani of her own shortcomings. *I've been critical and judgmental, Lord. I need Your forgiveness. I need Your forgiveness and Carter needs mine!* The thought shocked her for a moment. *Who do I think I am that I can withhold forgiveness? I am merely a sinner who has been granted mercy and forgiveness. Dare I do less for another sinner?*

Dani stood up, lifted her hands in the air and allowed the wind to carry away the pretty pink petals. *You've answered my prayer, Lord. I know what I have to do.*

She returned to the car and sat in silence as the decision she made filled her with peace. Joy invaded her dark soul, and she felt relief for the first time in weeks.

I don't know how this will turn out between Carter and me, Lord, but I know without a doubt that You have shown me the right thing to do. You have answered my prayer. Just like Abraham of long ago didn't know where You would take him, he believed You. Dani laughed aloud for a moment at the thought of her walking along with old Abraham. *I believe You, too! You are faithful. You love me and . . . You love Carter.* Dani realized she had said a kind of prayer for her husband. She knew she had to be on her way, although she didn't want to end the holy moments she had just experienced. She wanted to linger just a bit longer.

I think the Best Western is out on Springfield Highway, she thought, as she turned the car in that direction.

About the Author

I reside with my husband, Jack, and our funny and smart goldendoodle, Maxwell Smart.

I have four amazing children and two equally amazing step-children. Together, Jack and I have 16 grandchildren and 9 great grandchildren. Family is my treasured gift from God. When any one of them rejoices, I rejoice, one is hurt, I ache right along with them.

I am a graduate of Wright State University, Dayton, Ohio, and have taken courses in counseling and nursing as well as several Bible courses through my local church.

Primarily, I write for the Christian market and have been blessed to have many devotions, articles, poems, and stories published in a variety of publications.

I love hearing from my readers either on Amazon or via email at evacmaddox@outlook.com.

My Books (available on Amazon)

Eduardo Magnifico, An Unlikely Hero

For elementary school boys and girls. Eleven-year-old Eddie has no place of significance in his 5th grade world. His physical attributes are a source of shame for him and an excuse for teasing by classmates. When Eddie's dad leaves and his best friend moves away, his self-image plummets.

God in My Kitchen

A 30-day devotional book, packed not only with daily devotions, but recipes, puzzles, poems, tips and other useful information. Each day's reading is based on an ordinary kitchen item.

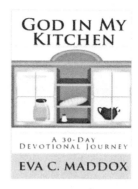

Roses for Betts
Forgiveness Series, Book I

A Christian novel. Follow the life of Dani Krieg as she experiences the depths of despair and ultimate healing in a way only God could engineer!

Come, Go with Me to Littleton Hill
Book I: A Berry Big Adventure

The first in a series of five learning modules for home and school based on adventures of ten-year-old Tessie Trumbull, a fun loving, tomboyish, and creative friend who will gladly share her experiences growing up in rural Kentucky during the 1950s.

Made in the USA
Middletown, DE
26 April 2024

53509298R00181